RETURN TO THE

A Kathleen O'Shaughnessy Mystery
By Ruth Raby Moen

Return To The Kill

By Ruth Raby Moen

ISBN 0-9635653-5-4

Library Of Congress Card No. 96-85085

Copyright 1996 by Ruth Raby Moen

Cover art and book format by 'Typer Tere' Watkins,
826 South 22nd Place #A, Mount Vernon, WA   98273

Kathleen O'Shaughnessy Mysteries are published by:

        Flying Swan Publications
        P.O. Box 46
        Sedro-Woolley, WA 98284

Before I begin . . .

I cannot release this book to the world without extending a note of gratitude to those who have helped me write it, in so many ways.

My daughter, Tere, whose personality and good looks serve as the prototype for the series character, Kathleen, is due a special thanks for her encouragement and unapologetic devotion to her mother.

Another daughter, Patti, has also lent her incredible self in support of her mother's endeavors, as the beautiful and courageous, fictional Patti, found in the confines of these pages.

My simple stories and descriptions can never give full credence to their love and loyalty.

I am also indebted to my longtime friend, Joe Bowen, Attorney and member of the Upper Skagit Tribe, for his invaluable advice and counsel. This book would never have happened without him.

And to my friend and editor, Paul Cocke, for his patience and careful diligence, making this story the best it could be.

Ruth Raby Moen, Author

To Jeffrey, the
best grandson that
ever was:
May you always
grow and learn
and be prosperous.

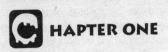

CHAPTER ONE

Saturday. It was a sunny, late-August Saturday. The type of summer day that only Washington State can produce if for no other reason than to forever dispel the wildly exaggerated tales of constant, dreary rain. And who should know better about the trifling now-you-see-it, now-you-don't sun, than a true Seattleite. It's here, as the *Seattle Gazette*'s newest and therefore most expendable journalist, that I labor over a hot computer keyboard, cooking up stories about boatshows or home shows or King Dome repairs that Gunner, the managing editor, assigns me.

This would have been my day off. A time to do nothing but jog or go shopping or clean the apartment. Today's plans had actually included doing some laundry and, later on this afternoon, a trip to the local mystery bookshop. But this weekend promised to be a real delight. Since Gunner had actually sent me on an assignment that sounded fun, and since this was such a fine day, I had called my younger sister and made arrangements to meet her.

Patti lived in a great little town in the Skagit Valley, called Eagle Ridge. It was a beautiful area a little more than an hour's drive north of Seattle. Together, we would prowl through the booths of the Skagit Wildflower and Forest Festival, take lots of pictures, and try to capture the feel and the fun of a small-town celebration on black and white newsprint.

It was early afternoon, about 12:30, when I pulled out of the parking lot and headed due north up Interstate 5, the ancient '76 Porsche in rare form from its recent overhaul. Exiting at the Burlington turnoff, I headed Northeast up Highway 20 another twelve miles, past Sedro-Woolley and about 2 miles this side of Birdsview, to Eagle Ridge. Once in town, the signs pointed the way to the fairground.

Although the town had almost doubled in size in the last

five years, it was still an oasis of feed and seed stores, fishing and bait shops, and the best place in the area to purchase or repair a chain-saw in a mostly logging community. Tall Victorian houses and ancient brick buildings, which had long since been turned into office buildings and retail shops, made up most of the commercial district. All eight blocks of it. Beyond that were homes, dozens of churches, a spanking-new Senior Center and lots of schools. And most every yard around had at least one rose bush heavy with blooms and overly-energetic sprinklers slinging half-moons of water into the streets. The air was heavy with dust and the scent of flowers and the sound of buzzing bees.

A pimply-faced teenager directed me to a spot in the back lot, where I parked and locked up. On the right, two huge cherry trees were packed with a hundred or more birds singing and squawking and making an awful racket. It was hard to tell if their exuberance meant that it was mating season, or mealtime, or if they were simply happy to be alive. Encircled by acres of sweet-smelling grass in a small town park, miles and eons away from the cities of cement and snarling traffic.

A number of families had funneled at the gate, waiting to get in and get their hands stamped. Baby strollers bumped along the uneven earth, and short-legged two-year-olds tottered beside their parents. The older grade schoolers, who couldn't recite a multiplication table to save a month's allowance or even remember their own lunch, had not forgotten last year's slurpies and were already begging their mothers for spending money.

Those finished with the festival looked relieved to be headed home, carrying most of the kids under five, cranky and candy-faced, as their strollers were piled high with prizes and diaper bags and Mama's single purchase from the arts and crafts building. One little girl sound asleep on Daddy's shoulder unknowingly posed a picture I couldn't resist. The shot was timed just as the string of a bright orange balloon escaped the confines of the child's grimy fist and soared its way to the heavens.

On the right, in a roped-off area, four self-conscious but terribly excited 4-H kids marched their sheep around the corral. Eyeing the blue ribbon on the awards table. The judges

2

stood in the center, murmuring to each other, checking their notes, ready to announce the winner.

Next to the judging area was a string of large barns, each devoted to a separate species of farm animals. The first building housed a huge sow nursing a passel of squealing new-born piglets. Across from her in another pen, an Arkansas Razorback glared through the slats with tiny, intelligent eyes and sniffed the air with his wet snout as I walked by.

Coming around the corner from the parade grounds, a six-horse team of Shetland ponies towed a haywagon full of townfolk. Quickly, before the lead horse managed to flatten my left foot, I scooted to the side of a building and let them pass by unhindered. As the sweaty beasts plodded up the hard-baked path, heads low, harnesses jingling, I heard my name screetched joyfully from aloft.

"Kathleen. Aunt Kathy! I'm up here." From atop the highest hay bale, my ten-year old nephew, Jeffrey, thrust a paper cup skyward and waved it as if it were a flag, rattling ice and slopping soda down his arm. "Come on up," he shouted. "This is really cool!" Laughing and shaking my head "no thanks", I motioned at the loading dock where he would undoubtedly disembark.

Keeping in character with his zest for all things fun, Jeffrey was the first to jump off and race down the plank, which the driver barely had time to set up for that particular purpose. He flew to my side, throwing his arms around my waist with great abandon, his freckled face buried in my midriff.

Although my nephew and I had always been on friendly and somewhat affectionate terms, I'd never been met with quite so much enthusiasm. Flattered that he was so pleased by my visit, I returned his fervor with a swing-in-a-circle hug. And with the bold and clever timing of a child who knew instinctively on which side of his bread the butter went, he looked at me with great imploring eyes and begged. "Can I have 5 dollars for some corndogs and a coke for me and Billy? Please, Aunt Kathy? Please, please, please?"

It wasn't until then that I noticed another child who had followed him down the ramp, a stocky Native American boy about Jeffrey's age. The boy's clothes were certainly nothing to write home about, a dirty tee shirt hanging to his knees over

3

a pair of torn Levi's. Under the shock of straight black hair and backwards baseball cap, glowed the marble-bright eyes of a wounded doe. He lingered just a few yards away, trying a little too hard to look "cool" and uninterested, a ten-year old version of the macho-male that would undoubtedly be perfected to an art form by the time he turned 20. With all eyes trained in his direction, he blushed and traced a pattern in the dusty earth with one very worn tennis shoe.

"Are you Billy?" I asked. Although the answer to that was obvious, the journalist in me needed that verification of names and faces. He nodded quickly, completely embarrassed by now, and jammed his hands into his pants pockets. "Sure," I said to Jeffrey, finger-combing his wavy, light brown hair away from his face and exposing a spattering of reddish brown freckles. And though he wasn't supposed to eat junk-food due to his new set of braces, I figured that just once wouldn't hurt that much. "Come on, kids. My treat." Still mindful of the warm reception, I gestured at an empty picnic table and suggested that they wait there while I ordered lunch.

Minutes later, while passing out corn dogs, cokes, and potato chips, I handed Jeffy a toothpick to help clean his braces and asked him about his mother.

"Oh, she said she'd pick me up about 3:00. What time's it now?"

"Not quite two-forty five." I was about to ask Billy the same question about his parents, when my sister walked up beside the boys.

Patti showed her Irish heritage in a little different way than I did. She had inherited the same flawless ivory complexion and naturally pink, apple cheeks as our grandmother. Which seemed even more striking as all of this was framed by the kinky spirals of her dark reddish-brown hair. Her eyes reflected not only the same color of brown but also the family clanship from that Emerald Green Isle, as there has always been a impish quality about her. Those round globes could shine and gleam from an inner light without warning, as if the leprechauns lived in their depths. And if one watched closely, you could see them on occasion, sparkling and plotting some mischievious act.

On the other hand, I had the same dark brown eyes as

4

Patti and the same headful of curls. Though mine were yellow blonde. Nevertheless, we were both born with hair that sprang from our heads in devilish tight ringlets and those who knew the family when we were young, laid bets that it was a sign of bewitchment. As if even our curly tresses had been hexed by the Irish temperament.

Who knows? They might have been right.

Having divorced Jeffrey's father some years ago, Patti had recently re-married and bought a five-acre lot with an old house that had been a part of a dairy farm, on the edge of town. It was time she and I caught up on some family gossip and I found out how she was faring in her new home. We hadn't spent a lot of time together since she'd moved upriver, and I missed her.

After the obligatory hugs and touching of hair, the inquiries into each other's health and sex life, my next question came out more like a comment. "Hey, Sis. What have you been up to? Man! You've really lost weight! You look good."

"Oh, thanks," she said, with an appreciative smile and several tiny dips of her head. "You look pretty good yourself."

About then, Jeffrey spotted his mother and ran up to her for more hugs and money for rides. She greeted him with all the usual comments about dirty faces and not eating too many potato chips, but somehow, she seemed to be lacking her usual spunk. Her natural inclination towards fun and excitement seemed to be replaced by a sadness that was not normal for sister Patti. When she raised up after wiping a mixture of mustard and candy off Jeffrey's cheeks with a Kleenex, a tear dropped from her eye and plopped onto the top of his dark-blond head.

I was surprised and momentarily caught off guard. My sister had never, in all her life, let anyone see her cry. Certainly not here with half the county to watch. For one thing, she didn't believe in making any kind of a fuss in public. It was humiliating to her and just something she did not do. But there she was, her dark eyes swimming with tears, her normally pale cheeks blotchy and streaked with mascara. And all the while, pretending it was just another day. "Patti. What's the matter? Are you okay?"

She nodded. "I'm fine. All this pollen in the air has my

5

allergies up. Kind of a summer cold." Bending her head, she brought Kleenex to nose and blew gustily.

She wasn't kidding anyone. *I knew that sniffle and the way she was avoiding me.*

"Patti, you don't have any allergies." Slowly, and with great affection, I brought up my sister's chin and looked directly into her eyes. "I wish you'd tell me what's wrong."

Digging into her purse for quarters, she mumbled quietly, "I'll tell you later. Let's just get Jeffy taken care of and get out of here."

"Okay. But you haven't heard the last of this, you know."

"I know," she said, the beginnings of a brave grin on her trembling lower lip.

It was hard, having to see her like this. But since I'd agreed to do the festival as a kind of assignment, and since she could use a little cheering up anyway, we took a turn through the yard and garden buildings before heading for home.

The tour led us past the arts and craft booths, more food vendors, and deposited us smack dab in front of the carnival gates. Of course, if we passed them by, it meant that Jeffrey would be terribly disappointed. And as Billy seemed to be glued to Jeffrey's side for the duration, it was agreed that both boys would be treated to a few turns on something called a Monster Mash and a Whirligig.

While we were waiting for the kids to finish with their rides and stagger back to the bench where we were waiting, I noticed a herd of sign-waving politicians who had mounted a platform and launched a campaign-stumping speech. "Who in the world is that?" I asked Patti, thinking I might as well snap a few shots to finish up the roll in the camera.

"Jebediah Winthrop, the Second. Everyone calls him Junior. Mayor Winthrop is his dad, who's on his fourth and last term. He's old and wants to retire. Of course, they all think its a great idea if his son carries on the Winthrop tradition. So he's running for Mayor this year. But from I've heard, his Daddy's popularity doesn't transfer too well with the voters. Different generation, different town. His bid for the Mayor's office was supposed to be a shoo-in, but I guess it's much more of a challenging race than they'd planned on."

Shortly after Patti moved there, I'd ordered a subscription from the town's weekly, the Eagle Ridge Report, and had managed to keep up with their more recent scandals. And one of the stories I'd been following, was this election. Evidently, Junior had leveled a fairly serious charge last week against his opponent, Zeke Larson, the Personnel Director of the Bastolak Casino and Hotel, for unfair hiring practices and mismanagement.

We watched while a local reporter, I guessed to be from this same newspaper, asked him a few questions. Naturally, Winthrop skirted the issue without actually answering, used the audience to hype the situation, and wound up repeating the offense without mentioning that it had not yet been proven. Junior was of a type that left me cold; a 40ish good ole' boy, office-soft and overly confident. I hated dirty politics and couldn't blame the voters for feeling disenchanted with him.

It was after 6 o'clock before we were out of there and on our way to Patti's house. But Billy, the little Indian boy, was not cooperating. We tried to help him, with offers to take him home or to any relative's house he wanted. I even offered to look up his address and phone number, if he'd just tell us his last name. All the questioning about his mother, his home, or his school did no good whatsoever.

He refused to talk. The more we tried to talk to him, the more he shrugged his shoulders, blushed, and looked to Jeffrey for help in dealing with these unreasonable adults. Of course, Jeffrey, always the faithful friend, stood up for him and his right to speak, or not to speak in this case, saying he was just bashful and why don't we leave him alone and he'll probably find his mother himself when he was ready, and maybe he was waiting to find a phone and didn't have the quarter it would take to call her.

It was beginning to look like Billy just might be a runaway. And like it or not, we needed to at least alert the local authorities. Immediately, this was met by a full volume of *you-can't-do-that's*, by an indignant Jeff, complaining that his friend had done nothing wrong and should not be snitched on like a common criminal.

On the other hand, Patti seemed awfully anxious to get home. She insisted that she knew the boy and that he lived just out of town on the reservation. "Why can't we just take him with us," she argued. "And let him call his Mom from our house."

I finally gave in. There wasn't much else to do other than take him to the police station, which Jeffrey would undoubtedly consider an act of treason. I reluctantly agreed to take the child home.

 **HAPTER TWO**

Patti's husband was an out-of-work logger. Of course, Dwayne's lack of a job was everyone else's fault but his own and he was angry about it. Angry at the government, the environmentalists, the voters, the owls, and his new bride of less than a year; Patti. When we walked in the house, he was stretched across the couch, sucking on a can of beer and cranky about dinner being late. He had obviously not expected her to bring any company home. I pretended not to notice his rude behavior as I didn't much care for him, either. I *did* care about how the whole episode was affecting my sister.

At the festival and on the way home, she had started to talk and act like the old Patti I knew. But now, with her husband primed for a confrontation, she was sinking back into that pit of depression before my eyes. If I knew her, she was mostly worried that he would show himself, in front of family members, to be the kind of brute that would abuse anyone who was smaller and weaker than himself. Of course, since he topped out at 5' 6" and 130 lbs. fully dressed, that left him little besides a small woman or a child.

For the next hour or so, we scrambled together a meal for 5 people while the boys watched cable television and Dwayne cranked his way through the rest of his six-pack. For the sake of appearances and the need to finish dinner on as high a note as we could muster, I was determined to keep the sarcasm down and not to push it. Billie was *still* following Jeffy around like a puppy dog.

We had just sat down and were passing around the tuna-fish casserole and salad, when a breaking-news broadcast interrupted a *Roseanne* rerun. A 30-something woman had been found dead in the park on the other side of town. Only about a mile away. There was no identification on her, but the sheriff said they had a positive ID and he added that she was an em-

9

ployee of the gambling casino. The chief of the Bastolak Tribe, Andrew Joe, had identified her as a member of the tribe.

KRSB Channel 2 showed a picture of a Native American woman who had been naturally beautiful in life. A life that had ended just hours ago. She wore no make-up, didn't really need it, and combed her long, black hair straight back. Free and flowing. Her name was Tiffany Redbear Jack.

There was something about the picture and the circumstances surrounding this afternoon that nagged at me. Something peculiar. And...something woefully familiar about the deep depths of her brown-black eyes. They were the same melancholic brown as the boy we had found at the festival. *Billy*.

It was the first time I had heard the kid utter a word. He was staring at the woman's picture on the television screen. When he heard her name, he began to sob quietly.

I grasped him by the shoulders and turned him around to face me. "Billy. Talk to me, Honey. Do you know this woman? Is she your mother?"

Billy raised his eyes, those incredibly deep and wounded eyes, and nodded 'yes.' Jeffrey sat beside him, looking from him to me, his reddish freckles standing in stark relief on his frightened face.

"Patti. Call the police. This boy is the son of that woman who was killed. Somebody better get over here, and I want to know why they let her picture be broadcast with her child running around the country scared to death."

After a quick dial to 911, she hung up and stared wide-eyed at Billy. "Officer Clancey's on his way. Are you sure about this kid?"

"Well, he certainly knows who his mother is." Behind me, the boy had started a peculiar kind of wailing, rocking back and forth in his chair. He was breaking my heart.

Patti knelt beside the boy and offered him her handkerchief. "Billy, we're so sorry. Sorry this happened and sorry you had to see it on TV, like this."

At that moment, the door slammed. Dwayne had finished eating and was stomping outside. Beginning to look mean. Patti immediately rose from the boy's side.

"I'd help you more," she said, nervously glancing through the living room window at her husband's retreating back. "But

Dwayne needs me to help him hold the tape measure while it's still light. The city council will be voting on the new sewer line this Monday night and we've only got this week-end to get ready for it."

"Then go. God forbid, that Dwayne wouldn't get his share of attention," I snapped immediately, wishing I'd stayed quiet.

She blinked, eyes brimming with mortification that a member of the family should see her in such a position. I was sorry she'd been embarrassed. But underneath that was something that concerned me even more. I could have sworn that Patti was scared of something, too. Or someone. She was absolutely terrified. So much so, that she couldn't even tell me about it. Nor tend to a child who had just been told that his mother was dead.

Dwayne must have heard his name mentioned from outside. He threw something into the bed of his pickup, stomped back to the house, and began to shout through the open doorway. "Damn it, Patti. Are you going to help me with this or not? Cause if you're not, you can take the whole damn project, land and all, and shove it up the Mayor's ass if you want. But we're either gonna get this done tonight, or I'm washin' my hands of the whole fuckin' mess! I'm tellin' you, Pat. I'll walk away and never look back. And don't think I won't."

Patti's look was more frightened than angry and I motioned to her that she should give the old grouch whatever he wanted and that I would carry on with the boy from here.

Watching Billy wipe his nose on his filthy tee shirt, was more than I could stand. And since I'd waited as long as I could to use the facilities, I handed him the last few Kleenex's and gave him a quick hug. Hopefully, there were more boxes in the bathroom cabinet. Patting him on the knee, I told him to sit tight and I'd be right back.

Big mistake. Leaving a severely traumatized boy in the room, alone. Especially one whom I did not know and was not effectively communicating with. Because in those few minutes that the bathroom door was closed, even investigative journalists need their private moments, the boy shouted something from the other side about having to leave. He sounded panic-stricken. Dwayne's little temper tantrum had not helped.

"Billy," I said, trying to hurry, wondering where in the world my sister's head was that she was not looking after the boy, mad that her husband considered his needs more important than a woman's life and a young boy's heartbreak. "I'll be out in a minute, okay? Billy? I'm coming. Just hold on a sec." The next moment, I heard the back door slam. Although the television still blared, the house was strangely quiet.

"Billy?" No more sobbing. No more shouting demands. No sound at all but the raucous voice of an advertisement. Cold chills settled around my shoulders.

When I came out, the boy was gone. "Jeffrey? Patti? Where is everyone?"

I ran the length of the hall. "Billie? Where are you?" Searched the living room and kitchen. He wasn't here. I shivered and peered out the window at a point where I could see several blocks down the road. A terrible wave of guilt and vulnerability flooded over me.

Nothing. No one was home, no one was in sight. It was too late. The boy had vanished into the dark night.

And so had my sister.

CHAPTER THREE

Chief of Police Clancey's car pulled into the driveway some fifteen minutes later. As the only one left at home, I answered his knock and asked him inside.

Clancey had a ruddy complexion, ringed by wispy reddish-blond hair. He was a big man, tall and broad shouldered, a good 60 pounds overweight, and wheezed slightly as if bothered on occasion with asthma. He introduced himself, took quick note of the room and its inhabitants, and asked if I was the woman of the house.

Quickly explaining that my sister Patti and her husband had gone off to stalk the back forty, I invited him to sit and assured him that I was the one who had found the boy and would answer as many questions as possible. After cups of coffee were poured and served, I proceeded to tell Clancey what little I knew about the Indian boy, Billy.

"I brought him home simply because sending him to the police station was only marginally better than leaving him there by himself. We knew he lived in this general area, somewhere. Plans were that after he ate, we'd get him to tell us where he lived or at least have him call his parents from our phone."

Jeffrey had wandered in minutes before, and Clancey questioned him too, going down on one knee and letting him tell it in his own way. When asked, Jeffrey replied that he had no idea as to where Billy had gone, if he'd ever attended school in this county or even what class he'd be in. He did explain to Clancey what little he did know about his friend and how they'd met earlier this summer. Evidently, both boys had been new in town, and a little out of place.

Billy and Jeff were friends in a way that only little boys can appreciate in a world of rushing rivers and deep forests and wild creatures. All just waiting to be discovered and tested against their own young wills. They had run into each other

13

when Jeffrey was trying to catch a fish in one of the creeks that fed into the Skagit River. His fishing gear had gotten hopelessly tangled in a low tree branch and he hadn't brought any extra line. Exasperated, he'd been tugging on the pole for all he was worth while trying out a few new cuss words, thinking that no one was around to hear.

Billy had come from the prairie in Eastern Washington, but had gone fishing with his father and other members of his tribe many times. The Bastolak Tribe had a rich heritage, centuries long, of fishing for salmon, steelhead, and trout in this same river. Who better than Billy to show Jeffrey the ropes when it came to catching a fish. Or experiment with some interesting four-letter-word combinations. The boys had played at the river's edge all summer, camping out every once in awhile and fishing. One of their favorite holes was not too far from the place where Billy's mother had been found.

As I walked Clancey to his patrol car, he handed me a card with instructions to call anytime, day or night. I said that I intended to report the incident back to my editor at the *Seattle Gazette* and would probably be assigned to cover it for at least the next few days. He then left.

I couldn't handle having to sit in my sister's house, doing nothing but watching Jeffy watch television. And although the police chief had promised to begin looking for the boy right away, I was awash with guilt for leaving the child alone in the room.

Meanwhile, the trail was getting cold. And since Jeffy knew the places where this young boy may very well prefer to hide, and since there was no way I was going to leave *him* alone in that house, I hustled my nephew into the car with a promise of letting him help me look for Billy. We left a note for Patti, saying we'd be back before bedtime.

For the next two hours I drove up and down each street at least twice, out to the park by the river, and rumbled up and down each and every county road and trail I could find. We stopped at a number of points known to be good 'kid' hangouts and most of the popular fishing holes. Billy was nowhere to be found. Finally, I parked at the park entrance, the scene of the woman's death having been encircled with bright yellow police tape and got out.

It wasn't long before one of the city policemen saw my car and stopped to ask me a lot of questions. I showed my ID and my press pass and had them check with their office. Finally, I got permission to stay as long as I promised to keep away from the crime scene.

A small trail led straight down to the river bank. And though I was sure they had covered this area already, I didn't see how it could hurt for us to look again.

Walking alongside the river bank, a bracing wind whistled past our ears and made knots of my long hair. I was shivering from the cold and the fact that a woman had been killed not far from here. We continued to poke into bushes and peer under logs for close to an hour. It was time to go back. We were both tired and it was getting dark.

On the way to Patti's house, I made another sweep of the neighborhood. The sheriff's car was up ahead, cruising up and down the streets, searchlight beaming into every alley and carport. I guessed it to be Deputy Sheriff Jack's patrol car. As the first Native American the county ever had for a deputy sheriff, Benjamin Jack was a little controversial. Although the articles I had read described him as thorough and well trained.

He's the one I need to interview, time permitting. If he, the boy, and the victim were members of the same tribe then the deputy would probably be the best one to head up a search party and might even be organizing one already. Finding nothing that even faintly resembled the trail of a little boy, I drove back to the house.

At least she was home. Her car was parked in the driveway and she had left the front light on for us. She greeted us at the door, hugging Jeffrey and I both. Dwayne was nowhere in sight. With any luck at all, he'd already gone to bed.

It was time she talked. I waited until she had hustled her son off to his room. Having an idea that she would once again evade my questions, I waylaid her in the hallway.

"Patti," I whispered, fingers crossed that Dwayne was a heavy sleeper. "If we're going to talk, we'd better do it now." With a slight shake of her head, Patti indicated the bedroom door. Okay, so Dwyane was *not* a heavy sleeper. In a voice just loud enough for him to hear should he be listening, I pulled her down the hall toward the kitchen, saying, "I got a chill out there. How about fixing us both some hot cocoa? You can tell me all about your life up here in the wilds of Western Washington while you show me where you hid the extra blankets."

Nodding ever so slightly, she gestured at the hall closet as we passed by. "Sure. The blankets are in here." Once out of earshot and over the steamy cups, we huddled together at the far end of the counter.

"By the way," she said. "I'm really sorry for not being more help with Billy. I thought he'd probably gotten in trouble at home, maybe put on restriction or something, and was rebelling. It's a stage all kids go through at one time or another. Who could have figured that this would ever happen?"

"It's alright." I told her about the visit from the Chief of Police and our fruitless search around the neighborhood. "The kid has to be scared to death. Think about it. His Mom's dead, and he might even know who did it. We can only hope that he'll either quit running or we'll catch up with him."

She hung her head, sniffled, and wiped her nose with a paper napkin.

I waited for a minute, expecting her to offer some kind of explanation. When that didn't happen, I asked her. "Time to fess up, Kiddo. I want to know what in the world is going on with you."

"It's nothing. We're fine. Really."

"Fine? You call this fine? Almost in tears at the fair, your husband biting your head off right in front of me, God knows what he does when I'm not watching, and you seem scared to death of him. This is not *fine*, Baby Sister." I tapped the kitchen counter for emphasis. "Now, it's time to get honest. Besides his verbal abuse, what else has he done to you? And what's the deal with your property needing to be measured and this bit about not getting a permit?"

"Well, Dwayne and I are having a few problems. But nothing that can't be fixed." She folded her arms. "He's had a rough time of it, getting laid off work and everything, and my paycheck doesn't quite stretch. And now it seems that the city has decided to put in a sewer along our property line."

Drawing a crude map of their five acre tract on a napkin, she indicated the position of the house and the proposed sewer line. The house sat on the back end of the lot. "They've planned

16

it to go all the way across the front of our property, way up here on Pine Road. The thing is, if this project actually goes through, it would increase the value of the land by five times what it's worth now. Which means that we'd have the right to subdivide it and sell off lots one at a time."

I made a wry mouth. "Let me get this right. The city is putting in a new sewer line across one side of your property, giving it a projected value of five times what you paid for it....within one year after you bought the place. And your husband sees this as *having a rough time*? If this is true, winning the lottery would be devastating for the old boy."

Patti stamped her foot and glared. "If you're going to insist on belittling Dwayne every chance you get, I'm not going to talk to you anymore."

"All right, all right. Just tell me the truth." I was dog-tired, and looking forward to having this settled before going to bed. "Why in the world is your husband upset that your property value has increased five-hundred fold."

Teary-eyed but still defiant, she stretched across the counter and plugged in the hot water kettle. "Because, to get to that point, we'd have to pay a $30,000 assessment fee. And as we live on the back half of a long rectangular lot, we're talking some 500 feet of our own sewer line, which means another $30,000. It would have to run all the way from the house to the road. Add to that, a $1,200 hook-up fee. And we're expected to hook up to it right away. What with all the fees and contractors to put in the line, we're looking at over $62,000. Cash. Up front. They've given us 90 days to come up the money."

She sniffled and wiped away a tear. "Kathy, we don't have that kind of money. With Dwayne out of work, we don't have *any* money. It looks like we might have to sell to the highest bidder on such short notice, and we won't get a chance to take advantage of the new development at all. Which means we lose everything we've put into it. Including the down payment." She rubbed her arms, looking absolutely pathetic. "It's been a real blow. Dwayne's taken it pretty hard."

Biting my tongue, I decided not to mention the fact that this dilemma had also happened to her and that she was also 'taking it hard' and didn't need an abusive husband to boot.

Instead, I stuck to the matters at hand...for the time being. "So, your property is increasing in value, but you won't see one bit of the profits."

She nodded, and touched the end of her nose with her napkin. "We're being forced off our own land. Can't get a loan with Dwayne out of work. Not even with the property as collateral. We'll have to sell out. For peanuts, or have it auctioned off. And you know as well as I do, that we'll never get a decent price. One of the developers has already given us an offer. Pennies on the dollar, if you consider what he'll be able to make off of it."

"Well, buck up Kiddo. I'm going to call my editor on Monday, to see if I can stay on for a few days and get the story first hand on this woman they found at the park and the little boy. If I can wrangle some time before I have to go back, I'll nose around a little and see what I can find. I'll bet you anything that there's lots of things that can be done. "

"It's no use, Kathy, we've already tried." Having finished the cocoa, she began loading up a coffee cup with Folgers Instant, hot water and a liberal helping of brandy. "The city has made up their mind and they could care less what happens to us in the process." With a gesture, she offered me one, but I turned it down.

"Oh, but you'd be surprised, Little Sister, what lurks in the heart of a city council member who just happens to own a little land. There's always something. Certain little laws on the books that the city forgot to tell you about. Old deeds, minutes from long-forgotten meetings, and tons of documents making a paper trail of back-room deals by all *kinds* of cigar-smoking, back-slappin', good ole' boys." I made a face, thought about it for a moment, and said, "I'll scout around in the county title office and in the records of the building department and see what I can come up with. Don't worry. Remember what Momma always used to say."

"I don't remember Momma ever saying anything about this kind of mess."

"Sure she did. Something about, 'If you can't beat them at their own petty little games, bury under enough paperwork to make 'em wish you had.'

"Don't you mean, 'If you can't convince them with logic,

18

then baffle them with bullshit?' Patti said, with a playful thump to my shoulder and the closest thing to a smile I'd seen all day.

"Same thing. Now, where did you say those blankets were? I'm tired, and I have an idea that tomorrow will be a long day."

HAPTER FOUR

⟨⟐⟐⟐⟩ **Sunday**. The next day, I was up with the birds and while Patti was still asleep, loaded Jeffy into the car and left her note. Ten minutes later, we were on our way to the Police Station. The Mayor wasn't in, but a young woman in a mini-skirt and long, painted fingernails handed me their prepared release for all press persons.

"I'd like to speak to Deputy Benjamin Jack," I said.

"The Sheriff's Department is across the street." She waved a crimson-tipped hand in that direction. Evidently, she was busy and had no time to be bothering with out-of-town reporters. A photographer that I guessed to be a freelancer was snapping pictures of everything in sight. Including her.

"I know where the office is. Already been there. They said to check over here."

With a surprised blink, she turned on the intercom and asked, "Is B.J. here?" Her answer must have been in the affirmative, as she held up one finger meaning she'd be right back, and disappeared around the corner.

Ten minutes later, the receptionist appeared back at the counter. "B.J. didn't come to work last night. I don't know when he'll be in."

Irritated that she'd kept me waiting a full ten minutes, I bit my lip, determined to hold my temper and said, "Do you know if there has been a search party initiated for the missing boy?"

"Uh, you mean that Indian kid? I don't know. Haven't heard anything."

And evidently, didn't care.

This woman was getting on my nerves. The racial slur and the attitude had me simmering. I was about to turn on my heels, when the Channel 2 news-team came bashing in the door. Shoulder-held camcorders scanned the room and every-

20

body in it. Their field reporter was not with them.

The woman didn't know much about lost little boys or missing deputies, but she knew an opportunity when she saw it. This group could put her on television. Showing the camera her best profile, she hooked that same handful of crimson-tipped nails, which I was now ready to bet big money that they were fake, on one hip.

"Deputy Sheriff Jack isn't home. Hasn't been home since they found the body. Actually, if you wanna know...," At this point, she pointed her chin toward the microphones which had been shoved in her direction. I was hoping they'd hit her in the mouth, saving me the trouble.

"I heard that the deputy has been taken off the case completely," she simpered. "Might even be going on suspension."

One of the cameramen shouted from behind his equipment. "Why? What are the charges?" Head reeling from the clerk's statement, I was amazed that the Channel 2 newsteam had come all the way out here without a reporter. These men were all technicians.

"No charges yet. Just might be, is all I said."

At that point, the journalist in me went to work and I began to conduct the interview. I whipped out a pad and pencil, and said, "Do you know for sure that he's been taken off the case? Has a reason been given for this illeged suspension?"

"Well, he didn't show up for duty last night. Hasn't called in....nothin'. And seeing as how his wife is dead, ex-wife anyway, and his kid ran away from home and won't have anything to do with him...," here she sighed with a dramatic pause, and actually touched her mouth with one of her red claws as if to demonstrate how much more she would have liked to tell but didn't dare, and gave an exasperated shake of her head. "They'll probably consider him one of the suspects. Anyway, he's long gone, now. Looks to me like he's headed for parts unknown."

Just then an older, rather hulky-looking cop took exception to the noisy crowd and strode to the counter, tugging at his trousers. "Is there a problem here?" The camera's swung in his direction.

"No problem that I know of," I said, making sure the entire episode was recorded on film. "I'm waiting to see the Mayor."

The woman was getting nervous. The Mayor was not only submerged in politics with a big election looming ever closer, he was also her boss. "You said you wanted to see B.J. I mean Deputy Jack."

"He's not at work right now. I'll settle for the Mayor."

"You'll have to have an appointment."

"Then make me an appointment."

Pretending to study his schedule, in a spot where I couldn't see it, she looked up innocently and said, "Mayor Winthrop doesn't have a time slot open until day after tomorrow."

"Too late. Try again."

"Sorry. 3:45, Tuesday afternoon. Shall I write it down for you?"

"Look," I said, hauling out my press pass from the *Seattle Gazette* and flashing it under her nose. "I'm calling in a story in about 5 minutes." Of course, my call would be to the newsroom at the paper and probably directly to Gunner, but she didn't know that.

"And these guys here will be broadcasting another report live, at about the same time. Then another at 3 o'clock this afternoon." Gathering momentum, knowing full well that what I had to say next would never air but would be quite useful in instilling a little respect for the media and garner some needed cooperation, I made my play of the day.

"Look. I don't care if the Honorable Mayor Winthrop has anything he wants to say about this travesty or not, and I could care less if he wants to spend his every waking hour politicking for Junior. I also don't care if he hasn't even heard about the homicide in the park or if he just hasn't come to work yet. Whatever has transpired from the time that woman was killed until now, I will report. And if the Mayor's work habits look a little questionable to the public, who do you suppose will have to answer for it? So, if you don't want to make your boss look like a bumbling nincompoop, I suggest you crank up that phone of yours and call him at home. And while you're doing that, I highly suggest you inform him that it will be even more beneficial to Junior's career if he gets a search party started looking for that little boy."

At the door on the way out, I looked at her over my shoulder and said, "By the way, one of your fingernails just fell off." Pretending to be horrified by it all, I gestured for effect and said in a stage whisper, "Middle finger."

After that, I left the City Hall in a huff, a vice-grip on Jeffrey's hand as we swept through the building and out the front door. My nephew was still wide-eyed, but seemed to be enjoying himself. Quickly, we made our way down the stairs past reporters and gawking onlookers. The Channel 2 news team was setting up, ready to go on air. They'd be broadcasting from the City Hall steps.

I hustled my nephew toward the car. "Jeffrey, what's this bit about Deputy Jack's boy being the missing one. Why didn't you tell me, Billy's dad is a Deputy Sheriff?"

"Well, yea. Everybody knows that."

"Everybody but your Aunt Kate." My first reaction was to remind him that I didn't live in Eagle Ridge, and apart from having a psychic experience, there was no way I could have known and that I relied on my family to keep me informed. But then, I hadn't asked. As I placed him in the car, a twinge of guilty conscience for having exposed him to the spectacle inside began to pinch the pit of my stomach. "So what do you think of your big-mouthed Aunt Kathy now?"

"I think you're pretty cool."

It was the first, decent thing anybody had said to me in days. Driving off, the Porsche rattling windows from its crumbling exhaust, I did a squealing U-turn on Main Street, mostly for Jeffy's benefit, swung into a teenage-type drive-in and asked him if he was hungry. After a quick meal, we drove back to the park where the body had been found.

The parking lot of the city park and the grounds were swarming with cops, a contingent from the Sheriff's department, and a handful of plain-clothesmen. A few of them looked out of place enough to be FBI.

Down on the boat launching dock, a number of Indians, whom I guessed were from the Bastolak Tribe, were crowding around an old pickup, easing three of their boats into the river. I was certain that they wouldn't be using the boats for fishing; they'd probably volunteered to help search the banks downriver for more clues. Ten or so of the plain-clothesmen seemed to be organizing the hunt.

I didn't want to disturb the murder scene, so Jeffy and I

wound up walking along dusty county roads that paralleled the river. The hike took us past a few dairy farms, some older country homes and a small orchard. Here, the river bed narrowed and there were some rapids. As the road petered out to a dusty trail, we dropped down the bank and started walking up the beach. About another hundred yards upriver, the sun glinted off a foil package. As I reached under a bush to look closer at it, I noticed a rag or piece of clothing had been draped over a low alder branch, as if someone had hung it there as a kind of outdoors closet.

It was a knit top. A ladies' knit top. Careful not to disturb the area, including any footprints or fingerprints, I eased back away from the area and called to my nephew.

"Don't touch anything, Jeffy. This could be some valuable evidence."

"Never saw that here before," he said, going around it and continuing on up the beach. After walking another twenty feet, Jeffy suddenly stopped, looking decidedly uncomfortable. His freckles stood out like red polka dots on his now white complexion.

"Jeff," I said, hoping he would continue to cooperate. "What's the matter? Are you okay?"

He nodded and shrugged, hands nervously wiping the fronts of his jeans. "I...think...maybe, we better go back pretty soon. Mom's gonna be mad if I don't..."

"I left your Mom a note, telling her that you were with me and that we'd be back later on." Taking a few more steps, I stopped and turned. Jeffy hadn't followed me, but seemed rooted to the same plot of ground, his cheeks red now from embarrassment. "Jeffy, what's wrong with you? Don't you want to help me find Billy?"

"Yea, well, sure. But, how'm I supposed to know where he went."

"You know his favorite spots probably better than anyone. Can't you show me some of them? You realize, of course, that that little boy is out there, all alone, probably without food or blankets and sick over seeing a newscast about his mother being dead. We've got to find him, Jeff. It's terribly important."

Touching a sore on his lip where the braces had been rubbing, Jeffy nodded again, seemingly having made some kind

24

of a decision in his young mind. "Well, we could go this way, I guess," he said, ducking behind a large boulder and scrambling up the bank. From there, a small trail led into a group of alders. No more than a hundred feet deeper into the trees, he gestured at a kind of fort built like a lean-to and grinned.

I was surprised. "Did you and Billy build this?"

He nodded, at once both proud of his accomplishment and embarrassed. I had an idea that the boys had some kind of oath not to reveal the place to anyone. Especially to a girl. And that was why he had been reluctant to bring me here. It appeared that even though I was pushing the age limits, I still qualified for the title of *girl*. Which meant that Jeffy had broken that vow by bringing me here.

Trying not to show too much emotion, I ruffled his dark blond curls and gave his ear a tug. "Thank you for helping, Jeff. I know it's hard, but we really do have to find Billy as soon as we can."

The fort looked like something a group of boys would have spent the summer building. A bundle of small logs, scraped clean of bark, had been laid out in a row. Some of them had been cut into 5-foot sections. It was obviously a wall section still in the making. They'd completed three sections, each of which had a row of small logs with both ends lashed to a perpendicular log with strong twine, thereby creating an almost solid log-wall. These three walls had then been lifted up and each corner tied to a tree, which created three sides of a somewhat squarish structure. An old blue tarp, cut to fit, provided the small shelter with a rain-proof roof.

Inside, there was evidence of a fire and some fish bones. Someone had been sleeping there. Could it have been the boy? A tramp? Some neighborhood kids out to enjoy the last of their summer? Or was it my own beloved nephew.

"Jeffy, Come here a minute, Honey." I waved him over, making sure he was looking directly at me. "Does anyone else know about this place? Tell the truth now. Has anyone, beside you and Billy, ever been here?"

"Uhm, I don't know. We got it hid pretty good."

"Looks like somebody built a fire and cooked some fish in the last few days. Do you know anything about it?"

Immediately, Jeffrey went into full denial. He started back-

25

ing up, shaking his head. "Uh, no. It wasn't me or Billy. I don't know who did it."

"Hey, kid. You're not going to be in trouble. I just need to know if your little friend might be staying here."

At that, he took his stance and looked me directly in the eye. "Well, I didn't cook no fish. Or make any fires."

"All right. Let's move along then."

The trail meandered along the bottom of a cliff, then veered off toward the river again and down the bank. We walked up-river for about a half a mile, along the water's edge. After awhile, the narrow, rocky beach dwindled down to nothing and the river water surged against the high bank wall. It was either go up the bank or wade. I climbed out at a spot where many others had climbed before, and evidently at least one other with little feet .

In a place where a tree root jutted out from the bank was a bowl of dry earth. It held a boy-sized footprint. Probably sneakers and though the edge of the track was well defined, the pattern on the soles was not, suggesting that they'd been made by a pair of old, worn sneakers. Could they have belonged to the boy? It was hard to tell, and it would have to be matched with another sneaker pattern, but it was my first lead.

I covered the area of the print with a large chunk of bark taking care not to smear the print. Scrambling down the bank, we clung to the tree roots and branches to keep from tumbling headfirst all the way to the river's edge.

Back in town, I delivered Jeffy to his home, thanking him and promising to keep him informed of all new developments. I then found a rack for the local newspaper and bought a copy of the latest issue. Most of what the article said I already knew. They knew where the woman had lived but weren't releasing the address. It appeared that she had lived alone. There was no mention of the boy.

My next stop was back to the police station. Chief of Police Clancey was on the phone when I arrived, with another line blinking impatiently. He held up one hand as if asking me to wait, and motioned to a chair. I mouthed the words 'be right back' and left to find one of the officers who was in a position to talk.

I found Officer Miller at the dispatcher's desk. He couldn't or wouldn't tell me much, other than that they had finger-printed the body and faxed it to the FBI fingerprint section in Washington D.C. "I just want to know if there's any evidence that she's been raped. Have they found any semen? And if so, are they going to type it for DNA?"

"That would be in the autopsy report, Ma'am. And since today is Sunday, I doubt there is anything they'll be doing on it before tomorrow."

"Are you saying that the coroner won't even look at the body until tomorrow? How can they determine the time of death if they wait for two days before they even look at it?"

"Oh, no. Doctor Sorestad has viewed the body and released a death certificate. We just won't be getting a report for another day or two." The officer flushed and fidgeted, mumbling something about getting back to work, and disappeared through a doorway on the far side of the counter.

Clancey's conversation was over, so I walked back into his office and plopped down in a chair. "Thanks for coming by," he said. "I'll need to get a signed statement from you detailing what you know about the Native American boy."

Speaking clearly into the tape recorder, I answered all the questions, telling him everything I knew as clearly and as completely as I could. I even told him about the boy seeing the dead woman's face on the TV, how he replied in the affirmative when I asked him if she was his mother, and how he freaked out over it. And how he went running out of the house while I was in the bathroom. The part about my brother-in-law was the only thing I left out. "You know," I said. "Since the boy seemed to be so scared, I would hope that there is a search party already starting to look for him.

"There is indeed. The Skagit Search and Rescue has already organized and is out there now, as we speak." I was relieved enough that it probably showed on my face. Clancey grinned, but said nothing.

Playing dumb about the newest gossip making the rounds, I decided to give the chief all the room he needed, should he need to maneuver around this next question. "How about his father? I hear his Dad is Deputy Sheriff Jack. Wouldn't he be the most obvious one to lead a search party?"

Here, Clancey chose his words very carefully. "It hasn't

yet been determined exactly what role Deputy Jack will play in the scheme of things. Or even confirmed the fact that the missing boy is his son. We do know that the victim and Deputy Jack had been married at one time and that a boy was born out of that marriage who might answer to the description you have given me. Because of the circumstances, Jack has been given some time off. He'll be out on compassionate leave for the time being. For now, that is all that has been officially determined."

"Does anyone know where he is?"

"You mean on a moment by moment basis? No, we do not. Nor have we determined that it is necessary that we should know. For now, Deputy Jack has been given paid leave for compassionate reasons."

Apparently, Clancey had either decided on his own or was following directions, on how much to tell the media. And he'd said all he was going to say about Deputy Jack. Knowing a brick wall when I ran up against it, I changed the subject. "How about Tiffany? Has anyone given any statements about who would want to kill her?"

Clancey nodded. "Those are questions that have already been considered. One of my best detectives has been sent to question the casino personnel director. Name's Zeke Larson."

"Isn't he the other candidate for mayor? Junior Winthrop's opponent?"

"Yes. I believe that is correct."

In my head, the list of questions that needed to be answered was getting longer. Tiffany's boss was also running for office. A coincidence? I could look into it, if there was time. "How about the casino? I take it Tiffany had worked there. Do we know who her friends were? Her enemies? Did she work in the casino itself, or in the office? What shift did she work?"

Clancey frowned, as if to demonstrate his displeasure at having to entertain my amateur attempts at detecting. "As I have already said, communications have already been sent to both the personnel director at the casino and the chief of the Bastolak Indians." He sighed, making it clear that the flood of press-persons, including me, were getting on his nerves. "Ms. O'Shaughnessy, everything that can be done is being done. If we hear anything more, you will be notified." He turned to

28

some papers on his desk, as if to dismiss me.

"Are the Indians willing to help? Isn't there some kind of an agreement between Skagit County and the Tribal Council, saying that they will cooperate in criminal investigations?"

"Yes there is. Very good ones, in fact. The Bastolak Tribe has always fully cooperated and we have no reason to believe that this investigation will be any different."

"Has anyone questioned any of her co-workers? As a pretty divorcee, you'd think she'd be quite popular. Does anyone know if she was seeing someone?"

"I repeat, all steps that can be taken at this point in the investigation, in so far as this is a Sunday morning, have already been initiated." The big man shuffled his papers in agitation of being told how to do his job. "Your tape will be transcribed within the next few days. At that time, you will be called in to review that transcription, and finding no errors, you will then be asked to sign it. As for now, this interview is over."

"Look, I've got to phone something to our newsroom for tomorrow morning's paper. You saw the body. What do you think was the cause of death?"

"I can't divulge that information at this time."

"Bull-hockey. The whole world already knows there was a homicide here. Channel 2 already told them. And there is a herd of media-jocks out there, just waiting to catch a headline. What did the body look like? Were there stab wounds? Bullet holes? A lot of blood? Did she drown? What?" I waited, while he pondered how much to tell me. He obviously wanted to, would probably relish the chance to expound on his prowess as a police detective. But for some reason he was holding back.

"This is the *Seattle Gazette*, Clancey. Your chance to tell the world what a great chief of police you are. And, unlike a mention on Channel 2 news, a newspaper article fits nicely as a back-up to your resume just in case you ever want to blow this town." Giving him a minute to reexamine his position, I pressed on. "Surely, Doc Sorestad took some snapshots when he first viewed the body. And you certainly saw it yourself. What's your educated guess?"

"Look. I've been on the phone with every reporter in the

state, and all wanting to know something no one else does. And I've had to tell them all the same thing." Blood rushing into his face and voice rising, he banged his desk with a meaty fist. "This is an ongoing investigation and I cannot divulge anything more at this time."

He was panting. "A summary of the coroner's report will be available to you all, when it is ready. Whether it will include pictures, I cannot say at this point. Now, the sooner you let me get back to work, the sooner I'll be able to find the answer to some of those many questions of yours."

"How about a copy of your notes at the death scene?"

"The interview is over, Miss O'Shaughnessy. My deputy will show you out." His big paw snatched the ringing phone from its hook and he barked into it, "Chief of Police." It must have been an important call, by the way he frowned into the phone as if it was responsible for this new set of problems. As he alternately snarled one or two word replies, I took a moment to scribble some notes on a pad.

For my profession as a writer, a method called 'free-writing' usually works as a way of getting in touch with my subconscious, letting that intuitive process burble freely out through my fingertips and down the length of the pencil. Many times, an amazing amount of creativity has appeared, as if by magic, upon the paper. Therefore, the act of writing those impressions down right away, was absolutely crucial.

I must have sat and scribbled for several minutes while Clancey conducted his phone conversation, when Officer Miller came running from around the corner. He was talking fast and didn't see me sitting by the wall. "They found a knife in the river, about 10 yards or so from where the body was found." Too late, Chief Clancey held up his huge hand to silence his deputy, gesturing toward me with a thumb the size of a sausage. "Oh," Miller said. "Uh, I, I'm sorry. I didn't realize... I thought she was long gone."

I wasted no time at all jumping on this new lead. "So. She was stabbed. And you think you found the knife. It it too late to get any fingerprints off it?"

Normally, I would have used my laptop computer to bang out the story right there in the office and begged the use of a phone from Eagle Ridge's finest to send it to Seattle. But by the venomous glare and jaw bunching of the illustrious police chief, I considered it best that I leave. This story would have to be written and sent from somewhere else. The closest phone was at Patti's house.

My story was already sent in, flashing by computer modem in millionths of a second to the newspaper computer system, when Dwayne came stomping through the house. He was wearing dirty battle fatigues with a beat-up bush-rifle in the crook of his arm and carrying a wooden box as wide as a bread box with the word *Remington* inscribed on the top in gold lettering. The sheath of a hunting knife the size of a small saber protruded from under his padded vest.

"Where have you been?" Patti asked. "I've been worried."

He brushed by her as if she were a piece of furniture. "Hunting," he grumbled. "Trying to bag a white-tailed buck or two. Groceries ain't gonna last very long around here now we got five people chewing on 'em."

My editorial mind required that the facts in this case, especially as they pertained to a homicide, must remain correct. Any exaggerations or inaccurate statements sent a kind of alarm off in my head. With Dwayne, it was a four-alarm fire. I felt a distinct need to remind him that since Billy was reported as missing, he would not be chewing on any of his groceries. Or anyone else's groceries, for that matter, as I was convinced the boy had gone into hiding in the woods and probably had little or no food with him.

Poor Patti had to be mortified at her husband's behavior, but she didn't say a word. And that was the hardest thing to understand of all. Though I'd always said he was a strange one, this was my first experience with this kind of hostility within the family circle. The obvious attempt at getting me to go away was pathetic. Especially since deer season didn't start until October, and even then the tags are quite limited.

Dwayne had stumbled to the refrigerator and was downing a can of beer. The moment he turned his back, I looked at her with a what-the-hell? gesture. Patti grimaced, rolled her eyes in his direction and with a tiny but terribly intense shake of her head sent me a non-verbal message.

Don't say anything to him or in front of him about it. Instead, we waited, silently, while he clumped down the hall,

31

counting the seconds until he was out of hearing range. Before disappearing around the corner, he glared at the two of us.

"You coming?" he said to Patti.

"In just a minute. As soon as I finish cleaning up."

As soon as he had finally retired and closed the door behind him, Patti and I went back to the counter. This time, she plugged in the coffee pot and I grabbed the brandy. She was still a little defiant, ready to defend her new husband at all costs, but at the same time embarrassed that he had been so rude.

I said, "So, what's with the Great White Hunter?"

She sighed, giving a sad shake of her head. "I don't know what his problem is. I thought the sewer line problem was bad enough, though once we managed to get through it, we'd be okay. But then, he joined this *group*. Some kind of anti-government organization where he and some of his buddies get together on the weekends, have these secret little meetings, and every once in awhile they do these *exercises* out in the woods."

"Exercises? What the hell kind of exercising do they do up there in the boonies? And why do they need so many guns? Bench presses in the dirt and leaves, maybe? Using a case of ammo for weights?"

"No. It's not like that at all." Looking like the cat who went to swallow the canary but got a mouth full of bird seed instead, Patti leaned on the counter and said, "You know, they do have a right to exercise their free speech and Constitutional rights."

"Rights to do what?"

"To bear arms."

"Oh, for crying out loud."

"Kath, it's their *right*. Their way of making a political statement." She sat down and chewed nervously on the inside of her lip. "Dwayne seems to think it's his duty to speak out against the government. They say the government's after them."

"Good God, Patti. We're talking about a militia movement here. You know that, don't you? The same kind of people who bombed Oklahoma City."

"Yea. I know. I know," she said, almost in tears. "How'm

I supposed to stop him? I've tried talking. Their leader says they're not to listen to anyone who doesn't totally agree with their position. He says that if anyone they know vocally disagrees with their little war games, they're probably conspiring with the FBI and therefore are to be considered an enemy."

"Who's this leader of theirs?"

"I don't know. He's keeping his identity secret. To thwart off any attempts at assassination, they say."

"Patti, presidents and governors get assassinated. Nitwits like these get thrown in the pokey for the criminally insane. Oh, brother. Kiddo, I don't think..."

"That's the whole...." Suddenly, she jerked to attention, eyes wide and swinging toward the hall. "Shhh", she whispered, finger to her lips and listening intently. "Let me handle him."

One heart-stopping minute later, Dwayne slammed the door open, shouting. "Don't stop talking just cause I'm here. You telling your dear sister about the Forces For American Arms and Liberties?"

"Not exactly." In a sudden switch of temperament that should have nominated her for an Academy Award, Patti moved to his side and wrapped her arm around his waist. "I was explaining how it's every citizen's right and responsibility to stay politically aware and in good physical condition."

I was numb with disbelief. Anyone who hadn't spent their childhood watching this little pixy waltz through life, amazingly untouched by life's subtle pranks, would have thought that she was quite comfortable with her husband's stunts. But I knew better. "See there?" she said, grabbing a chunk of tissue-thin skin from somewhere under his T-shirt. "Not an ounce of fat. Dwayne really keeps himself in good shape. Sweetie here, can go...," she gave him a passionate thump in the ribs, "...all night long if he wants to. And he seems to *want to* most of the time." Pacified, he leaned over and kissed her lightly, his wounded pride seemingly on the mend.

Again, I was shocked. The Patti I knew would never had made such a disgusting display in private, let alone in front of me. I'd heard enough. "Well, I'm going to bed and leave the countertops to you two lovebirds. The *Gazette* wants me to

33

keep a daily tab on the developments of this homicide. See you in the morning."

HAPTER FIVE

Monday. My first stop was at the Sheriff's Office. They were not releasing any information on Deputy Benjamin Jack nor answering any questions about where he was or when he'd be coming in. The dispatcher made a show of calling Jack's car phone, which he, of course, didn't answer.

While I was there, I also ran around the side of the building and popped in to chat with Police Chief Clancey. I truly wanted to work with him and to help them find the killer. I even permitted him to keep me waiting for ten minutes and even then, after I was escorted into his office, I got to stand in front of his desk and wait again while he finished a phone conversation. Minutes later, still standing, I had to wonder if my punishment for overstepping my bounds yesterday wasn't being stretched just a little too thin.

Finally, I was shown a brief summary of the coroners report from Mt. Vernon. The autopsy revealed the cause of death. She'd been shot, then stabbed numerous times shortly thereafter. "So what's next?" I asked.

I had to admire Clancey. Contrary to my concerns, he was all business. A professional doing his job, not allowing personal grudges to get in his way. He paused a moment, thick fingertips touching a small scar at his hairline while he studied his notes. "There's the other matter of the boy. Your statement mentions that he ran out of the house when he saw the victim's picture on TV. Have you seen or heard anything since then? What about the other boy, your nephew? Has he heard anything from Billy?"

"No, we haven't."

"How is it that these two boys wound up alone at the fair? Did they know each other previously? Say, from school?"

"My sister lives here in town. If you'll remember, you interviewed me at her house and her 10-year-old boy, Jeffrey,

35

who is a friend of the missing child. He and Billy are close to the same age. They wouldn't have known each other from school, since my sister only moved here this summer."

I paused, thinking it through before I answered. "The best I can figure out, is that they hooked up down at the fairgrounds. Whether they'd planned it that way, I don't know. They had been friends before that, I'm not sure just exactly for how long. But I can ask Jeffrey."

"What do you have that will help me to make a positive ID on this kid?"

"Well, let me think. He drank out of a Pepsi can at the house. I could probably dig that out of the garbage. It'll give us his fingerprints. I gave you his description. What else do you need?"

"I need to be absolutely sure that the name we were given is the correct one. Did he tell you his name himself? His full name?"

"No. My nephew did."

"The other ten-year-old."

"Yes."

"How about the first name, *Billy*? Did you refer to him directly by that name and did he respond?"

"Uh, yes. I did. The first name only. Not the last."

Clancey eyed me intently. I realized that he might use anything I said to back an indictment against the deputy sheriff. A man I had yet to meet. It would destroy the man's career, if not his life. Guilty or not guilty, I didn't want that on my conscience. Checking my watch, I noticed that I had just an hour and forty five minutes before I would have to call in to my editor. Time to go.

"Thanks for the information, Chief. I won't be taking any more of your time." Turning to leave, I added one last comment over my shoulder. "Let me know if there's anything else you need."

"I need a snapshot."

"Sorry. I wish...wait a minute! I do have some pictures from the fair. Dropped them off at the drugstore, yesterday. I think I can get you a perfectly good and recent picture as soon as they're back."

"That'll be fine. For now, until I'm sure there is a link

36

between the boy and the victim, we'll have to handle it as a separate investigation. But it will carry a high priority." Fingering that same scar, Clancey seemed to be pondering a decision. "I will tell you this. As the missing boy seems to be connected to the homicide and the probability of foul play as it concerns a ten-year-old is greatly increased, I've decided to handle the investigation as a possible kidnapping."

"So, what does that mean?"

"It means that I will have some of the best law enforcement this country has to offer, working on the case. Kidnapping is not only a state, but also a federal crime."

He handed me a form with three copies. "If you can take this with you and fill it out within the next day or two, I'd appreciate it. Write out the boy's description, as fully as you can. Try to think of all the little things. In detail, right down to the color of his socks. And I'll need to know everything that happened, from the time you first saw him up until he disappeared. If you like, you can even include any impressions you had at the time and any deductive reasoning. Let us decide if what you tell us has any bearing on this case or not."

Kidnapped. I crossed my arms as an uncommon dread scampered up my spine, playing havoc with the hair on the back of my neck. "He didn't want to go home. To the point of refusing to tell us who his parents were and where he lived."

Clancey jumped on that like a junkyard dog on a bone. "Would you say he was *afraid* to go home?"

Thoughtfully, I pondered that possibility. "I'm not sure I'd say that. But he did seem to be afraid of *something.* Or someone. I'm not sure just what it could be, he just wouldn't talk. Every time my sister or I tried to ask him a question, all we got was a blank look and a shrug. He'd end up everytime, staring at the floor. Of course, once he saw the broadcast about his mother, it was all over. The child was absolutely terrified."

"All right, what about his appearance. Did he appear to be well looked after? Had his hair been washed recently?"

"Well, that's another thing. He was scruffy, and definitely needed a bath, but he seemed....uncomfortable being so. For instance, when I called the boys to come and eat, he went first to the bathroom and washed himself. His hands, face, you know, really scrubbed himself and combed his hair. Without being told. And although he was obviously half-starved, his table manners were quite good. Even waited to be offered a second helping. How long's it been since you saw a ten-year-old kid with decent table manners?"

"Okay. I'll send out an ALL WEST on teletype for the boy. By the way," Clancey's hand closed around his coffee cup, almost obliterating it. "The fingerprints from the body of the victim have gone off to the FBI fingerprint section and to the Washington State Patrol ID section, to check against prints that are not already automated." He took a sip of coffee, his brow furrowed with worry. "A search of the downtown and the surrounding areas has been initiated, to see if the boy is living in the streets — so to speak. There's only one street in town, and the roads leading out of it. I've got several patrolmen already checking the alleys and storerooms of the stores which have a back delivery door. Some reports have been released to the media, asking for people to check any unsecured motor homes, shacks, and garages where a boy might hide." He leaned forward, his old office chair squealing from the effort. "I'll need you to get me those pictures and bring in that can. Be sure to pick it up by the very edge with pliers or something so the prints won't blur. Better yet, let one of my deputies come after it."

I needed something to run next to my story on Tiffany. "How about a picture? Anything. A high school yearbook, the employment records at the casino."

"Uh, sure. Let me see if I've got any copies," he said, rummaging through a file on this desk. He pulled out a 5 x 7 glossy portrait and handed it to me. "By the way, I'm going to ask you to go easy on any information you release as far as Billy is concerned. Let's face it. What we have here is a ten-year-old boy who may be the only one who can identify the killer, and might even have been an eyewitness. Add that to the fact that this victim was his Momma ...," Clancey shuddered at the thought. "He might not only know who killed his mother, but they could *know* that he knows and be hunting him down themselves."

He gave me a menacing look. "That's why it's important that you hold off on some of this until we can be sure the boy is safe." Our eyes held. He made a wry mouth. "I don't want to find out that what I have just said is plastered all over your front page."

"Hey, we figured that out, long ago. Don't think that you're the only one who cares about the safety of this child."

"Good. Then we understand each other."

There was just time to call Gunner before the next deadline. As much as I hated to, without interviewing him first and getting his side of the story, I'd have to mention the possible link between Deputy Sheriff Jack and the boy. The new classification of kidnapping would be the main slant of today's story, and I would certainly *not* be using what Clancey said about Billy being a possible eyewitness. I wouldn't even tell my editor.

Going down the front steps of City Hall, I spied Mayor Winthrop and Junior lurking next to my car. It looked as if they'd prepared an ambush. They'd certainly gained a whole new attitude since the scene with the receptionist yesterday morning, and were demanding to be given an interview. I agreed to talk to them this afternoon, and we made an appointment to meet in his office.

The next stop was the grade school. We were guessing that Billy was 10 or 11 years old and had probably attended fourth grade. Although classes would not convene for another 3 or 4 weeks yet, most of the office personnel were there, setting up for another school year.

The secretary showed me last year's class picture and the year before that, pointing out all the boys of Native American heritage. None of them were Billy. My description of him didn't ring any bells. Neither did they recognize the photo of the victim as a parent, other than having seen it on TV.

Marion Bell, the school's vice principal, seemed to be the most savvy and most helpful. I asked her if she had any ideas that could help us find this child. She thought the mother might have had some strong feelings about the so-called 'white man's school' and didn't want him to attend. It was an intriguing possibility.

"What happens if a kid just doesn't go to school?" I asked her. "Say, maybe the parent doesn't register him, do you have any way of keeping track of a child who just never shows up?"

"You know, that's a very touchy subject. Right now, the

schools don't have a provision for anything like the old-fashioned truant officer. It's entirely possible that a family could move here from out of state, and simply never enroll their children in school. We like to think that every parent with a school age child would have that child registered by the next school year. And most of them do. But, unfortunately, there are some exceptions. Native American children who live on the reservation are just like anywhere else. It's up to their parents to see that they get to school, one way or another. All we ask for when they enroll is the physical address, the parent's names, and proof that the child's immunizations are up to date."

"Is there any other way of fulfilling the education requirements other than going to this school, here?"

"Well, he could go to a private school. But, since there aren't any private schools in this area, it means that the child would have to live in another city with a friend or relative. Or they could place him in a boarding school. That can be quite expensive, especially for a kid that young. There's some talk about home schooling, the Governor just signed another bill. I haven't seen the exact language on it yet, but it basically means that a child can learn at home as long as his studies meet certain educational requirements. There's a lot of that going on, but they're supposed to be registered with the school board."

A teacher's lounge was at the end of the hall, with several middle-aged women relaxing on a couch. Quickly, I showed them Tiffany's picture, asking if they had ever seen her around the school or anywhere else. No luck. They'd never seen her before.

A quick check at the casino also drew a blank. No one was there except the janitors, who wouldn't let me in and advised me to come back in the late afternoon. They either wouldn't or couldn't give me the names of the Tribal Chief or any of those who sit on the Tribal Council. There was nowhere to go but back to the park where it had all happened.

When I arrived, the murder scene and the entire park for that matter was crawling with cops and reporters on the run with a cameraman huffing along behind. Parking had become such a problem that the State Patrol was out directing traffic.

Clancey was at the murder scene, blocking a particularly insistent reporter from ripping right through the yellow tape in order to get a close-up of the blood which had puddled in the wet grass. He turned at my tap on the shoulder and shook his head when I asked if there were any new developments on the case. He was obviously frustrated, as were the rest of us. We all knew that with every passing day the odds were tapering off that this crime would be solved and the killer brought to justice.

I sauntered over to the river, letting its whispering rush calm my nerves while I went over the events of the last few days. Checking my watch, I noted that it was just 1:30. I could probably put Gunner off for another two hours before deadline, *if* I had a good enough excuse. I hated having to rehash the same old things from the last few days, and using the *alleged* incriminations about a Deputy who had yet to be offered the chance to defend himself really bothered me. I needed something more concrete. And stuffy old Mayor Winthrop wouldn't add much.

I'd been walking along the edge of the mighty Skagit River for some time, when I noticed a spot on the bank where a boulder and a pile of old driftwood had been used as a kind of stairway to scale the twelve-foot-high bank. Scrambling up the sandy incline, it wasn't long before I was on the same path that Jeffrey and I had trod just hours ago. It was cooler here in the shade by a good 10 degrees, and offered a lovely tranquillity.

I slipped under the graceful boughs of a huge cedar tree, bending almost double to keep its tiny needles from prickling my bare neck. When I looked up, a man was standing directly in the path....and the very force of him made me stumble backwards a few paces and draw a startled breath. Though he was not in uniform, there was no doubt as to his identity.

Deputy Sheriff Jack was a stout and heavy-shouldered Native American somewhere in his early forties. A tangle of black hair as thick and untamed as a wild horse's mane protruded from under a baseball cap. There was an intenseness about him, a personal power so strong that I could almost see it rippling around him like heat waves.

I took a jagged breath and said, "I've been looking for

41

you." The deputy stared for a moment, as if angry at me for interrupting his privacy and for who knows how many other sins: for poking my nose in where it didn't belong, for being vitally alive while someone he had once loved was dead, and maybe even for being white. He motioned to a large log where we might sit.

It didn't take long for me to wish that I had met Deputy Benjamin Jack under different circumstances. Although he'd never be considered handsome, he was good looking in a rough kind of way and, I trust, from the occasional slide of his bright black eyes, didn't seem to mind having to look at me either.

I briefed him on the same information I'd given Clancey and confirmed the fact that Billy was indeed his son and that the victim was his ex-wife. He was mostly sullen and noncommunicative, seeming to take more interest in an up-turned leaf and the slightly damaged bark of an alder tree than anything which I might be able to tell him. He asked no questions nor seemed to making any judgments about my presence. He simply accepted the fact that I was here and that I was talking...at that particular moment.

I blamed this on his mourning for the victim and a deep concern for Billy. He turned slowly and for the first time looked at me straight on when I began to explain how I first met Billy at the fair and that he and Jeffy were playmates. Eager to show him the spot upriver where I'd found the footprint, I said, "Come on with me. I want to show you something."

Maybe he saw my excitement as a cheap, flirtatious way of extracting information that the other reporters didn't have and maybe he didn't. Or maybe his human need for an affirmation of life in the face of such a horrific death, had overshadowed his ability to think clearly. And maybe it was simply time I got back to civilization. But the moment I mentioned that we might venture deeper into the forest together, he replied, "You reporters will do anything for a story, won't you?"

I resented the audacity of this man. Whether it was the slow rumble of his voice that admittedly had me ready to swing from the maple branches, or his agony over the missing boy, I wasn't sure. He was, after all, a public servant of the same judicial system that had yet to serve him much justice. And that didn't seem fair. But the astonishing part was that none of this showed outwardly but seemed to quantum leap from his heart to mine. It all meant that this guy was bothering the hell out of me, and he seemed to be mocking me for it.

Momentarily stunned, a sudden burst of self-deprecating emotion exploded in my gut and I was overcome by a need to prove my worthiness as a reporter, a woman, and God-only-knows what else. "There is some evidence out there," I said, ever so righteously. "...which, I believe, may be crucial to the search for your little boy. And I thought you might want to look at it with me before I turned it over to the hordes."

Giving me his full attention, *finally*, he said, "What kind of evidence? Where?"

"It's a foot print. Looks like it belongs to a child. Jeffy and I spotted it last night just before dark. Which, incidentally, does *not* match his shoe but is consistent with what I last saw Billy wear. An old pair of tennis shoes. All my efforts to get you on the phone were to no avail. Haven't you ever heard of an answering machine?"

I was beginning to sort through the surge of hurt feelings, and realized that I was steamed in more ways than one. Yes, he did exude a kind of chemistry that definitely affected my body temperature and, yes, a long walk with him up a quiet river bank would certainly fire up a certain sensation that I'd have trouble keeping hidden. But he had acted like an ass, and even reporters, or at least *this* reporter, had her pride. "And I highly resent your inference that my offer to point this spot out to you, as a cheap way of getting a story."

His cheeks would have shown a flush, if they hadn't already been the color of well-tanned leather. "I'm sorry," he said. "Wasn't thinking straight. If you'll show the way, I'll be happy to look at your evidence."

For the next 15 minutes or so, we walked in a strained kind of closeness with only the crunch of gravel beneath our feet and the occasional snap of a twig to break the silence. Occasionally, our shoulders would touch on the narrow path, sending shivers along my spine and causing my throat to constrict. In the most difficult places, his hand was warm and strong as he helped me climb up and over a fallen log or scale a pile of boulders.

Perhaps I should have kept my mouth shut, or used more diplomacy, but I'd had relationships before which had started out on a mostly sexual attraction and I was determined to never again try something so stupid. His face showed nothing of the torment I was going through, and I had to wonder if I had blown my one and only chance to really know this man. Or perhaps he was so totally consumed in his concern for his son, it left him with little ability to concentrate on anything else. It made me painfully aware that he may never feel anything for me but a momentary physical attraction that had already faded to indifference.

Even so, it was still better than a cheap affair, doomed before it began, with no heart or soul invested into it. From here on, I wanted a relationship with a real chance to develop into a solid commitment. Or nothing at all.

We reached the spot where the shoe print was imbedded into the dirt. Benjamin carefully removed the large round of bark that was covering the print and stared at it for a few minutes.

"Do me a favor," he said, carefully replacing the chunk of bark. "Have you met Police Chief Clancey?" At my nod, he said, "He's a fair man. Honest. As far as I know, you should be able to trust him. Tell him about this print and that you think he should get a plaster mold done."

"But..."I thought you'd be the one to..."

"At this point in time, he'd be able to expedite matters with a lot less hassle than I can. What's important here is that the mold is done right away before the print gets too dry and crumbly."

At that point, Deputy Jack loomed over me, setting all my sensors on high with little energy left over for my brain to work. My breath caught and my heart raced as I knew that with only the slightest provocation I could have been deep and warmly kissed. I waited, wondering what would happen if indeed I....

Ben's deep voice interrupted my fantasies. "I'll be in touch," he said, squeezing my hands, his black eyes lit up with controlled passion. "Don't worry about finding me. I'll find you." Already backing away into the depths of the large cedar, he added, "And don't tell Clancey or anybody else that you saw me." Then he was gone, retreating into the somber sighs of the forest.

Drawing myself upright, I realized that once again I just had time to get to a phone before deadline. But this time, thanks to Deputy Sheriff Jack, I had something new to say.

Most all of the major stations had set up in the park, preparing to shoot live for their 6 o'clock newscast. Channel 2 had set up close enough to the crime scene that the tree under which the victim had been killed could be seen in the background. Mayor Winthrop and Junior were standing by.

At once, Bernie Goldman, a photographer from our paper, stormed to my side.

"O'Shaughnessy. What the hell's going on? I come all the way out here to get some shots for your Indian kid story, and you're not only late but you look like something the dog drug out of the river. Gunner's gonna have both our hides."

"Get me a telephone."

"You're going to call a story in? Now?" He was incredulous to the point of sputtering. Any moment now, he'd lapse back into the Yiddish he'd learned at his grandmother's knee. "You should have been here hours ago. Every newspaper in the state has a story on this, except for the *Gazette*."

"Oh, yes we do." I proceeded to the little log structure that housed the restrooms, and dropped a handful of quarters into the pay phone.

Gunner answered on the first ring. I didn't let him get started on me, but simply talked louder when he started complaining. "Look, have you ever thought that the reason why I'm late is because I have been tracking down some important leads? We're talking breaking news here that no one else has got, Gunner. No one."

"O'Shaughnessy, I'm sorry. Tomorrow's paper's already gone to press, and we can't afford to hold up the run now. And as far as your Eagle Ridge assignment, I think you're too damn involved. I understand that this is your family, but you've gotten too emotional over that kid. We're gonna have to replace you on that project. At least until you can learn to be on time."

"Gunner, if you'd stop complaining long enough, I could have used Bernie's laptop and had the thing written by now.

I'm telling you, this is some stuff that even the authorities aren't aware of yet."

"Then what is it? Tell me."

"Damn it, Gunner. I talked to the Deputy Sheriff, okay? The father of the missing boy. There's a lot of new leads and I damn sure don't have time to argue with you about it. You either trust me or you don't. So, fire me now and I'll call the Herald in Everett, or get out of my hair and let's get the show on the road here."

"Kathy, you know I hate it when you're like this. Mayor Winthrop called, said he and his son have been promised they'd be interviewed and you haven't even talked to them yet."

"Screw Winthrop! Besides, I've already got a few quotes from him." I looked at my watch. "Theoretically, we've got less than three minutes left before the press starts to roll, and you know as well as I do, that they're always a little late." I winked at the photographer, all the while counting seconds. "Come on, Gunner. Take a chance, just this once." From the corner of my eye, I could see Bernie shaking his fat head, looking absolutely woeful.

Gunner barked into the phone. "You know very well I can't make a decision like that. We'll talk it over after you get back."

I snorted. What he actually meant was that he'd report me to the publisher, who answered directly to the owners, and who looked upon any extra expense with extreme criticism.

"Fine. But you're going to look pretty silly when your own reporter gives the biggest scoop of the year to the Herald. And you're still putting out some garbage that isn't even true! Tell *that* to your damn publisher for me. Not even you, Gunner, can suck up good enough to make up for that kind of boner." I paused, then said in a tone of total resignation. "Look. It's too late now, anyway. I'll see you when I get back. Okay?"

"I'll expect you here, in my office, by 5:30. Maybe Webster, from Accounting, will stop in."

"I won't be there."

He breathed into the phone, an uncomfortable moment. "When, then?"

"I don't know. This is my family, and I won't leave until I'm sure they're okay. And I'll be damned if I'm going to let this tribe take another rap for something they didn't do."

"You could lose your job over this. You better think about it, if a bunch of damn Indians are worth it."

I was really starting to simmer and that last crack, a racist slur if I ever heard one, was about to push me over the edge. "I might *quit* my job over this, and explain to your precious newspaper association, in detail, why it's impossible to work for a boss who's also a bigot."

I could hear him grinding his teeth, agonizing over his decision. Either way, it would cost the paper some money and make them some money. Replacing a story at this late date meant they'd have to delay the press run until I was finished writing it, and start all over again. A hard call to make.

"All right, dammit! I'll give you five column inches. No more. And this better be good, Kathleen, if you want to work as a journalist in this town, *ever again*." He slammed down the phone.

I looked at Bernie. "Where's your laptop? I've got two minutes, tops."

When I'd finished, I strolled back to the rivers edge, felt the sun on my face, the cold spray as I tossed a rock into the water. Bernie had followed me with his Nikkon, even though the need for it was no longer required.

I'd never felt so alive. I'd never before felt the top of my head tingle or the thrill of walking two feet off the ground. And I'd never before known that the reason every eye at that park was on me, not because I wrote articles for a Seattle newspaper, but because there was something shiny about me that had never shone before. And that something had happened in this last hour that had never happened before and it had changed me forever. And that Bernie's camera, in its filtered kindness, would capture this moment and keep it for me forever.

Besides having the scoop of the century, I had met a man who thrilled me down to my socks. An *extremely* interesting man, who'd touched a place in my heart that, before now, I hadn't even known existed. It's no wonder that they headlined my story on the top half of the front page, and after the paper hit the streets, Channel 2 paid a pretty penny for a 5 second spot.

CHAPTER SIX

Hours later, Clancey caught up with me in the building department's archives, researching some of their old ordinances. He was not happy. I really couldn't blame him, as our newspaper had hit the streets about Deputy Jack's flat out denial of the inferences, he had not, after all, been charged with anything yet, before the Police Department had been informed. It had been necessary that I wait that long before telling him, in order for my scoop to be fully effective.

I held up one hand as if stopping traffic. "Before you even start, you have to let me explain."

"Then start explaining. How do you know what Deputy Jack said and where was he when you last saw him?"

"I never said I *saw* Deputy Jack. I left a message with your office, that I had received a statement from excellent sources and that he categorically denies all charges, inferences, and rumors that he had *anything at all* to do with his ex-wife's murder and his missing son. That he will not only be searching for the boy, but also for the killer of his ex-wife. He will do this in his own way and on his own vacation time. And that may or may not include his law enforcement training, his Native American beliefs, or any combination of the two. And I, for one, think it's silly that you don't have him lead the search." My statement only served to make Clancey even more unhappy.

"That is contrary to the conditions of his administrative leave and an affront to an on-going investigation. And even though he has not been charged as a suspect, I will not abide his interference in this case. Not even in the search for the boy. Tell him that when you next see him."

"I repeat, I never said I saw him nor do I now state that I have seen Deputy Benjamin Jack. And I have made no plans to see Deputy Jack at any definite time during this investigation." By Clancey's ominous stare, he was only too aware that

48

no journalist will willingly reveal a source.

Clancey's face was red as a beet and I was beginning to worry about his blood pressure. "But," I said, hoping to make peace. "Should I just happen to see him, I'll be more than happy to give him your message." I let him think about that for a moment, then added, "By the way, I also left a hand-drawn map with explicit directions to a spot on the river bank that had a footprint consistent with the look and size of Billy's shoe. I hope you got the message and will make a plaster cast of it."

And with that, having done enough damage to the mental health of the esteemed police chief, I fired up my old Porsche and sped off to my sister's house. There were a few loose ends I still needed to tie up for today.

At my arrival at Patti's house, I found her and her husband preparing to go to a meeting of the city council. They'd hoped to leave Jeffy with me.

"There's a public meeting tonight at the Community Hall," Patti said. "They're going to be voting on the sewer and on the new road. Somehow, we've got to convince them that they can have their damn sewer and their road, but they're going to have to do it without driving us off our land. Wish us luck."

"Luck, hell. Think I'm going to sit here while you two are having all the fun? I'm going too."

The hall was already packed by the time we got there. The three of us and Jeffy, found seats toward the back of the room.

"Okay," I said to Patti. "Point out who each of these people are, and how they relate to you in everyday life. Who are they when they're not in here, where do they work, and where do they live."

"See those six lined up on the long tables, over there on the left? That's the city council. The first one owns a real estate company here in town and is in partnership with his brother, as a developer. They'll be building a large apartment house on the sewer line, which means that the sewer going in is absolutely essential to them getting a permit to build."

"And he's sitting on the city council?"

"Yea. He might actually sit out the vote, which doesn't mean a hill of beans because he's been there for the last two years or so. Plenty of time to make the deals and to buy up

49

what land they need insofar as knowing what will be developed next and what will come after that. The whole time it took to plan the details of exactly where the sewer line would run and who would be putting it in. His name is Rafferty. I see here...," she thumped the agenda sheet put out by the city, listing the items that would be discussed and voted on tonight. "...his brother, Rafferty, the developer, will be making his pitch tonight. Probably be taking the initial steps to get things started."

"I can't believe these guys. Man oh man, talk about cronyism. And no one's stepped in to say anything about it?"

"Not yet."

I almost understood why Dwayne had been so upset with the city's management of the sewer affair, although I could never agree with his choice of targets on whom he vented his anger.

Police Chief Clancey and one of his patrolmen had taken their positions at the entrance where we came in. It was doubtful that any of these hillbillies would stage a ruckus as they all seemed very reserved and almost shy. But should a knock-down-drag-out brawl break out, their long arm of the law was ready to pick them up by the scruff of their necks and lock them behind bars.

Patti had gone on to the next councilman. "The second guy is retired. Used to work for the Forest Service. Next to him, the third guy is our neighbor. He also owns half interest in the bakery in town and, I think, part interest in another big apartment complex they just built last year. It hasn't been quite the going concern they seemed to think it would be. Evidently, only about a third of the apartments have ever been rented out."

She paused, her attention momentarily on Dwayne. He was squirming in the hard metal seat, complaining that they were too far back to hear anything. She pacified him with an assurance of a loud-speaker system, then returned to her appraisal of the council members. "The next guy and his wife own the drug store and he is the main pharmacist. She runs the register. Oh, and by the way, their grown daughter works in the Police Department as a clerk." She eyed me. "I believe you already met her." I rolled my eyes upward, remembering the blond snit in the mini-skirt. Patti poked me in my side, then went on to the next member. The guy next to him is a retired dairy farmer. I don't know much about him but I guess he used to own a dairy farm just out of town. He sold the farm about a year ago."

An older man wearing a worn pair of bib overalls over a ragged thermal undershirt was sitting on my right. He smelled of the soil and of a life of hard labor in the hot sun. By the way he was working his gums, it was plain to see he had overheard our discussion and would soon burst at the seams if he wasn't allowed to join in.

And they say that women *like to gossip.*

I bent over to ask him if he knew anything about the council member in question.

He did, and with a toothless grin and a lick of his brown, leathery lips, the old-timer shook our hands and introduced himself as McClusky. Mac, for short.

"The little lady there was talkin' about Ole Man Smitty. Well, there's more to that story than most people in these parts would like you to know." At this point, the old-timer pulled a square of Red Devil chewing tobacco out of his overalls pocket and sliced off a wad the size of his thumb.

"Yes, of course. We'd love to hear it."

One bony knee hooked over the other, the wad making a bulge in his left cheek, the old man settled in for a little storytelling. "Well, Old Smitty, he used have a dairy farm just about 5 miles or so out of town. Over the years, the town just kept growin' and growin', and before you knew it, they'd annexed his land into the city boundaries. Course, that changed everthing about running a farm and caused Smitty all sorts of headaches with all the new rules and such. Couldn't keep up with all the finicky requirements they got now for having a working dairy within city limits, let alone the dad-blamed taxes. He tried, and worked, and done everthing a man could do. Couple years ago, he gave it up. Fought it for a long time, went to court 'n all. Finally, he just threw up his hands and sold out. He and his wife moved into a house right on the edge of town."

"How big of a farm?"

"Oh, he musta had twelve or fifteen milk cows. And with

51

that many cows, there's always some calves and a few ponies for the grandkids. Add that to the machinery, you know, tractors, hay-baling equipment, tools and saws and such, it all adds up. Course, there's no doubt the machinery was old and wearing out, no money to buy replacements you know, but, knowing Smitty, they was probably in damn good working order. But you know how it is, nowdays. You don't keep up with the requirements, they gonna get you in the end. And sure enough, the whole damn farm was auctioned off. Everthang. One day he was a farmer, the next day he wasn't. A man's whole way of life, finished." He snapped his arthritic fingers, albeit it took two or three tries. "Just like that."

"What did he do with the proceeds of the sale? "

"I don't rightly know if he ever invested any of the money or not. Or even had any left over to invest. There was all them back taxes and attorney's bills to pay, let alone the doctor's bills. I do know that it just about broke Smitty's heart when he had to sell out. That farm had been in his family for three generations. His grandpappy homesteaded that place back when there wasn't nothing here but a lot of Indians and a few old Tarheels workin' the shake mill. I do know for sure that he'd always promised it to his older boy once he got married. All that's over now, and the kids all grown and scattered. Oldest boy moved to Seattle little over a year ago and the last I heard, he'd got hisself a drug problem and died of an overdose."

The old farmer shook his head sadly, and spat tobacco juice into an empty tin can he'd stored under his chair.

"Like to finished poor ole' Smitty. Wife never has got over it. The boy was kind of her favorite. Surprising part of it was when Smitty ran for city council. Nobody that knew his predicament woulda ever believed it. But, there he sits. Don't miss a meeting, either. I kind of always wanted to believe that he was tryin' to make sure that they never do this again to any other unsuspecting family."

Just then, with a minimum of pomp and ceremony, the Mayor started the meeting. This was followed by the city engineer who read a short statement, outlining tonight's purpose. Junior Winthrop was there, looking like he would gladly leap into his father's shoes at a minute's notice, never mind the pesky notion of having first to go through an election.

Only one man, besides the Mayor, was dressed in a suit. He looked tall, even while sitting down as he thumbed nervously through a handful of loose papers. After a few minor items, the Mayor announced that the public meeting was in session and asked if anyone wanted to speak.

As the tall, well-dressed guy stood up and approached the microphone, Patti poked me in the ribs and whispered, "That's the developer who's trying to put in that big apartment complex, up the street from us and is brother to the councilman. Name's Rafferty."

Rafferty cleared his voice and hunched over the microphone in a kind of hungry position. "Eagle Ridge is growing by leaps and bounds. Everywhere we look, people are moving in, businesses are starting up and there's even some businesses coming in from out of state." He waved the handful of papers at the council, and proceeded to declare the town dangerously close to drying up and blowing away without his sightful input to attract new businesses and bring unprecedented prosperity to its citizens.

"This can mean more jobs and more opportunities for the residents already living here and more revenue for the city," he crowed. This was delivered with much finger-waving and podium-thumping, along with some dire warnings that, without his help, the next rain would surely wash Eagle Ridge downriver and overflow most every one of their septic tanks.

"And when the rains do come, those old septic tanks are not going to be able to hold all the extra water. Which means that the yards and roads and ditches will be flooded with... well, let me just say, some stuff that shouldn't oughtta be laying in the middle of anybody's front yard. Let alone, a front yard where children play."

The upshot of his lecture was that the council should pay him top dollar to put in a new sewer line down Pine Road. Patti's street. He nodded to the council and gave his brother, the council member, a longer-than-necessary look before sitting down.

Several other people got up to speak, mostly concerned over the cost of the hook-up fee and sewer assessment. And though each one of them professed the lack of funds to pay for a sewer line, none of them was a strong enough speaker, and

probably more than a little intimidated by the long row of au-
thoritarian figures staring back, to evoke any kind of a response from the city council. Only one citizen, probably the
same one whose broken-down septic system was flushing into
their front yard, urged the council members to take action,
saying they desperately needed the sewer and would they please
get it going.

I purposely stared at Dwayne and said, "Aren't you going
to say anything?"

"Naw," he whined, scrunching down into his chair. "Won't
do no good. You can tell they already made up their minds."

Patti's attempt to goad her husband into action also served
no purpose. "Then I will," she announced, rising up out of her
chair.

This only served to infuriate Dwayne. "Sit down," he
hissed, gesturing in an almost violent manner at her. "I said
sit! You ain't sayin' nothin."

Patti did as she'd been ordered, her face red with embar-
rassment from the commotion Dwayne's anger had caused and
the looks from the other people sitting nearby.

Frustrated by his apathy, I pleaded for a nominal effort.
"Dwayne, if you don't at least try, and put your objections on
record...."

The Mayor picked up his gavel. "Anyone else? Any more
speakers?" He was ready to bring the public meeting to an
end. "Last chance."

He damn sure won't stop me from talking. I jumped up
and reached the microphone in about five steps. "Mayor
Winthrop, I have something to say on this subject."

The mayor's expression was sour as he recognized me as
the out-of-town reporter who had already caused him a lot of
grief. "This is for the residents only, who will be personally
affected by the project."

"I'm speaking for the Hickman's, who live at 1412 Pine
Road."

"Are you saying you represent Mr. Hickman?"

"At this moment, yes."

Deferring to the city attorney, the Mayor covered the microphone, and began what looked like a heated, though whispered, argument. He seemed to be pressing a point, causing

the city attorney to shake his head, saying 'no' with every bit of body-language he possessed. The city attorney knew, as well as I did, that they didn't dare refuse my right to speak at an open public meeting. I was certain though that the mayor was trying to block my statement anyway, regardless of the consequences. He covered his face with one hand, in an obvious attempt to keep anyone from lip-reading his arguments.

Talk about a railroad. Moments later, mouth twisting as though he'd been eating lemons for a living, the mayor rapped on the table and said, "Go ahead."

"Members of the council, Mayor Winthrop, good evening. I hold here," I said, "...a letter from the building department, stating that a proposed sewer is about to be voted on. This sewer will stretch across some 1200 feet of my sister's property." I then repeated the figures I'd been given by Patti, in excess of $60,000. "I wonder if your office realizes, or any of the council members realize, the full extent of what you're asking for. You see, you are making it absolutely impossible for this young family to live on their land and in their own home."

"In other words, they are being forced to sell off their own property to the first man-Jack to make an offer. Somehow, I feel that land cannot help but fall into the hands of one of these developers. Now, I am willing to give you the benefit of the doubt and understand that the council may not have realized that this development would cause this young family such a hardship. But, I also feel that now you have become aware of this travesty, you will most certainly take steps to correct it.

"Council members, please vote this measure down. Please, do not jerk their....," with a sweeping gesture, I indicated Patti and Dwayne. "...home away from them, only to be razed by the bulldozers and chopped up into building lots. There are deer on that lot, not to mention the trees. Trees that incidentally, are not native to this area. Trees that were planted some forty years ago. Council members, to vote this measure into law will simply mean one thing. That Eagle Ridge cares more for the deep-pocketed developers than for tax-paying citizens. That some stranger blowing into town in his rented car and borrowed money has more weight with this administration than the voters. And how, pray tell, can that be? If this should be

55

true, there can be only one answer. That the building permits, fees, and bloated taxes mean more to this governing body than do their own citizens. Can you afford this, Mayor Winthrop? Can your son's political career afford it?"

Some council members were astonished, not only by the statement I made of local politics but also the hard facts of this project and how it hurt this young family. Others were poker-faced, not allowing me to read their inner thoughts. And yet others were obviously mad as hornets. I had definitely made a few friends, and a whole lot more enemies

The vote was put off until the next meeting in two weeks. Police Chief Clancey glared at me on my out of the building.

CHAPTER SEVEN

Tuesday. The casino was an impressive three-story structure, with the gaming rooms and restaurant off to the right and a 3-star hotel, which occupied an expansive area to the left and most of the top two floors. The decor outside was an interesting combination of logs and Native American art affiliated to this tribe.

Positioned over the double-wide doorway was a swimming salmon in deco art. Crafted by hand in good wood, it had been painted black with white, ghost-like eyes and looked as if at any moment, it might thump its strong tail against the wall and leap to a nearby stream. On both sides of the door, totem poles stood guard against evil spirits with carvings of a raven and a coyote, two of the more important mystical characters in much of Bastolak Tribe's culture. And though the area would be sufficiently lit up after dark, there was none of the glitz and glamour of Las Vegas or Reno.

My first stop was at the office. After several requests and a little arm-twisting, which included the use of my press pass as leverage, I was admitted in to see the assistant personnel director. His boss, Zeke Larson, was out campaigning.

Ethan Tibbs was a middle-sized man, his appearance not necessarily Indian nor any other ethnic origin. His main identifying trait was a pencil-thin mustache lining an even thinner upper lip. I asked him about Tiffany's background. "Tiffany came to us last November," he said. "From the Yakima area. She was a good worker, always on time, and a big favorite with all of her co-workers."

"Did you know her personally?"

Tibbs' mustache twitched with a downward pull, in what I could only suppose was his way of demonstrating grief. "I wouldn't say that. With over a hundred employees, it's impossible to know each one of them on a personal basis. But I knew *of* Tiffany and that she was a very personable young woman. Bright and friendly. In fact, she won Employee of the Month last March. We're all going to miss her."

"Do you know who her friends were? If she was dating anyone? Any old boyfriends lurking about?"

"I have no idea. I don't get involved in an employee's personal life."

"Surely, you'd have noticed a scorned lover hanging around, getting drunk and loud. Running up a big gambling bill."

"Not that I recall." He checked through her employment records. "There's nothing in here that would substantiate such a claim. And, I'm sorry to say, even if there was, personnel matters are confidential." He closed the file and stood, indicating that the interview was over.

I made a move as if I was more than happy to comply with his unspoken request. At the door, I suddenly turned as if I'd just remembered something. "I take it she lived on the reservation in Yakima. Was she originally a member of the Yakima Tribe?"

"I would have no idea."

"Can you tell me how long she's been here in Skagit County?

"No, only how long she was employed here at the casino. Tiffany was hired on when the casino first opened, about 15 months ago. She's been here ever since."

"Did she have any friends other than the people she worked with?"

Tibbs was shaking his head. I wasn't sure if it meant that he didn't know or that he refused to say. "I'm afraid I've told you all that I can. Sorry I can't be of any more help." He showed me out.

Lured by the aroma of a hot cappuchino, my next stop was the coffee shop. As I walked down the hall, I couldn't help but notice a room off to the side, which had been reserved for a museum of sorts for the Native American tribes of the Pacific Northwest. The Coast Salish and a number of their clans.

A quick peek revealed several glass cases that housed some very old artifacts made centuries ago by different tribes within the Central Coast Salish region. In one case were several mountain sheep horn rattles, carved with intriguing human-like faces. A sign next to them indicated that they'd been used as a cleansing device by shamans of the Cowichan clan.

Along the far wall were display cases and shelves, devoted particularly to the Bastolak Tribe, which owned the casino/hotel. Tattered baskets, both coiled and twined types and woven with interesting patterns, took up most of the space in one of the cases. Next to it was a separate case, holding a carved length of cedar, looking like a flat rolling pin with handles. The sign next to it indicated that shamans had believed, long ago, that it inhabited a spirit of its own, the *s.xpaya'xubiq*. A kind of peace-making spirit that inspired anyone who would hold it or even to be in its vicinity to express what was in their heart and to tell the truth. It had been used as a method of settling tribal disputes and was called a *s.qwedilic* board.

I moved on to the coffee shop. It was a part of the larger restaurant, called *Emma's Place*. The cook, a long-haired blond guy in his thirties, eyed me from around the kitchen corner. "Good morning," he said, as I took a seat at the counter. "What'll you have? Coffee? A bite to eat?"

Ordering a double-shot cappuccino, I told him I was from the *Gazette* and doing a story on Tiffany Jack. Obviously impressed, he shook hands and introduced himself as Brian Biringer. "Yea," he said, sweeping away the paper place setting and serving my coffee with the full china set-up, including the cloth napkin normally reserved for the formal dining room. "I saw your story in the paper."

I nodded, and immediately plunged into an interrogation about the murder victim. Had they been friends, had they socialized, and how much did he know about her personal life?

"Sure, I knew her and liked her. Everybody around here liked Tiffany. A couple of times she brought the boy in with her. On her days off, to pick up her check and stuff."

"Did you ever go out with her?"

"Me?" A smirk played around the corners of his mouth. "Uh, no. Never did date Tiffany. We were good friends, was all." In a gesture intended to change the subject, he offered me a fresh toasted bagel with cream cheese. "I'm the only one around

59

here that eats them. You might as well help me get rid of these before they're all dried up." I accepted with much thanks, realizing that I'd forgotten to eat breakfast and was hungry.

While I ate and sipped the hot coffee, behind him in what I guessed was a walk-in pantry, I heard a few thumps and the sounds of metal scraping against floorboards. The unpleasant sound gritted my teeth, but since Brian seemed to shrug it off as part of the daily routine, I did the same.

I tried again, rewording my former questions. "Certainly, a woman that pretty and personal to boot, is bound to be popular. Do you have any idea who she was hanging out with after this place closed up? Anyone ever give her a ride home?"

"I can't really say. How's that bagel?"

"Can't? Don't you mean won't?"

"Look, I'd like to help you. Really I would. I mean, it'd take a real slimeball to do something like that to anybody, let alone someone like Tiffany. But, friendly as she was, Tiffany was pretty private about her personal life. Seldom said where she had been on her days off. But when she worked, she worked hard and was always pleasant to be around."

Just then, a group of politicians and their mayoral candidate, Junior Winthrop, came trouping through the kitchen and dropped a handful of campaign buttons on the counter. I believed he was the same one I'd heard stumping for votes at the festival. Brian was replacing the tablecloths on the small tables under the window when they came in and he brightened considerably as they trouped through his dining area.

Junior acknowledged him with a high sign, and a sneer for me. I didn't really mind the snub, as a discussion with one of these fanatics would be about as stimulating as an enema. Heading for one of the back rooms, they all wore some stupid-looking hats and carried signs that claimed: "*A Vote for a Winthrop is a Vote for Fiscal Responsibility*."

Brian did his best to explain their behavior. "They have a breakfast here every Monday morning at 10 o'clock. Kind of a pep rally."

I shook my head, and said, "It's amazing what some people will do, in order to be elected. Isn't it? Absolutely amazing."

His reaction to my comment was surprisingly sour. "What do you mean by that?"

"Well, the stupid-looking hats, for one thing. Carrying signs everywhere they go. Willing to say anything, and I do mean *anything,* to get their guy elected. *Hello.* Am I the only one here that sees this behavior as a little radical?"

"In a democracy, voters have the right to support the candidate of their choice."

"Of course, they have the *right* to do it. They have the *right* to jump off a bridge if they want. I just said they looked stupid. Evidently, you don't agree." He simpered a bit, but seemed to be placated.

"Let's get back to Tiffany," I suggested. "How about her wardrobe? Did she dress well?"

"Oh, she'd show up in nice clothes now and then, evidently just having returned from a shopping trip. No one at casino asked her about it though, since she let it be known that she didn't want to talk about anything personal. Whatever went on before or after her shift, she just didn't talk about."

I pushed and I begged for some kind of clue I could sink my teeth into. But none of my efforts helped. Brian had begun to act very odd. The crack about the sign wavers must have touched a nerve. Where only minutes before, he was happy to share the last of his bagels, he now seemed decidedly uncomfortable about talking to me. Even where it concerned Tiffany. When I asked again if he hadn't seen the victim being escorted by a male of any kind, he snapped at me.

"No. I never saw Tiffany with anyone. You'll just have to take my word on it."

After that, he flatly refused to give me any more information, growing more and more nervous with each question asked. Some ten minutes later, he expressed a desire to go back to the cleaning of the stove...a chore that I found hard to believe would carry more merit than a discussion about a recent homicide of a professed good friend of his. He was saved by the ringing of a phone in the back. As he talked in low, somber tones, I paid my bill at the cashier in the front office and popped back in to leave a sizable tip on the counter with my business card. Quickly, I scribbled Patti's home phone number on the back, waiting a moment to see if he'd turn around.

Brian was still on the phone, facing away from counter. "No, I'm here alone. Susan didn't show up." The rest of conversation concerned some hamburger rolls that were too old, melons too green, and avocados that were hard as rocks. He didn't see me approach or leave.

I vowed to come back to the casino, this time at night when the dice were rolling. Perhaps in the smoky atmosphere of fortunes won and lost at the simple act of turning a card, someone existed who would be enraged enough at her murder to drop a few names and details. No matter how dangerous those details might be.

Tiffany's address wasn't in the phone book but had been on the police report I'd seen in Clancey's office. It was on Cedar Hill Road, not much more than a gravel road winding up into a mobile home park, surrounded by trees. Her place turned out be a fairly new double-wide in a string of assorted mobile homes and trailers. As I expected, the police had closed off that area with yellow tape.

Kids were everywhere. Digging holes in the yards with tiny shovels, racing from tree to shed in a game of hide-and-go-seek, and splashing through the dog dishes. Three toddlers played on a rusted swing set and took turns on an old tire with a squeaky chain. Still more shouts and hurrahs in the distance suggested that there were more games with the older kids in the wooded area just beyond the last trailer.

At the end of the dirt road that ran the length of the park, I spotted an older single-wide that looked like there was someone at home. A fairly recent Ford was parked in front and the strains of a morning TV show could be heard from inside. A little girl, I guessed to be about four, peered out of the front door. Her bright black eyes blinked and stared in unabashed wonder from under a shock of even blacker straight hair.

I entered the toy-strewn yard, conscious of several older kids speeding past on their bicycles. The oldest did a wheelly, screeching to a halt barely a foot or so away and glared at me. He then did an amazing thing. From a full stop, he hoisted the front wheel up and balanced for a breathless moment on the back tire in a great imitation of a rearing pony before letting it crash down with a thud.

I nodded and grinned in appreciation of his skill and continued walking toward the house, conscious of the many sets of eyes boring into my backside. My arrival seemed to be the most interesting thing to have happened all morning. Certainly the most hazardous, for me. Having elicited my full attention and apparently satisfied that I'd shown the appropriate amount of respect due a talented twelve-year-old, the boy turned his trusty two-wheeled steed to the streets and sped off after his friends.

As I approached a small front deck that led to the open door, the little girl seemed surprised that I had survived thus far and bobbed out of sight behind the door. My knock was answered by a sleepy-eyed heavyset male, a Native American I guessed to be in his fifties.

I identified myself and was invited in. He immediately called his wife from a back room then sat back down, drawing the four-year-old girl onto his lap. She was a cute little thing, terribly shy, peeking out from under her father's arm. Thumb in mouth, she continued to stare at me.

Her mother wore a necklace of hand-carved charms. From across the room, I made out a bear, a salmon, and an animal with a big fat tail. Probably a beaver. I took a chair in front of the picture window. As it was still early in the day, the warmth of the sun felt good on the back of my head. We introduced ourselves all around. Their names were Dan and Cassandra Deepwater, and Molly was the four-year-old.

I began the interview. Yes, they had known Tiffany: her son Billy had played with their children many times. Tiffany seldom had friends at her place, and if she was dating anyone they hadn't seen him.

"Tiffany wouldn't do that," Cassandra explained. "I mean, she'd never just bring a man home, around her boy. One thing about Tiffany, ever since her divorce, she was always worrying about the boy. Was he missing out on too much, wishing they lived closer to her own tribe so he could learn some of their ways while he was young. She grew up on the Yakima reservation, you know. I'm afraid it's been a little hard for her. A big change in cultures. When you've only known one way all your life, then everything suddenly changes and all of what was familiar is no longer there, it can be awfully hard on a person."

"But, she stayed here on the reservation, right? I was led to believe that she had lived here, with...with people of her own kind. I'm not sure what you mean by, *change in cultures*."

"Oh, well, no reservation is that much like another, since each one is primarily inhabited by a separate tribe. Each tribe is a sovereign nation unto itself. Each one with its own beliefs and customs. You see, the Yakima, they're Plains Indians. You know, like with the horses and the buffalo? Bows and arrows? Where here, on the coast, we're considered the canoe Indians. Our ancestors lived primarily on fish and clams. Occasionally they'd snare a rabbit or some venison."

"I see. So, would that influence her son's education? I mean, his *formal* education? I checked at the grade schools, but they don't seem to have any record of Billy."

"No, Tiffany was very particular about that. She was afraid he'd experience uh, well, nowadays they call it 'racial tensions.' Which is just another name for hateful ways. You know, children can be terribly cruel when they've not been taught any better." She said this with a lip-tightening frown, drawing herself up in a way that meant she had firsthand knowledge of the evils inherent in bigotry. "She didn't like what she heard about the things going on at school with the other kids from the res. You know, the name-calling and teasing. She took him out of that school while he was still in kindergarten and started him on home schooling."

"She'd get up extra early in the morning, just to go over his homework from the day before. Making sure his education included plenty of talk about his Indian heritage. Both Bastolak *and* Yakima. And then there were the pow-wows and different things going on at the Tribal Center. She always tried to see that he went to those, too. Lots of times, if she had to work, we'd take Billy with us."

"Did you ever see her with anyone? Say, a ride home from work? An outing on her day off?"

Cassandra shook her head, 'no'. "Not here at the house, around Billy."

"Is that her car?" I pointed to an old green Datsun, the back fender blackened with a crust of smoke. "Was this her only form of transportation that you know of?"

"No. She bought a new car, just recently. It must still be over at the casino."

Although Dan also worked for the casino, he had kept

64

different hours than Tiffany. Glancing at his wife, Dan moved uncomfortably in his chair and said, "We already told all of this to the policeman, yesterday. And I've got to get ready for work pretty soon."

I nodded, indicating that I was preparing to leave. "By the way, do you know a Benjamin Jack? Deputy Sheriff Jack? I hear he was Tiffany's ex-husband."

Standing up with Molly still riding one hip, Dan smiled. "Sure. I ought to. He's my cousin."

I moved towards the door. "Now that you mention it, I do see a resemblance." I wanted to blurt out that I had almost been kissed by this man of their tribe, was in a state of infatuation and blithely, wonderfully aware that the possibility, no, the *probability* existed that I would soon find myself falling head over heels for him. And I hoped that they wouldn't look upon me as one of the biased white-man pigs. But I held back, knowing it would take more than a lot of chest-thumping to make friends with these people who had been treated with such intolerance for so many years.

"What can you tell me about Billy? Do you have any idea where he might have gone? Did *he* have any friends he might be staying with? Obviously, the boy is frightened. I'm hoping he might have found shelter here on the reservation with some of the other tribe members."

"No one I can think of. Everyone knows that his father is looking for him, not to mention the Eagle Ridge Police Department."

I let my glance swing from Cassandra's face to Dan's. "The authorities have listed his case as a possible kidnapping. Do you know of any enemies Deputy Jack might have, who would be vicious enough to hold the boy against his will?"

Cassandra glanced at her husband, then looked down. I could have imagined it, but it seemed as if there was a certain resoluteness about the look that passed between husband and his wife. A look that had passed between husbands and their wives since time began. And here, in the home of a Native American family, it seemed to reflect the age-old prowess of a warrior rising up to defend his family and tribal members against the hosts of enemies outside their small village.

And she met his look with the raised eyebrow of a woman

who'd rather keep her man at home. Safe. *Keep quiet. We don't know this person. She's not one of us, and besides...she's white.*

Dan shook his head. "No one we could really mention at this point."

I stepped out onto the porch.

"Nice to have met you, Molly," I said. She smiled shyly, around a thumb so entrenched in her mouth that it was gathering drool, and clutched her father's shirt. During the entire time I'd been in their home, the child had continued to stare at me. To her mother I said, "You know, she is the cutest thing, but I can't figure out why she's looking at me that way."

"It's your hair," Cassandra said, a tiny smile digging dimples into her rounded cheeks. "Molly has never seen anyone with hair quite like yours."

Immediately, my hand went to the unruly mop. "Oh, I washed it this morning, but didn't have time to pin it up before I left, just ran a brush through it and let it fly. I must look an awful mess. No wonder I've gotten so many strange looks." I could feel the hot flush of embarrassment redden my cheeks as I drew the hair into a fluffy ball at the back of my neck and tried to stuff it under the collar of my blouse. Finally, feeling like a total fool, I rummaged through my purse to find a business card.

"I really have to go. If you think of anything else later on, *and I do mean anything*, please don't hesitate to call." With that, I started down the porch steps, fully prepared to bid them a hasty goodbye and race home to a shower and a giant dose of moisturizing conditioner on my notorious curls.

Cassandra reached out, as if to stop me from leaving. "No, no. It's not *bad*," she explained, a hand fiddling nervously with the charms. "Your hair, I mean. Please don't think I meant that there was anything *wrong* with it. Kathleen, your hair is fine. In fact, it's really quite lovely. Especially when you have the sunlight behind you, like it is now. It shines around your face like a halo. It's just....different. So yellow-blond, and so very curly. Molly's never seen anyone with blond *and* curly hair, that was so long." She shook her head and blushed, then clasped her hands over mine and pierced me with a look of great sincerity. "Your hair is beautiful. The color of the sun. Long ago, when the white man first came to the Northwest, our people thought anyone with hair the color of the sun had to be a god."

Feeling a little better, I thanked her and left. At the road, I was forced to unsit some teenagers who had clambered onto my car. Starting the Porsche, I let them listen to the engine for a minutes, revving it a few times just to let them hear its power, and promised to take them for a spin the next time I came around. Gearing into second, the little red car boomed and vroomed all the way down the hill.

Though no longer humiliated over my hair, I still felt some-what uneasy. There was something there that just didn't fit. For one thing, even though she had been a mother, it wasn't quite normal for a woman as attractive and friendly as Tiffany to not have had a single friend to invite home. No dates, no boyfriends, no parties. But she worked at a casino as a dealer. Maybe it was just me. I could be making a lot of value judg-ments about a woman who'd simply been trying her best to raise a child as a single parent.

Plus, I couldn't get Benjamin Jack off my mind. He'd be doing what he could to find the boy. But where could that be?

Turning onto Pine Street, I headed for Patti's house. There were calls to make. Gunner would have to be filled in on the recent disclosures, and I needed to start on tomorrow's article. I pulled into Patti's driveway, just as she and Dwayne were preparing to leave. There was only room for two cars, with the second sitting directly behind the other. I pulled back out and let them by. My sister waved as her passenger window came even with my driver's side window.

She waited for me to roll it down. "Hi, the door's unlocked. Jeffrey's home, feel free to make the both of you some lunch. He makes such a mess when he's on his own. We're going down to talk to the city engineer. He seems to be open to hear-ing our side of the story. Says he'll work with us on this sewer project, in any way he can." I nodded, noticing that Dwayne seemed to resent even this short exchange between sisters.

"You two can gossip later on," he grumbled. "After I'm out of earshot. That's the way you like it anyway. Talking about me ever time my back is turned." Patti turned away in embar-rassment, one hand covering her mouth. Sneering, evidently happy that he had ruined his wife's day, Dwayne shifted into gear and stomped on his gas pedal. Ripping up the road, his Toyota pickup threw gravel on the takeoff and peppered the hood of my Porsche.

I simmered for a few minutes, checking the paint job to see if there were any new nicks. Then went inside.

Rather than have Jeffy watch some soppy talk show, a teenage hooker was trying to tell her mother she had AIDS, I coaxed him into turning the television off and helping me make lunch. We decided on grilled cheese sandwiches and iced tea.

"I take it you and Billy camped out in your fort there by the river," I said, flopping the sandwich over in the pan. Jeffy looked up from the ice cube tray, scared. He'd been filling the glasses with ice. "It's all right." I paused, hoping he'd make a comment about the camping, wondering just what in the world was he afraid of. Or whom. I had a good idea, but wasn't sure how to approach it.

"I'm not going to rat on you, Jeff. I wouldn't do that. I just want to find Billy, that's all. If he's hiding and scared, we want him to know that it's okay to come home." I reached for a loaf of bread and a package of cheese. "Did Billy ever say anything to you about what his life is like on the reservation?"

Jeffy shrugged, and turned on the cold water to refill the ice cube tray. The child wouldn't speak.

"Did he seem to be happy living there?" Same thing. I poured the tea over the ice. "Do you know any other kids he was friends with? Anybody at all he played with, besides you? Come on, Jeff. Talk to me. This is your Aunt Kathy, remember?"

He swallowed, heaping two huge spoonfuls of sugar into his tea glass. "He used to talk about a dog. His Mom used to take him to somebody's house and he got to play with this dog."

"Did the dog belong to one of his friends?" He shrugged. "Think, Jeffrey. Was this at a boy's house? Or was it at one of his mother's friend's house?"

"I don't think it was another kid. Billy would have said if it was. Probably a grown-up. He didn't say anything about them, just the dog. It was like, a wolf-breed or something. A really cool dog, with one blue eye and one brown one. Smart, too."

We had sat down to eat, but I didn't have much of an appetite. I needed to see Benjamin Jack again. Not only did I have to talk to him about this dog Jeffy had mentioned, I wanted to ask him about Tiffany's family. Did they still live in Yakima? I'd need her maiden name to be able to find them in the directory. Her funeral was the day after tomorrow. Certainly, they'd been notified of her death. But they also would have an opinion about their daughter's murder and should be given the opportunity to make a statement to the press.

And yes..., I really needed to see Benjamin. I had to know. Would what I had seen in his eyes still be there? Or had I really seen anything? The man's son was missing, his ex-wife dead, and he could still be considered a suspect in the investigation. Not much basis there, for a romance. Who knows? Once this is all over, I may mean nothing more to him than that 'loud-mouth blonde from Seattle.'

My daydreams were interrupted by the sudden ringing of the phone. Bernie, the *Gazette's* photographer, was returning my call. He had been given an assignment to do a photo spread on the area, including some of the tribe's elders. The owners of the *Gazette* also owned a magazine that featured Washington State. I was to interview Chief Andrew Joe, of the Bastolak Tribe, and he was supposed to go with me.

Before leaving again, I'd need to check the recorder for messages. There was one from Gunner, demanding that I call in immediately. I sighed, and called in. He had just stepped out. "Is Anna, his secretary there?" They put me through. "Anna, tell Gunner that I'm putting a story together that features life on the reservation from the viewpoint of a few tribal members. The victims' neighbors, the casino, with a little folklore thrown in to make it interesting."

To Jeffrey I said, "Just keep on letting the recorder take all the messages. If there's anything for you, you can pick up." On the way out, I noticed that he'd begun to pick at his food, crumbling the bread crust onto the table. "By the way, a team of Little Leaguer's are having try-outs today. Why don't you go on down and play some baseball? Come on, I'll drop you off."

The body had been found in a lovely little park, fronting the Skagit River. There were a good two acres of well-kept grass and a few shade trees. Picnic tables had been set up here and there and a larger shelter with a brick pit large enough to barbecue a whole pig was attached to the other side of the restroom building.

Normally, the park was quiet, a nice place for a picnic or a lunch-time break. But the scene there today could hardly be considered normal. The crime-scene tape had gotten a little ragged from the breeze blowing up from the river. A hundred tramping feet had pummeled most of the grass into the ground and cigarette butts, hamburger wrappers and other litter had been strewn all around the garbage can and into the road.

Patrol cars still packed the parking lot and detectives wearing rumpled suits still gestured, took notes and mumbled to each other. A crew of lab technicians was vacuuming the grass in search of minute particles, which would hopefully provide them with more evidence. I walked around them and down to the water's edge. Then headed upriver. Jeffrey's fort was less than a twenty minute walk from the city park.

Inside the forest, there was a whole different world. The lean-to hadn't changed at all from yesterday, from what I could tell. The logs were where they'd been dropped, the rocks which had held the small fire looked cold and barren. Beyond the fort, I followed the trail back to where it joined the river again, found a fairly dry piece of driftwood and sat down.

A breeze had come up, blowing off the Skagit River and making frizzled knots of my ponytail. Overhead, the screech of a bald eagle gave rise to a rash of goose bumps up my arms. The huge bird dove straight down into the water, plucking a small salmon from under the cold ripples. Its wriggly meal clutched in its sharp claws, the bird soared away to the other side of the trees.

It was a cruel fact of life, I supposed. The idea that one life must die so that another might live. Watching the last ray of sun play on the water, my head dropped to my hands. *Please....if there is a God, don't let them hurt Billy. He's just a boy. A little boy.* Later, when the sunlight no longer reflected off the cold ripples, a sharp blast of cold wind swooped down from the north to buffet that side of my face. I found myself to be suddenly besieged with shivers.

Time to go back. Hurrying to my car, I checked my watch. There was just time enough to change clothes and get to the casino, if I wanted to watch the Channel 2 news team broadcasting live from their doorsteps. Many times, the TV reporters could attract some very important informants, simply by the excitement of seeing themselves on the screen.

On the way through town and onto the reservation, I kept an eye peeled for anything out of the ordinary. Anything that might lead me to that little boy. But there was no sign of Ben, or Billy, or anyone else for that matter. The streets and roads were almost empty.

I parked and proceeded to the casino's front door. Slowed by a woman in a wheelchair struggling up the ramp, I stepped out of the way – giving her husband and the casino doorman room enough to maneuver. In the two or three minutes it took them to get her situated, I paused and looked up to the surrounding hillside.

Out of the corner of one eye, I'd detected a slight movement in the trees. Not much, but as I was still spooked and a little shivery, it was enough to set my senses on high alert. Pretending to brush some lint from my dress, I chanced another peek in that direction. But whatever it was, was gone. Just the wind remained, which had picked up even more since my hike along the river. Once again, I felt a tremendous dread for a little boy who was all alone, possibly cold and half-starved. And once again, I yearned for the strong warmth of a man who resembled a bear and who made me feel as if the perilous world stopped where his arms began.

Just for the heck of it, I looked for dog tracks in the gravel parking lot or any piles that hadn't been scooped up by the gardener in the grassy area on each side of the sidewalk. A

71

few cigarette butts and a toothpick were all I found.

The Channel 2 newsteam was just winding up their broadcast. A man who I recognized by his photo in the papers had just been interviewed. Zeke Larson, the casino personnel manager, had hired Tiffany Jack and possibly knew things about her no one else could. He was also Junior Winthrop's opposition in the Eagle Ridge mayor's race.

Elbowing into the crowd that had massed around him, I hoped to make an appointment for the next day. But my hopes to interview him for the *Gazette* were soon dashed. After quickly shaking hands all around, Larson leapt into a waiting sedan and sped away.

The casino was crowded, the blackjack and roulette tables doing a brisk business. Mingling with the crowd, I ordered a glass of bottled spring water, then wandered over to the tables to watch. The dress I'd plucked from Patti's closet was black velvet and satin and I seemed to have caught the eye of most every male in the house. So much for my efforts to remain incognito.

An older man dressed in levi's and rundown cowboy boots placed a chip on a red square and won. His winnings went onto a black line running the length of the table top, which he lost. And on and on it went.

I was getting bored with it all, having no money to gamble with, when a rather heavy man I guessed to be in his late forties, handed me a pair of dice. "There you go, gorgeous. Bring me some luck and I'll buy your dinner."

"Bring you some luck, you say?" I laughed, thinking how I would love to have a little chat with old Lady Luck myself. "And how do I do that?"

"Blow it a kiss and toss it out there for me." And though the man was at least 100 pounds overweight, there was a kind of polished, suave look about him. His hair was the whitest blond I'd ever seen that didn't come out of a bottle, his eyes the crisp green of newly minted money. He was undoubtedly a man who'd seen it all so many times, he'd rediscovered his sense of humor. He introduced himself by the name of, "Montana."

I rubbed the dice between my two hands as if to warm them to the game the way I'd seen done in several old movies, then tossed them onto the table. "Like this?" The dice rolled and stopped, landing with two dots on one and five on the other. The dealer handed me some chips. I turned to my blond escort and said, "Now what?"

"Let's try this one," he said, and guided me to the roulette table. "Here you go. Now help me make this bet. You're wearing black, so we'll go with that."

I tugged at the skirt, suddenly self-conscious.

"Next thing we need is a number," he said. "Since it was straight up 7 o'clock when that dress of yours first knocked my eyes out, let's go with a black 7." An almost imperceptible nod to the dealer and the roulette wheel did a whirl, the balls clicking and jumping from one slot to another. They eventually landed in a black slot marked with the number seven. Montana didn't even look surprised. He *did* look pleased. "What do you think? Stay with it or move to another number?"

I wanted to squeal and jump up and down like a kid who's been given a blank check for her birthday. Taking a deep breath, I made myself count to five before answering. "Oh, I wouldn't stay there. Uh, maybe 9?"

He placed a little over half of the winnings on the red 9. Once again, the hypnotic roll and click of the ball. And once again, my new-found friend and I won. "See there? I knew you'd bring me luck." We played for another half-hour or so, winning and losing about the same amount each time, the original winnings still intact.

"Well," he said, "Now that we've tainted you to the sins of the gambling halls, and since my Momma taught me never to break a promise to a lady, I would love to buy your dinner. Are you ready? This dining room all right? Or we could blow this joint and find something more, shall we say, suitable? Would you prefer to go elsewhere?"

"No, no. This is fine."

We took a seat next to a large picture window, where some cleverly hidden flood lights heightened the light from a half-moon, giving us an incredible view of the forest edge at night. Twilight had descended like a big, blue blanket, but it wasn't quite dark yet. In an open area just beyond the circle of light, a 4-pronged buck stepped daintily out of the shadows of the trees and began to feed on the tall grass. Minutes later, a doe and a yearling followed him.

73

As our drinks arrived, I turned my attention to my dinner partner. "What is it about gambling that for some people, no matter how much money or possessions they lose, it always seems to have a hold on them. A kind of fascination."

Montana folded his well-manicured hands on the table and nodded knowingly. "Most people come here once or twice a month for a night out on the town. A chance to try their luck, to imbibe in the ambiance of big money. Every once in awhile, they'll get a decent win and for a little while they get to feel *invincible.* Larger than life. A guy who's been a loser all his life, suddenly becomes a *winner.* It's one hell of a high. A rush like none other you've ever felt. Like falling in love, you know? With an incredible focus, so that nothing else exists. They can be taking your car and your house and your kids can be hungry, but for a little while, the game is the only thing that's really *real.* Everything else fades in comparison. On a subconscious level, it's as if you've just been told that you're gonna live forever. You'll never get old and you'll never run out of money. And sometimes you can like, *smell* this... this essence, this thing we call luck, so thick you can hardly breathe and you'll wanna scoop it up and stuff it in your pocket."

For a moment, Montana seemed lost in his philosophical mood as his jaw set and one well-manicured hand swooped through the air, taking a swipe at an imaginary bit of gold dust. "Pretty powerful stuff. Some people seem to have a greater need for that than others, and it gets away from them."

"I hear there are people who actually make their living gambling?"

He shot a green-eyed glance in my direction, no doubt as a warning to be careful. My questions were hitting a little too close to home. But he nodded briefly, and said, "There are a few who've had some measure of success. Not here in the casinos, but in private games. Games where some dude with money wants to take on a professional. Had a few lessons, read a few books. Thinks he knows something." Montana shrugged. "Even then, most of them go bust within a week. But for the average working stiff looking for a night out at the casino, he'd be better off staying away from the machines. You know, like the slot machines and the roulette wheel. They don't leave you a chance to turn things to your own advantage."

"Such as?"

"Cards. Poker. Anything that will allow you some room to maneuver. That way, if you got a little skill to start with and you know how to count the cards, you just might have a chance. In other words, you want to separate the numbers into say, five or seven groups. Low ones, next to low ones, and so on till you get to the tens and higher. That way, if you can keep tract of which cards have already fallen, you'll have a shot at guessing which ones are coming up. Its pretty simple. Then, you can bet or not bet, accordingly. You do that, and as the dealer works through the deck, you just might be able to play a few hands without loosing your shirt."

With one raised finger, he flagged a passing waitress and motioned that we were ready for another round. I wondered how he did that. Usually, and especially if I'm dining alone, I find myself reduced to waving my arms like a maniac or threatening to trip her on the return run before I can get waited on. And, the part that I liked the best, my bottled mineral water was ordered with the same amount of aplomb as his whiskey sour.

When they were delivered, scarcely a minute later, we ordered dinner. Montana selected a huge, half-raw steak- *why was I not surprised*- and I wanted the broiled salmon. *Also no big revelations.*

That done, Montana returned to the fascinating world he moved in. "Don't get me wrong. The *Maverick* days of going from town to town and living high on the hog are just a big romanticized notion that no longer exists, if it ever did. Especially here in these reservation casinos." He grimaced with a look of great disgust. "They've taken to running six decks together, making any kind of card counting just about impossible. Don't even call it gambling. These are *gaming* houses. Ever heard of such a big bunch'a bullshit? *Gaming houses!*"

I was preparing to ask him about Tiffany, when Junior Winthrop strolled in, backed by three other guys I took to be bodyguards. Daddy Mayor must have been left at home, catching up on some shut-eye, or soaking his corns, or whatever it is that old politicians do this time at night. Junior seemed either excited or agitated, with him it was hard to tell, and didn't notice the two of us over by the window. Leaning away from the candle-lit table, I crossed my fingers that he wouldn't see me.

Montana gestured with a fat thumb, causing the diamond on his pinky-finger ring to glitter in the candle light. "Here comes the favorite son of Eagle Ridge."

"Spare me. We're not going to be subject to another round of hand-shaking and baby-kissing, are we?"

"I take it you don't care for Jebediah Winthrop, the Second."

"Besides his being a bore and a snob, you mean? I'm still trying to decide if he was born a jackass or if he took lessons. Will the locals really *vote* for this guy?"

"Well, I don't know, Kathleen. He and his dad before him have been the major power-brokers here for a long time. They're pretty well known for cutting deals and favor-doin's. Got a lot of friends in this neck of the woods."

Junior had walked directly to the window where one can buy chips to play with or cash in what chips they've won. A mild commotion ensued. Junior was arguing with one of the men on the floor. There was a short discussion, all in hushed voices, when three more men hurried down the steps from the offices above and circled Junior, shoving another man, whom I took to be his bodyguard, to the side.

Although it was hard to see much from where we sat, the bodyguard stood out in an odd way. He was taller than the others and had a shaved head and a red beard. From somewhere inside the group, I heard a squawk. The men had separated him from Junior and had him pinned against the wall.

Suddenly, the games stopped and the customers stared. A pock-faced security guard came pounding down the stairs, two more arrived from the area by the door. The three of them converged on Junior, although it was all in hushed voices. They made quite a gathering. I bit my lip, wishing I'd brought a camera.

Soon, with hardly a ruffled hair, Junior was marched up the stairs to the executive offices while a tall, gray-haired guy with a cigar waited, leaning against the rail. The lead security guard and a few of his buddies followed close behind.

I turned to Montana, "What's going on?".

Montana chuckled. "Looks like Junior's due for a reality check."

"I don't understand....."

"Simple enough. According to the grapevine, Junior's been operating on credit. Running up a big gambling bill. The guys upstairs say it's time that bill was paid."

"I didn't know you could do that. Gamble on borrowed money? To the point that you can't pay your bills? Sounds like a pretty dumb move for a man who's trying to run for office."

"No one has ever accused Junior of being bright."

My face had to be registering shock, as my brain did a fast-forward to the possibilities this held for Junior's career as a public servant. I also knew that it would never appear in print without undeniable proof of what he'd done. But considering that the personnel manager of this very casino was his opponent, the chances the man was taking with his own career were unbelievable.

Montana sipped his whiskey sour, made a face and smacked his top lip. "Well, to be totally honest, gambling on credit is not really that easy. I'd venture to say that damn few people are ever given the opportunity. First, you're bound to sign a promissory note, to get a letter of credit issued. And even then, it'll only be for just so much and not much time to get it paid. I've never heard of anyone going for more than a few days, a week at the most, before they're going to want their money."

"What are they going to do with him up there? You think they'll break his leg? Beat him up?"

"You've been watching too many old mafia movies." Montana downed the last of his drink, and fixed his gaze on the balcony where Junior had last been seen. "They'll just talk to him. Probably scare him a little. Get some kind of agreement that he'll be bringing the money in, directly."

The waitress brought our dinner and took Montana's order for a refill.

"So," he said, leaning back in his chair. "Now that I've answered your questions, how about you returning the favor?" Underneath Montana's skill at cards had to be an uncanny sense that allowed him to read people. Know what they were thinking, thereby judging their next move. He'd know if I was fudging at the edges of the truth and I didn't really want to, anyway.

I decided to cut to the chase. "What do you want to know?"

"You're not here for a night out on the town. Or to pick up any stray gamblers. Do you mind telling me exactly what you *are* doing here?"

"I'm a reporter for the *Seattle Gazette.* Here to do a story on Tiffany Jack."

He nodded. "And you thought I might know something."

I shrugged. "You play cards, she was a dealer. I doubt that there's much of anything that goes on here, that you're not aware of."

The waitress returned with his refill. He took a long swallow, grimaced, placed it squarely on the napkin, and said, "Shoot."

"Have you ever seen Tiffany date or hang out with anyone? Someone who say, spent a little money on her? Took her shopping?" With a grin and wink, I added, "Bought her dinner? "

Instead of responding to my botched attempt at humor, Montana rubbed his chin, the strain of his mourning for a murdered friend showing through his poker-faced mask for the first time since we'd met.

"I was wondering when you were going to get to that," he said. His gaze ran darkly from his drink to Junior, who now appeared at the top of the stairs, still surrounded by the casino employees. "Yes I have, in fact. Now, this one's gonna stick in your craw. I know it sure did mine. Tiffany was a beautiful woman, a good mother, and a friend to most everyone in here. And I'd hate like hell to see whoever killed her, go scott free."

He breathed deeply, seeming to draw strength and self-control out of his desire to help find the murderer. "I've never been one to rat on anybody. Never snitched in my life. But in the interest of justice, I will tell you that Tiffany was seen on more than one occasion with none other than our boy, Winthrop." At this point, Junior had begun his descent, slowly and a little shaky but still in one piece. He seemed to be arguing, stopping every few steps to turn and talk to the pock-faced man behind him.

"You're kidding. Junior?"

Tiffany had been a beautiful, vibrant woman. She was single, in a position to meet lots of men, and I had no doubt hat she could have gone out with just about anyone she'd wanted. Junior was about the last man I ever would have considered. "But, why.....?"

He shrugged as if he found it hard to believe, too. "Who knows? Maybe she thought his beer belly was cute. Maybe she likes prematurely bald men. Or maybe, just maybe, seeing as how he was the one who bank-rolled her shopping trips, co-signed for her mobile home *and* the new car, she decided that all of that wasn't that bad a trade-off."

Montana cocked an eyebrow, scowling darkly. "Now, mind you, I'm not saying that there was anything wrong with it. Tiffany was single and had every right to go out with anyone she wanted. I'm just saying that she wasn't as bad as all this sounds and I wouldn't want anyone to insinuate any different."

"I understand. And let me assure you, that I'm not here to judge Tiffany for the sake of sensationalism. All I want to do is report the facts of this case, assist the authorities in what ways I can to apprehend her murderer and if possible, find that little boy."

He nodded with his eyes closed, several quick little jerks, as if he was content with my answer and hoped never to have to discuss that part of Tiffany's behavior, again.

"The word is out that one night when she left work, a guy spotted her getting into a car. He don't know whose car, but could only say it was a black, fairly new model, four-door sedan. She walked straight to it in the shadows and got in. Evidently, someone had been waiting for her. Light inside the car didn't turn on when she opened the door, must have been broke or turned off."

"And who was the guy that saw this happen? Could I talk to him?"

"That, I'm afraid, I cannot say."

I fiddled with my napkin a minute, thinking. *He is trying to tell me something here, without having to state it out loud.* "Does Junior have a car that would match the description you just gave me?"

Montana spoke carefully and clearly, obviously wanting his answer to carry more weight than the words alone would allow. "I believe he's been seen in a car that sounds pretty close. A '95 Honda, four-door, black."

Suddenly, a disturbance on the stairs, and a dull thumpity-thumping sound, caused a hushed pall to fall over the entire casino. Every game stopped, every conversation halted, and every raised dinner fork was held in suspension. Junior had slipped on the stairs, and was tumbling the rest of the way down. And though literally every security guard and bus boy in the place rushed to his side, they were too late. Everyone had witnessed Junior, prostate on the floor, belly down, his nose digging a trench in the carpet. Within minutes and after a groan or two, he was up and being whisked away to the exit.

I would have laughed if it had not been the most ridiculous display I'd ever seen. I felt angry, for some reason, and terribly embarrassed. Which was odd, because I normally don't feel a lot of empathy for someone I don't like.

Montana watched with a keen, if somewhat hardened, interest. He leaned back in his chair and seemed to be enjoying himself. "Some people have a longer learning curve than others," he said, digging a cigar from the inside of his jacket lapels, and lighting it from the candle on our table. "This calls for a brandy. Care to join me?"

I sighed, and turned my attention to Montana. "A brandy sounds great."

Again, the waitress appeared as if by magic. She brought the ticket to our table, took the order for two apricot brandies and began clearing our dirty dishes away. Jeffrey had mentioned a dog that Billie had played with. I asked the waitress for a doggy bag for the bones from Montana's steak. It prompted a quizzical look.

"By the way," I asked him. "Know anyone who has a dog? Probably an Alaskan Husky, or kind of a gray, half-dog half-wolf mutt with one brown eye and one blue one?" He indicated that he didn't know, but would ask around. We chatted for another half-hour or so, swapping war stories which ranged from the gambling halls to the newspaper proof-reading floors. It was time to go. Gathering my purse, we prepared to leave.

While we were waiting for a valet to bring my car, Montana said, "You know, this whole setup reminds me of Watergate. Nixon's historical downfall. Remember what Deep Throat said to that journalist?"

Just then, the valet arrived with my Porsche and Montana

held the door for me. Just before he slammed it shut, he mumbled the phrase that would reverberate through my head for the next few weeks. "Among other things, the famous informer said, 'Follow the money.'"

On the way home, Montana's comments did little but make me even more confused. The only sign of big money I'd seen since this whole travesty took place, was the incident of Junior's reprimand over his unpaid gambling bills. And his co-signature on Tiffany's loan.

When that thought circled my head so many times it threatened to scramble what little gray matter I had left, I turned my attention to the affair between Junior and Tiffany. She had divorced Benjamin Jack and later, took up with Junior. A loosing situation, no matter how I looked at it. Again, I had to wonder about the woman's state of mind when she died.

Walking into the house, I fielded a cutting remark from Dwayne. He was watching some shoot 'em up western on TV, the ever-present beer in hand.

"Where the fuck you been, this time of night," he boomed, his speech coming out slurred and slobbery. "And wearin' my wife's dress to boot! You look like a fuckin' hooker."

Several comments came to mind as I circled a wide berth around him, going directly to my room. But it was best to ignore him. It looked like he was already being punished in the worst way, having curled up on the couch with a blanket and pillow. Undoubtedly, Patti had had enough and ordered him out of her bedroom.

Way to go, Little Sister.

CHAPTER NINE

Wednesday. The next morning, I awoke on the end of a dream that was so real, that I could almost taste the remnants of a kiss. A kiss bestowed on me by none other than Benjamin Jack. It had been one of those nights that I slept so soundly the hours seemed to vanish, yet feeling like I hadn't been asleep at all. My heart was racing from a mixture of anxiety, perhaps a little fear of the unknown thrown in, and definitely some unfulfilled passion.

Shaking my head in an effort to clear it and bring all of my facilities to bear, I stumbled to the kitchen for coffee. Patti had cleared an old desk in the corner and set my laptop on it. A cord from the kitchen phone hook up was dangling close to the modem, giving me the ability to link up with my office. No more excuses for not keeping in touch, or sending in a story on time.

I sat down and started drafting an article about life on the reservation for the modern, casino-employed Indian. First I had to decide how much of what I learned last night I was willing to put on paper. In fact, how much had I actually learned, and how much was speculation? And how much could I say without endangering the investigation or being sued for libel. This article could not be finished without more information.

I took a shower and got dressed. My next stop was the Tribal Center.

The Bastolak Tribal Center was larger than I expected: a main hall with a big dining room and several offices, and a maintenance building with a carport where several pickups and cars had parked. A house which looked like one of those pre-fabricated structures that had rolled in on a set of wheels, sat next to the garage. Probably for the maintenance man and overseer. On the far side was a large, auditorium-sized building where, I supposed, the tribe performed many of their spiritual rituals, including pow-wows.

An old man, his face the color and texture of a worn leather glove, relaxed in a lawn chair outside the dining hall. He greeted me when I walked by, a big grin exposing the gums of one who would have nothing to do with either bad teeth or dental plates.

I explained who I was and that I was investigating the murder as well as trying to find the little boy. He commiserated with me, saying that the whole tribe had been looking for him.

"Look, do you mind if I ask a few questions?"

The old man worked his toothless gums and spat over the edge of the porch. "You can ask anything you want. But I don't live on this res, and don't have many answers. Be better if you talked to the women inside." He swept one hand toward the door. "They're all in there."

The old man posed a classic, Native American profile. I would have loved spending the afternoon, talking, learning, and studying him. But there wasn't time. "How about a few pictures?" I asked, hoping to take something of him home with me.

"Suit yourself," he said, straightening a little in his chair and passing an arthritic hand over a two-day stubble.

Snapping off five or six good shots, I thanked him, then turned to enter the dining hall. Wanting to be polite and not break any long-standing rules of etiquette, I thought it'd be best if I didn't barge into the room, uninvited. Poking my head in, I rapped and said "hello," to no one in particular. Five women were working in the commercial kitchen and by the size of the pans they were using, preparing what looked like a big meal for a number of people. They all looked up expectantly but kept on with their chores. No one returned my greeting.

I walked over to the counter, looking directly at one of the older women, and said, "I seem to be intruding, and I'm really sorry for that. But I'm investigating Tiffany Jack's murder and her little boy who appears to be missing. If someone here could answer just a few questions, it would really help me do that."

The one I'd spoken to carefully put down her knife and walked over. She didn't seem to be angry or even distracted by my meddling. Evidently, they were so overcome with grief over Tiffany's death that there wasn't much emotion left. It suddenly dawned on me that this was probably the day of the funeral and that these women were preparing for a wake of sorts, afterward. A sickening, sinking sensation tightened the pit of my stomach. "What do you want to ask?" she said, wiping her hands on her apron.

"Look, my nephew and little Billy are the same age. They were, and still are I suppose, good friends. I gave Billy a ride up from the fairgrounds. He was in my sister's living room, in town, when he saw the newscast, that his mother had...well, you know, what had happened to her. And it was from that house, that Billy ran away from. I feel terribly responsible, and...I don't know. I just thought we could talk, share what knowledge we have with each other, and perhaps, together, we could find this little boy."

The woman turned to look at each of the others, their eyes silently communicating. I also looked at them, begging with my heart for assistance. But no one spoke. Either to me or to her. They simply went on with their work, seeming to take little notice of my presence. One woman, who had been chopping vegetables, brandished a big knife and stared at me for a moment, then brought it down on a head of celery with a big 'whap.'

Becoming extremely nervous, I began to look for a way out. "This is obviously a bad time. Here's my card, the phone number of where I'm staying is on the back. If any one of you has anything to add to what I've just told you, please, *please,* give me a call. I'll come to you, anywhere, anytime, and do anything I can to find that child." I left, a blush of uneasiness still on my cheeks. I couldn't remember a time when I'd felt more uncomfortable. Driving away, I realized I hadn't asked about the dog.

Did I dare question their Chief? Perhaps I should wait another day. But as Police Chief Clancey said, whoever killed that woman may also be gunning for the boy. And with everyone concentrating on the funeral, a sick mind would find ample opportunity to rid themselves of a nuisance. Did I dare wait another day? Could they already have found him and be holding him now, waiting for a chance to dispose of his little body?

The Highway Patrol and Sheriff's Department were watching the roads, checking most of the cars that came and went, but they couldn't stay there forever. Eventually, the search for Billy would slack off, the authorities would get tied up with other tasks, and even the media would go on to other things. And the memory of a little boy named Billy would fade away in all but his father's heart.

I couldn't let that happen. Billy *had* to be found...alive.

Bernie, the photographer hadn't arrived yet today, but we could always come back later for a few good shots.

Chief Andrew Joe's home address was in the phone book. It was on the road leading out of the reservation. It would mean barging in once again, but I was running out of leads.

Driving down the hillside, I passed several small farms whose pastures were thick with dairy cattle. Willow trees bordered a stream that zigzagged through the well-kept countryside, disappearing into the foothills of the distant Cascade Mountains. Overhead, a bank of cotton-ball clouds was rolling in from the Southwest. It was cooler today than this time yesterday, and smelled like rain. Maneuvering the Porsche through a tight, gravelly turn, I spotted the cause of the cold air out of my side window. Nudging over the horizon from the west-northwest, a dark-gray cloud mass threatened us with a sudden shower, if the wind blew it this way.

The Chief answered my knock and listened carefully while I explained my mission. After asking for identification, he showed me in. Guessing his age to be sixty-something, the worry lines grooved across his forehead and the bags under his eyes made him look older than his years. He had to be under a tremendous strain.

A teenage girl got up to leave the room. A young man in his early twenties, who I took to be his grandson stayed. He was introduced as Joseph. Arms folded across his chest, chin jutting forward, Joseph Joe demonstrated his highest priority without uttering a sound. He would stay in order to protect his grandfather from the contaminating influence of the white man's world. Meaning me.

"I'll only be a minute," I said, nodding to the young man and taking a seat on the couch. "I realize that many young people, especially a single mother such as Tiffany, would be encouraged to speak to their elders about anything that was troubling them. I was wondering if she might have said anything to you or to anyone else that might move this investigation along."

"I've already told the sheriff and the police chief all that I know. Which is not very much."

"I'm sure you have. But, sometimes a little different perspective will prompt a different result, and you could wind up knowing a lot more about this killer than you'd think. Most homicides occur by some slight of a relative or a close friend or neighbor. The victim usually knows their killer and many times trusts them implicitly. Which means that, chances are, you also are acquainted with the killer."

I let that sit for a moment, watching him digest what I had just told him. "This is not to point a finger at any member of your tribe," I added. "But whatever his social standing, the killer has probably been on the reservation many times and is probably well-known around the casino." The chief nodded, indicating that my point was well taken.

I leaned forward. "How well did you know Tiffany?"

"Only from the casino and seeing her with the boy at some of our tribal functions."

"Did she ever mention being afraid of anyone? Was she ever threatened in any way?"

"Never told me about it if she was. I've thought a lot about this, ever since this started. Haven't come up with much." He placed his feet on a small stool, slowly and deliberately. For a moment, I wondered if he wasn't listening to a distant drum that was audible to his ears only. A tingle ran across the back of my shoulders, making me shiver.

"I don't have a lot of say when it comes to the casino," he said. "My responsibilities as chief of the tribe are more administrative. I lead the meetings and vote on different things as they deal with the tribe itself."

As he talked, the Chief didn't look straight at me. He seemed to be more comfortable looking out the window. I didn't mind, as it probably helped him bring the things to mind that we needed to discuss. "In our tribe, it is customary that one of the duties of a chief is to look after the children. Especially, a child who's living without a family around. You know, to pro-ect them and teach them all of the things a child needs to now as they grow up."

"But he had his mother. And, I'm sure his dad visited him uite often."

"Having a mother who lives in one place and a father who ves somewhere else, isn't enough. He needs a whole family. Grandparents, aunts, uncles, all of them in order to learn. When hose parts of a family are missing in a boy's life, the tribe teps in fill in the gaps. Know what I mean? Though a mom nd dad are his *principal* teachers, all the other tribal mem- ers act like parents too. That's why, when Tiffany died, it vas the same for us as it would be if you lost your sister."

A jolt shot through me, at the very mention that Patti may e in danger. These people were known to be psychic at times, evering their spiritual leaders. Did he know something I idn't? Was he trying to convey this to me? I vowed, then and here, that Little Sister and I would be having a heart to heart efore the week was out.

His gaze dropped to the floor. "Tiffany was as good a nother as she could be. And she did the very best she could vith what she had," he said. His expression was so sad, I hought my heart would break. The Chief felt responsible for er death and I doubted that anything I might say could change hat. "It was up to me," he said, head drooping. "...to see that er boy was given what she could not. I'm afraid I have failed."

Across the room, Joseph Joe seemed to be receiving a big- er lesson in maturity than he'd bargained for. His youthful efiance paled in response to Andrew's advocacy for personal esponsibility. It was probably the reason his grandfather had ermitted him to sit in on our talk.

I had to admire this tribe for their dedication to each other, nd especially to their children. Did we, with all our efficien- ies and prized work ethics, have anything equivalent to their ense of community? As the Chief explained, in their tribe, ne health and well-being of *all* of their children was the re- ponsibility of *all* of the adults. Outside of this reservation, nat attitude of moral obligation was damned hard to find.

Chief Andrew Joe's eyes had fixed on something outside ne window. Thoroughly curious by now, I followed his gaze nd noticed a small brown bird flitting among the leaves of a large, yellow dahlia in full bloom. A bird flitting through the flowers would not have been unusual except for the way the bird was acting. It was twittering nervously, leaping from one flower to another, chirping plaintively as it hopped along the stem, then up onto the windowsill to peck at the glass.

"Her name," he said. "...Tiffany's name in her native Yakima language was...," here, he made an interesting series of guttural sounds and hand motions. "In English, it would translate into Little Bird."

At that point, the archangels and nymphs could have spirited me away to the Happy Hunting Grounds and issued me a set of feathery wings, and I would not have been more surprised nor spooked. My feet were so hot I could have been standing on a stove and my skin felt as if a flood of tiny needles had washed over the top of my head and cascaded down my back. I was dizzy and torn between wanting to stay and afraid I'd black out if I did.

A moment later, the sensation was gone and I was left to wonder if it had ever *really* been there. I excused myself and asked to use the facilities. After rinsing my face with cool water I thanked him for his time and gave him my card. Before leaving, I did remember to ask him about the dog, a half-wolf Husky with one blue eye and one brown. He hadn't heard of such an animal, but would keep his ears open.

As the old man walked me to my car, I'd been trying to decide if I should ask him about Benjamin Jack. He might throw some light on what I'd learned at the casino and he needed to know about the dog. Evidently, this dog was owned by someone who lived off of the reservation. But if that was so, what was a young boy doing away from home and who took him to that house, and why?

The temptation was too great. I had to see Ben. Trying to keep a level head and look as professional as possible, I met the Chief's gaze head-on. "Last question, and then I'll go. Can you help me find Deputy Sheriff Jack? It's important that he be aware of some new leads I've turned up. Can you tell me where he lives?"

Our eyes locked. He made a wry mouth, then looked down. The old man was reluctant to give out Ben's home address, but would get word to him.

From there, I drove out to a small lake on the reservation. It was a pristine, snow-water lake that caught the blue of the sky and the breeze ruffling the mirror smoothness of the water seemed to reflect the icy-whiteness of the glaciers on the distant mountain peaks. It looked a lot like the place from my dream the night before.

Off to the left was a grassy knoll. Retrieving a blanket from the trunk, I scrambled up the hill. It overlooked the lake, while being sheltered from the wind and warm with the baking sun. A great place to meditate on the events of the last few days and where possibly, some of my inner turmoil could be settled.

A lot had happened this last week. A little boy was missing and his mother dead. The women from the kitchen were angry about it, and I couldn't blame them. Given the same set of circumstances, I would have thrown the rude intruder out on her ear.

And my poor sister. Whatever was I going to do to help her predicament? The marriage that never had a chance, the land investment going sour. It was affecting Jeffrey, too. Something had to be done. It was with these misgivings that I fell asleep with jerky visions of drowning and vicious wolves lurking in the shadows, that dominated my dreams.

I awoke to find Ben looking down at me on the blanket. "Oh. It's about time you showed up," I said, squirming under his stare and noticing that my backside had gotten damp and chilly. I yawned and stretched, thinking that if he wanted to look he might as well get an eyefull. Ben helped me to my feet.

We walked along the lake, as I told him of my visit to the casino and Montana's revelations. "It seems that everywhere I go, Junior's name pops up. And I'd bet a pretty penny that the casino is crawling with people who know things that they haven't revealed. I was hoping that you could get them to talk a little better than I've been able to."

"Actually, we do have several informants on the staff out here. I wouldn't hurt to check back with them."

My curiosity aroused, I noticed that his shirt and shoes were damp, and not in a way that would suggest perspiration. "So, I guess you've been busy tracking Billy. Have any luck so far?"

"Actually, I've been on a vision quest by fasting and swimming in the lake." He paused, stooped to pick up a small, flat stone.

I was puzzled. *What did all this have to do with finding his son?* "I take it, that this vision quest is a very important thing to you."

"It's an old tradition, necessary before any spirits can be called upon for help." He shot a sidelong glance at me. "You're probably wondering why I'm doing vision quests instead of being out there, beating the bushes. To someone outside our circles, it probably looks like a waste of time," he said, chucking the stone in a way that made it skip across the water.

"You know, Kathy. You've been a powerful friend in helping us find Billy. No one, even here on the res, has worked harder at trying to find him than you have. For this, if you're interested, I'm going to tell you some of the things that we believe in." He looked at me, quizzically.

I indicated 'yes', with much nodding and a tight smile. For some reason, every time this man was within arm's reach my voice couldn't be trusted.

Ben cleared his throat. "You see, it's an old tribal belief than one must fast for days and bathe in a clean lake to obtain a particular spirit power, called '*s.qelalitut.*' Or it can be passed down to a relative, at the death of a certain spirits' owner, much like the white man passes on his wealth when he dies. In this case, I'm trying to make a better contact with one already have. You see, when my grandfather was a boy, probably around fourteen, things could get a little tough now and then. It was a lot different back then. There weren't any Safeway stores around to pop into and pick up something for supper.

"One winter, during a terrible storm, a war party from the north attacked them and stole all their food. They had nothing to eat. Grandfather said nothing, but went out into the storm, taking a simple bow and arrow that his father had helped him make and killed an elk with it. He ate only the heart for himself, thanking the spirit of the animal in the way of our people, then dragged the animal all the way home over the snow. It took him two days to bring the carcass home, but the hide was amazingly intact when he got there. It was said, from then on

90

that he had the spirit helper of the hunter.

"This became very helpful when, later on in the spring, Grandfather led the war party to retrieve the tribe's belongings. Due to his successful strategies, few lives were lost, as they hunted the raiders down, took back their canoes, much of their food, and all of their women. That next spring, he was sent out on a spirit quest and received another, very powerful, spirit. A shamanistic spirit, called the '?ayiyus.' It is similar to the owl and known for finding things or people who are lost."

Ben's face seemed frozen in the past. As if it held a memory so precious that he was almost afraid to share it lest it dwindle away. "You see, my grandfather sent me on a spirit quest when I was just ten years old. Shortly after that, I also began to show some abilities to hunt. I learned to track game at a young age and brought down several deer and a lot of rabbits, myself. The old people assumed that I also had the spirit helper of the hunter."

I could have listened to Ben's disclosure of his tribe's spiritual beliefs all day long. As he pronounced the spirit names in the sounds of the ancient Lushootseed language, they rumbled from his throat like the wind blowing in from a far-off thunder. Accompanied by the hand gestures, it was at once the most fascinating thing I'd ever seen and heard.

"Then when grandfather died, I inherited all of those who had belonged to him. His shaman spirit of the owl and his lay spirits. His *s.qela'litut*. Theoretically," he said. "I already have his spirit helpers. But in order for the spirits to...wake up, so to speak, and for me to receive them properly, the body must be clean inside and out. In other words, the belly has to be empty, and the outside body scrubbed with leaves and small twigs." He sniffed his hands and the inside of his elbow, as if checking for body odors. "I've been doing exactly that, ever since I saw you last, by the river."

"So, do you have this owl spirit now?"

Our eyes met. "Frankly, I've never had to test it to this degree, before." He looked down, as if he were ashamed. "In my job, I've been using my formal law-enforcement training, almost exclusively. Like a white man. An unbeliever." He paused, his gaze scanning the lake and the trees. "I'll soon know if it's still there. The time has come for me to call on it."

"So, what's this other spirit? The one of the hunter that makes you such a good tracker today, as a Deputy Sheriff?"

"It is the one of the wolf," he said. "It is called, *stakayu*."

The intensity of Benjamin's spirituality, his strength, and his inherent goodness boosted my respect for the man. It also made me so self-conscious, I felt like a nervous teenager. We walked for a while on the edge of the lake. Shoulders close, touching now and then as we climbed over large pieces of driftwood and skirted around a dead fish. Suddenly, his arm moved. I jumped...thought at first, he was reaching for me. But he was only tossing another rock into the water.

Studying him while trying not to stare, I couldn't help but notice how his skin looked incredibly smooth, like a fine grain of leather. Would it feel as good as it looked? I wanted to touch him....decided that it wasn't a good idea. He was supposed to making himself pure with cold lake water and sticks. I couldn't compete with that if I'd wanted to.

Preparing to leave, he promised to keep in touch. He didn't say when or where.

Driving back to town, I flipped on the radio and turned to a local country-western station. They were playing the classic song by Dolly Pardon, *"I Will Always Love You."* It had long been one of my favorites. Familiar words, describing a special feeling. A feeling that always seemed to happen to everyone but me.

Windows down, the Porsche hugging the turns on the small country road, I sang along with Dolly, so what if my high notes were a little off key. There was no one here to notice. I thought about Ben, ignored a sharp twing in my chest, and hoped his spiritual efforts would help him find his son.

As the song closed, the station interrupted the moment with a breaking news broadcast. Zeke Larson, the personnel manager of the casino and Junior's primary opponent, had been found dead. His car had run off a bridge, which spanned the Skagit River. The cause of death would be determined by an autopsy. The authorities were refusing to speculate if his death was by drowning or by some other means.

Well now. A coincidence? I don't think so.

Larson's poll numbers go up and he dies. Flicking off the

adio, I shifted into third gear, eliciting a loud ka-boom out
he Porsche's rear exhaust, and sidled into town. A quick stop
t the police station to pick up their latest news release and
ny gossip that might be floating around out there on the grapevine, and home to pound out a scorching piece about small-
own politics for tomorrow's edition of the *Seattle Gazette*.

This time, I was taking on Junior and his shockingly
shoddy campaign. As far as I could go. Perhaps the personnel
assistant I'd first interviewed would be ready to act as an anony-
mous source.

Will this mean that Junior carries the election without an
opponent? Even if Larson's death proves to be the product of
foul play? I wasn't all that familiar with Washington State
campaign and election laws. Would there still be time for someone else to register? Perhaps a better question was, were there
were any locals left who would *dare* to register.

It was almost dark by the time I rumbled past the local
Baptist Church. I slowed to allow an old pickup and driver
complete its left turn into the parking lot while flipping the
dial on the radio to try and find another newsbroadcast. In the
shadows, I barely noticed a man with a package under his arm
sprinting toward a small shed in the rear of building.

Probably choir practice.

Around the corner, I pulled onto Main Street and entered
Eagle Ridge's idea of a rush-hour traffic jam. It never fails
that when I'm in the biggest hurry to get somewhere, that is
the precise time that everyone else in the county also wants to
go somewhere and they all have to poke along at ten miles
under the speed limit and they all have to be in front of me.

I braked quickly to let some old man in an ancient Pontiac
lurch backwards out of a space, of course the old fool never
once glanced in the rearview mirror. Too busy grinding gears.
While my Porsche and the Pontiac backed up enough traffic to
set the horns to blowing, a familiar-looking man crawled out
of a pickup and entered a tavern on the next block. Waiting
for Pops to find the brake, the clutch, AND shift into first, I
tried to remember where I'd seen this particular guy.

Ah, ha. *Last night at the casino.* He'd changed from the
pinstriped suit he'd been wearing to filthy jeans, wide suspend-
ers and the heavy boots of a logger. But it was him. The shaved

head and reddish beard gave him away. He'd been the bodyguard hovering around Junior. The same guy whom the bounc-
ers had slammed up against the wall and evidently told to keep
his trap shut, as he hadn't moved again until Junior made his
now-famous nosedive down the stairs. This time, he was driving a new, red Ford pickup, complete with a rifle across the rear
window and a big, black dog in the back, tied to the cab with a
short rope. The dog was standing guard over a beige, canvas
tarp which had been thrown over some bulky-looking boxes.

This was too good an opportunity to waste. A chance to
spy on one of Junior's cronies. I found a space across the street,
facing a service station, and pulled in.

Acting as if I had every right to do so, I checked the dog
to make sure it didn't have the blue-eye, brown-eye combination. He didn't. The beast was solid black, including his eyes.
A kind of streamlined mutt with a mangy tail that I guessed
was probably part Labrador.

Satisfied that this was not the one Jeffy had mentioned, I
walked straight up to the rear of the truck and peered under
the tarp. The dog immediately went crazy, barking and clawing, his nails gouging huge grooves in the red paint.

Figuring that I had less than a minute before the dog's
frenzied barking brought the owner out, I quickly pawed
through the nearest boxes. They held an assortment of fliers
in different colors and copies of printed articles. Keeping one
eye peeled for the tavern door to open, I grabbed one of each.
I'd look them over, later on.

Suddenly, the sounds of a line-dancing song blared into
the street. *Here he comes.* Quickly, I stuffed the contraband in
my shirt and ducked down under the truck, crawling between
the two back wheels.

Of course, the moment the guy came out, the dog's sav-
agery redoubled, clawing and covering the cab, the tarp, and
himself in foamy slobber. Instantly, what had been a fairly
tame pooch became a black, fanged beast full of white-hot fury
and jaws the size of a shark's. A wild brute that snapped and
barked ferociously, threatening to chew completely through
the thin rope that restrained him from diving after me and
biting my head off.

94

It wasn't long before I began to doubt that the dog belonged to the driver of this pickup. The destruction of his truck's paint job became the guy's only focus. This idiot had no idea of what kind of animal he had or what the beast was trying to tell him. He shouted at the dog and must have slapped him around quite a bit as the barking immediately stopped. Replaced by loud whining and a hurt whimper.

This added to my anger. *The poor thing was only doing his job.*

After giving the dog detailed instructions of behavior, which included not bothering him while he was drinking beer, the driver added: "Blackie, goddamn it. I'll beat you to a pulp and throw your ass off the same bridge where Larson croaked, you go to clawing at the cab one more time." He then stomped back into the bar. At least, he'd subdued the dog, discharging him from his truck-defending duties.

Remembering the doggy bag I'd left in my car, I fetched the bones from Montana's steak and tossed them to the dog. He backed up, snarled menacingly as if to warn me not to come too close, then proceeded to crush them in his powerful jaws.

Better those bones than mine.

After that, the dog knew he'd found a friend. Though still somewhat reserved and back-offish, his tail thumped a few times and his snarls were replaced by a shy whine and some wet snuffles. Telling myself not to be scared, I reached over and gingerly scratched his ears. This was also met with an eager yip and much sniffing and licking of my hand and fingers. I didn't know that all that much about dogs, but any fool could see that though this was not a full-breed of any kind, he was still a valuable animal in many respects.

But for now, I had to get my spying done. I patted his massive head, promising to do what I could about getting him away from that creep, and went back under the tarp. Crawling closer to the front end, I wanted to check out what was in those other boxes when suddenly, the cab door opened, the driver flopped onto the seat, and backed the pickup into the street.

It wasn't long before the pickup left the highway and began a jouncing, bumpy ride over a gravel road. He drove for what seemed like hours, the hard ribbed metal of the truck bed making permanent dents in my behind. It was hot and stuffy under the tarp as I clutched the hasp of the truck's toolbox, fearing that the next teeth-rattling jolt would cast me into a ditch. We were definitely driving uphill most of the time, into the Cascade foothills, as it was getting harder and harder to stay in the front part of the truck bed. My body kept jiggling to the rear and lodging up against the boxes.

Where could this lamebrain be going?

Finally, the truck stopped and the guy got out. Listening as closely as I could, it seemed that he asked another guy if he had a longer length of rope to tie on the dog's collar. Evidently, he was taking Blackie with him. *Maybe he's returning the dog to his rightful owner. This guy didn't deserve, and probably would never earn, the love and loyalty of this animal.*

Several other cars arrived and there were shouted greetings between them. I huddled under the tarp, praying they wouldn't find me, and nursed my bruises. My knees and elbows had taken a beating over the rough, washboard trail. This guy drove like he had the devil behind him, an euphemism which was probably closer to the truth than anyone realized. As the voices faded away, I crawled out of the truck bed, cramped and disheveled. It was dark by then, and I was able to move around with more ease.

The guy with the beard had gone into a fairly large, two-story log house. Lights were on and due to the warm night, the front door and several small windows had been propped open. From the parking lot, I could hear a man inside, speaking.

Blackie had been tied to a tree on the far side of the park-

96

ing area. The minute I emerged from the truck bed and began to move around the cars, the dog noticed and whined expectantly. He knew it was me and probably wanted some more bones and a little affection. Poor thing was starved in more ways than one. Come to think of it, so was I. My only source of nourishment today had been a morning cup of coffee. Circling the compound, staying in the shelter of the trees all the while, I eventually made it to where the dog was tied.

Blackie was ecstatic when I knelt down beside him. He licked my face and hands, wriggling and whining with delight as I scratched his ears and told him what a good boy he was. Thinking I'd check to see how well he would mind me, I motioned for him to sit and to stay. He immediately obeyed, tongue lagging out and panting his eagerness to please. This was a nice, well-trained dog. And again, I wondered where the creep with the bald head and chin whiskers had gotten him.

I then tiptoed around to the darker, back wall of the house, as the sun dropped under the ridge. From there, I could hear the speaker without being seen. There was some kind of meeting going on, mostly a lot of men complaining about the government. After awhile, I was beginning to wonder if this wasn't more of a rally.

The speaker seemed intent on whipping his audience into a frenzy, his wrath directed mostly against the Federal Government. Evidently, they were angry that the president hadn't given them permission to level every tree in the state, including the National Parks, the wetlands, and my front yard. Different members were called on to speak. Each time, they'd fall back on their favorite chant: the president had to go. If they couldn't find a way to get him impeached, they'd have to hope somebody shot him. As vicious as they were, I was getting bored from hearing the same accusations, over and over again. It was too stupid to take seriously.

After a few minutes of hearing a new guy spewing his hate from the podium, I realized that this particular brand of venom was emanating from an all too familiar voice. Peering around the corner far enough to see through the window, the shock shook me to my very toes.

Good grief! The speaker was none other than my brother-in-law, Dwayne! And this was his militia meeting! As quietly as possible, I pulled the fliers out from my blouse. It was a box full of propaganda! They were being urged to buy up every gun in sight and form an army that would *take back their country*. The meeting had moved past the point of being mean and nasty. They were actually laying out a strategy, using the guerrilla tactics of any militant aggressor to gather support for a coup.

To eliminate the Commander In Chief.

Execute the President of the United States!

Assassination. A term well-known around the Dwayne Hickman household.

These idiots were hostile to the point of being dangerous. Not only to themselves, but to the rest of the country. Becoming weak-kneed from the implications of their sick little war games, I leaned against the back wall for support. And it is well that I did, because someone else who by now had become increasingly familiar, eased out of the back door. Junior was not only there but also seemed to be a militia member in good standing. He was followed by Rafferty, the tall, hungry-looking developer from that city council meeting I'd attended and where I'd gone to bat for my sister's property rights.

And for Dwayne's too, I might add.

I leaned into a rhododendron bush as they passed only feet away from me in the dark. Blackie had resumed his barking, the howls now sounding more like a cry of alarm. He didn't like these men coming that close to me any more than I did.

They continued walking about 30 feet, into the parking lot. Although there were no lights out there, the moon, away from the shade of the evergreens, did a fair job of keeping things illuminated. Most of their conversation was in hushed voices and I couldn't hear much. What little I did catch, sounded like a wrangling for money. Had Junior still not paid his gambling debts? Was he having problems trying to get the money?

Junior was getting excited and his voice was on the rise. "...get the bid on Pine Street. Just add 10 percent to the bid and I swear to God, I'll see that you get it."

Rafferty was close to shouting. "It'll never happen," he said. "There's no way I can underbid the locals by adding that much on and still be awarded the contract."

"Never mind," Junior replied, stamping one foot and waving his arms. "I said you'd get the job, and you'll get it. All's I want is a measly 10 percent. You give me that much, right now. Today. And I'll give you my word that you'll get the contract."

Ohmigod. Junior's really getting in deep. He's offering payola! Kick back, for crying out loud!

"Your word, huh? You're giving me your word that I'll get that contract, no matter if it's twenty or even thirty thousand dollars higher than the locals." Rafferty had hunched his shoulders as if the wallet in the inside pocket of his suit coat was in dire danger and he felt an instinctive need to protect it.

"And how you gonna do that? On a late-comer's agreement? Bullshit! You know damn well the city council members will never go for that. And that includes your Dad, who by the way, is still the Mayor and will be the acting Mayor until the end of December."

"Dammit, I said you'd get the job, and you'll get it. Get me my money now and you'll get confirmation of the damn contract by the first of the year. I swear to God you will."

"No way. You get me that contract first. In writing and in a way that the council can't veto it later on. How do I know you're gonna win the election? The way you've been screwing up lately, Larson's more of a shoe-in than you."

"Not any more he ain't," Junior said, bitterly. "Larson's dead. His car did a swan dive into the Skagit River. Early this morning." He sniffed, letting his implications sink in. "I'll be running unopposed."

Evidently, Rafferty had the savvy not to ask too many questions. After a long pause in which I couldn't see or hear much of anything, he started walking back to the house, saying, "All right. You get me an exclusive agreement passed and approved by the city council, and I will get you the money. You can hurry it along by using some of my soil tests off the yards and ditches of those older houses."

Just yards away, Junior clamped him on the shoulder and spun him around. "You give me the damn money, *now*," he demanded. "Or you can forget getting any contracts ever again in this town. Either on that sewer or on your apartment buildings. And don't think I can't sink *that* permit. I don't get that money by tomorrow morning, no later than noon, I'll black-ball you, you son-of-a-bitch! I want that money, *pronto*. By tomorrow, you hear me? A cashier's check, made out for ten thousand dollars."

The heated exchange only served to excite Blackie even more. He'd been barking quite a bit. He now lunged against the rope, teeth fully bared, growling and snarling like a wild beast.

"Don't threaten me, you little twerp," Rafferty replied. "It's not my problem that you've gambled all your campaign funds away. You got any idea what I can do to you if the word gets out about your little sex games? How about that lover of yours working in the casino kitchen. All I have to do is drop a few hints here and there with the town gossips, especially some of those religious right-wingers, and it'll be Katie Bar The Door, for your election. I can always go elsewhere with my investment capitol. I'd hate to see you have to make your own living without Big Daddy picking up the tab."

Junior had become apoplectic. "Just try it. JUST TRY IT. And see if you don't end up the same way as Larson." And with that, Junior stomped away, headed back to the house.

I was hoping they'd end it there. The shouting and the dog's barking had alerted the men from inside the house and threatened to break up the meeting. Many of them were at the windows or had come right out in the yard, toting an assort-ment of guns, including assault rifles. And since I was still huddled under one puny little bush, the idea of their proximity to me was more than I wanted to think about.

But the arguing had gone too far. Not only their liveli-hoods but their 'standing in the community' had been threat-ened. The two men continued to intimidate one another until the quarrel turned into a shoving match. Rafferty stood a good foot taller than Junior, making his reach a considerable ad-vantage. Each time Junior tried to take a swing, the developer simply stiff-armed him, his palm pasted on Junior's forehead.

After about three swings during which Junior collided with nothing more solid than thin air, the onlookers began to mut-ter and a cheer rose up from the rear. By now, most of the spectators were outside. One of the men began taking odds that Junior would give out before he'd landed a single punch.

100

Exasperated past the point of hysteria, Junior let out a bawl like a sex-crazed bull. He dove under the arms that had caused him so much torment, landing somewhere around Rafferty's thin thighs. Pummeling and kicking the man's stick-like legs, Junior reminded me of a four-year-old brat in the middle of a tantrum. A cheer rose up from the crowd that had by now gathered in the small yard, and more odds-making was made, the ante going up with every ineffectual swing. Except for Junior, who seemed to be in the fight of his life, the men were enjoying themselves immensely.

Suddenly, Rafferty literally picked Junior up by his shirt front, talk about an adrenaline flow, and threw him toward the log house wall. Junior ended up in the flower beds, flattening the rhododendron bushes.

Their wall, their bush, my hiding place.

A hush fell over the crowd as I eased out from under Junior's weight, stood up, and brushed myself off. Nobody moved, they were obviously unsure of how much I'd heard.

What will they do with me?

In that moment, a number of scenario's ran swiftly through my mind; I could be lynched. Shot at sunup. Drowned in the river. Or they could simply cut my throat in the same manner as Tiffany and leave me to die on the cold ground. Whatever they decided, I would probably not leave here alive.

Three of them had pulled their sidearms and aimed them at me. One guy had actually cocked his. I looked around, trying to grin and said, "Hi guys. We really *have* to stop meeting like this. Whatever will the neighbors think?"

Before anyone could respond, Blackie went crazy. He'd witnessed the fight between Junior and Rafferty, and now they dared ransack my hiding place with me in it. He was savage with the fury of a caged animal, pitching against the rope and barking so ferociously that foam was gathering around his jaws. I would have given anything to have him by my side instead of being tied to a tree some twenty yards away.

At that moment, and as if some force had heard my feeble wish, Blackie broke loose from his rope and hurled across the clearing. On impulse, Junior threw his arm up, protecting his throat. The snarling beast lunged, going straight for the jugular. Missing it, the sharp teeth ripped a broad swath from

Junior's jacket. He cursed and kicked a glancing blow at Blackie's head.

The fight between man and dog had distracted the attention of the militia men just long enough for me to get to my feet and stumble into the woods. Luckily, I landed on a fairly good trail. Several men shouted and would have followed me in hot pursuit, but Blackie's onslaught was holding them at bay. Each time one of them moved, it was he who received the dog's fury. Hopefully, there was too much of a mix-up of man and beast for anyone to attempt to drop the dog with a rifle shot. I ran for 50 yards or so, mostly downhill. A branch scraped my face, a fallen log tripped me.

Out of nowhere, a piercing whistle ripped through the forest and stopped the dog's barking. I continued to run, sides aching, lungs threatening to burst. Too tired....still I ran.

Had to keep going.

Before long, Blackie came loping after me, his head nosing into my hand. My hand curled into the hair on his shoulders, letting the dog pull me along.

After another 10 or 12 yards of lung-wrenching running, Ben appeared. He caught up with the dog in three easy strides, then reached for me. Never had I been so glad to see anyone. I couldn't stand up, couldn't get enough air. Ben caught me as I collapsed, sobbing, my knees shaking like jello. Gently but firmly, he guided me to a log on the side of the trail.

"Don't try to talk right away," he said. "We're safe here for the time being." Blackie was twisting and panting as he rubbed against my leg, expressing himself the only way he knew how. From his tiny concerned whines to his happy yips and sloppy licks, the big dog demonstrated his happiness. He knew he'd done something grand, and his big, muscular chest trembled from the praise he was receiving.

When finally I could breathe without pain, I looked up at Ben's face shadowed in the black woods. While Blackie and I cavorted and cooed, Ben was listening intently to the forest sounds. The rustle of a dried leaf, the chirp of a tiny bird, the whip of a cedar branch in the breeze, all meant special things to him. His head was cocked to one side and I could have sworn he was sniffing the scent of those men on the wind.

"You're the one who set Blackie loose, aren't you? How

102

did you know the dog would protect me?"

He sat down beside me on the log, giving Blackie an affectionate rub. "The minute he saw you, he started wagging his tail so hard I thought he'd wet himself. Then, when those men started to fight, there was no holding him back. Where'd you find this dog, anyway?"

"In the back of a truck. Isn't he something?"

"Whose dog is he?"

"I don't know. He belongs to somebody. Not anybody here, I'll tell you that much. The man who drove that truck up here was there at the meeting. The big bald dude with the red beard. But if he's this dog's owner, I'll eat your hat. I saw him box Blackie's ears for barking when someone was rifling through his stuff in the back of his own truck." No need to mention that that 'someone' was me.

There was something else I'd been wondering. "Now that we're asking questions, how'd you know I was here?"

He grinned. "You don't really want to know."

In no mood for silly games, I said, "Oh, but I do."

"Truth?"

"Truth."

"I didn't know. I knew these guys would be here. They have a meeting here every first Tuesday of the month. I've been watching them for a long time now, hoping to catch them in a criminal act. Hoping they'd make a mistake. Hoping they could lead me to Billy."

"Well, at least we've remedied that."

"What do you mean?"

"What they've done to me. Aren't you going to arrest them?"

"Did anyone of these men actually hurt you? Intimidate you or threaten you in any way?"

"Well, no. But they would have if it wasn't for Blackie."

"Sorry, Kate. We can't arrest anyone."

He paused, and rubbed his forehead. "They still haven't broken any laws. Actually, you were trespassing on their property."

I was aghast. "What about treason? The last I heard, that was still a federal crime. They were in there, making plans to assassinate the president. This meeting was kind of like a rally.

Did I tell you that Dwayne Hickman, my brother-in-law, was one of the *leaders?* He was spouting all sorts of propaganda about how the feds are going to start controlling the weather and form one huge world government. That would be a real task, when they can hardly decide to stop killing each other. Oh, and don't forget, the government's still trying to take their guns away from them. God forbid, these fools would no longer be able to stomp around the woods, shooting at trees with their assault rifles."

Ben's rich, deep baritone was reassuring. "You must have gotten a real earful tonight. Would you be willing to make a statement to that effect?"

"Damn right I will. I've even got dates and places. There's a bunch of them planning a trip to Montana, any day now. From there, a hand-picked contingent of sharp-shooters will be driving straight to North Dakota. The president is making a swing through there speaking to a big university. They think he'll be especially vulnerable at that particular time, for some reason. They were bragging that they could recreate Kennedy's infamous trip to Dallas. They've got it all planned. I'm telling you, these guys are some real kooks."

"An FBI agent I know'll be real happy to have your state- ment. For now, let's get back." They swung off down another path, Ben leading the way with a small flashlight. He stopped beside a huge cotton-wood tree, where a horse was tied.

"Don't tell me, this our only transportation."

"How do you think I've been moving around without them hearing me? A car is too easily heard and too hard to hide."

"Should we be riding around in the dark? What if this horse stumbles over a log and breaks his leg?" Placing myself at the mercy of a semi-tame creature, should it decide to leap off a cliff, was *not* a good strategy in my book.

"Relax," he said, swinging into the saddle. "I grew up in these woods. Know every trail and tree like the back of my hand. I'll take you to a place where you can hide for the time being. There's an old logging road not far from here that goes right up to it. Won't even have to use the main highway."

Ben's horse was a large, heavily-muscled gelding the color of mahogany. Blackie wasn't sure what to make of the horse, but after much nose-touching and inquisitive snufflings, the two beasts seemed to decide that they could tolerate the situation for the time being. I wasn't nearly so convinced.

Ben was ready to pull me up. "Put your foot in the stirrup. No, the left one. That's it. Now swing your right leg over behind me."

I knew that. It's not like I hadn't *ever* ridden a horse. In fact, just last year I'd uncovered an illegal nuclear waste dump not that far from where we were at the present, and had ridden a horse all over the Cascade Mountains. It had just *been* awhile. I was a little out of practice.

"Hang on. It's not that far to the reservation."

"Is that where you left your car?"

"No," he said and, with a click with his tongue, he nudged the horse into a slow walk. "I'm taking you to my mother's house. You'll be safe there, until we can figure something better. There's no way you can go back to your brother-in-law's house."

I wrapped my arms around the strong bulk of Benjamin. His reassurance, along with the steamy rock and sway of the horse, calmed me down to the point I was half asleep by the time we left the shelter of the evergreens and was cutting across an open field. The grass here was quite tall, the dry, wheat-like stalks brushing against our legs and tickling the horse's belly. At one point, a wild, brown rabbit bounded away in haste, giving rise to a startled snort from the horse just seconds before a large hoof landed in the spot where it had been hiding.

We came out on an open, gravel road. After a few minutes, I recognized it as the road that led up to the mobile home park, where Tiffany and her son used to live. About a mile short of the park, we entered a long driveway.

His mother lived in a lone house, surrounded by a forest of cedars. A light was on in the living room. By the time we had crossed the porch, a short, gray-haired woman was standing in the open door. I instantly recognized her as the feminine version of Ben. Like her son, she had a well-sculptured profile with a smile that, given happier circumstances, was probably used quite often.

I was again struck by the attractiveness of this tribe. They were pleasant, intelligent, and downright *pretty*. She was also the same woman I'd spoken to that day in the kitchen at the

Tribal Center. Her name was Darlene.

Ben explained the problem to her, putting much emphasis on the fact that I was heavily involved in the case of Tiffany's murder and that my efforts in trying to find Billy had put my life in danger.

Darlene seemed neither pleased nor displeased to have me or even Ben in her house. She simply nodded, and said, "You're welcome to stay." With one plump, coffee-colored arm, she indicated the kitchen. "Come to the table after you've washed up and I'll serve your supper. It's still hot."

How did she know...? Ben pointed out the bathroom with a 'ladies first' gesture and a playful wink. He would have some explaining to do when this was all over.

Supper was a kind of fish stew, hot, filling, and absolutely delicious. I had no idea I was so famished. When I'd all but licked my bowl clean, on the second helping, I began to look for a graceful way of staggering to my bed and sleeping the sleep of the dead. My feet had been tingling for some time, there was a dull ringing in my ears and my eyes wouldn't stay open. This was a phenomenon for me, as I've never before sunk into a semi-conscious state while still standing, without benefit of too much brandy.

Blackie had been given some dry bread and the scrapings of the soup pan, of which he promptly wolfed down, also licking his bowl clean. We had a lot in common, Blackie and me.

As dogs weren't allowed inside, Ben had tied him to a corner of the porch with a rope long enough to reach the window outside the room where I'd be sleeping. Ben's old bedroom. Just the thought of him having slept here, grown up in here and played here as a little boy, made my head whirl.

Ben was leaving. I didn't have the energy to ask him where, as he obviously no longer lived at home. Tottering to the yard on legs of rubber, the horse ride had stretched the muscles inside my thighs to the point that they were no longer willing to hold me up, I asked him what he thought our next move should be.

"Tomorrow morning," he said. "We'll sit down and plan our strategy. I think it's best if you stay here for awhile. We don't know what those guys will do next. They have to know that you heard them, and that you will probably report it. They also will know how far to push it and stay within the letter of the law, and how they can use the First Amendment to get around it. Probably have their attorneys all lined up for just such an incident. Which means they'll know what their next step will be, but we won't."

I patted the horse's strong neck and looked up at Ben. He was certainly an enigma. Friendly yet standoffish, protective while still disinterested. Combine that with being quite literate and smart, while at the same time hindered with deplorable communication skills, he was a hard man to understand. Perhaps it was time I gave up on him as a romantic interest. Cut my loses and went on with my life.

I sighed. *And perhaps, love was just not in the cards for either one of us.*

Thanking Ben for saving my hide, I bid him farewell and told him to be careful.

With that, I went back inside, the smell of hot, perked coffee luring me into the kitchen. I couldn't resist having at least one cup and the chance to talk a little more with my hostess.

She was waiting for me, hands trembling slightly as she served me a cup. "Do you know if the police or any of them have figured out where Billy is? The whole tribe has searched every bit of the reservation, around town as much as we can, and all along both sides of the river as far as Mount Vernon."

It was one of the hardest things I'd ever had to do, when I told her we still hadn't a clue as to where the little boy had gone. Fear lay like an unspoken shroud of gloom around us. "Everyone, including Eagle Ridge's Police Force, the Sheriff's Department, and even the FBI are searching for Billy," I said. "There's an All West out, which means that every law enforcement agency in the western half of Washington, all the way up to the Canadian border, will be on the lookout for him."

I wanted to reach for her wrinkled hand, to cover it with my own...but wasn't sure if the gesture would be welcomed. This culture didn't seem to go in for a lot of sentimental demonstrations. At least not with an outsider. Even so, Darlene was Billy's grandmother and had been mother-in-law to Tiffany. If my heart ached with the need to find this boy, the pain she was going through must be staggering.

I wanted to give her something. Hope, maybe. Empathy. A feeling that she wasn't alone. These were all human needs, transcending cultures and generations.

"My nephew, Jeffrey, is a good friend of ...." Suddenly, a cold dread gripped me like a vice. "My God! Jeffy. Patti." My face must have mirrored the horror I felt.

Darlene stared, big-eyed and holding her breath.

I tried to explain. "It was my sister's husband, I saw tonight. They were....oh, its too complicated to go into. They're in *danger*. My sister and her boy. From her own husband...and he could be coming home....any minute now. Lord only knows what he'll do to them."

Darlene gestured at her telephone on the wall. "You better call her then, right away."

Patti answered on the first ring. Literally snatched it off its cradle, as if I'd caught her in the middle of an argument. "Oh," she said, disappointedly. "It's you."

"Thank God you're home and you're okay," I said, then added. "You are okay, aren't you?"

"I'm fine," she snapped, panting emotionally.

"Has Dwayne come home yet?"

"Been here and gone. He's cleaned out our bank account, some crap about having to go to Montana on a trip with his militia gang. I told him, if he left me like this, not to *ever* come back. He is such an *ass*. I've *had* it with him. Oh, and guess what else? When I got here, he'd been pushing Jeffrey around. *Jeffrey*. Said he was taking him on the trip, up in the woods for crissakes, to teach him how to be a man. A *real* man. Can you just imagine that? Haw!"

"Will he be coming back tonight?"

"I suppose. I truly doubt they'll get any farther than Red Dog Saloon tonight. Besides, he's still got some stuff in the barn. The tent, camping gear, things like that. He'll probably take off tomorrow morning. Plus, the *big man* will probably order his *slave* to make up sandwiches and a thermos of coffee for the gang. If he thinks he's getting *laid* before he goes, he can just think again."

Oh, Little Sister, just wait until you hear the rest *of the story.*

The Forces For American Arms and Liberties members had no idea how much I had overheard, but they would have

108

to go with the presumption that I not only knew what they were up to, but would keep very little of it to myself. They seemed to think their right to carry guns superseded everyone else's rights, including the rights of little boys to grow up in a safe environment. Taking Jeffy into the woods could well be an act of hostage-taking.

"Patti, if you've ever listened to me before Honey, listen to me now."

"What's wrong?"

"There's some bad stuff going down with that whole militia bunch. And I mean some *bad* stuff, concerning Dwayne. You and Jeffy are *not safe*. You've got to get out of there. Totally away from him, for now. I want you to come here with me for a few days until we can regroup and decide what to do. Okay? Grab Jeffy, and bring him with you. Do you still have the van?"

"Yea. It's right here."

"Good. Get Jeffy in the van, grab a few blankets and enough clothes to get you through the next few days, and get out here! You are not safe, there with Dwayne. I'm not making this up, Kiddo. Do you hear me? *You are not safe.*"

Her deliberations took no more than a minute, although it had to be a painful minute for her. In the space of an evening, she'd gone from hurt, to anger, to shock, to incredible disappointment. This was, after all, her new husband. And now she was being faced with fear for their lives.

"Patti! This is *important*. Are you coming?"

"Yes. Yes, of course. Just tell me where you are."

With Darlene's help, I gave her the directions, making her repeat them to me so she wouldn't get lost. At the last minute, I added a few personal needs to the list of things she was to bring; the laptop sent to me by my manager, the printer with paper, and my cellular phone. This house would serve as a kind of command post for the safe-keeping of women and children. After that, the only thing left to do was wait and hope that she got out before Dwayne came back. By the look in Darlene's lively black eyes, I wouldn't be waiting alone.

Over a second cup of coffee, I asked Darlene, as gently as possible, about Tiffany.

Placing herself in an old wooden rocker, the old woman

pulled a shawl close around herself, more to keep her hands busy, I thought, than any chills from the night air. She confirmed that Tiffany had been an adequate mother, while giving me the impression that the woman had been a bit uppity. Without saying so, she obviously blamed her for the breakup of the marriage with Ben. Evidently, Tiffany's greatest sin was that she didn't visit very often. In other words, didn't bring Billy over as often as she should have, and when she let him come on his own, he couldn't stay for more than a few hours. I assumed that Billy was Darlene's only grandchild, as I didn't believe that Ben had any sisters or brothers.

"Can you tell me a little about Billy's habits? Who were his friends? His baby-sitter, while his mother was at work?

The rocking motion of Darlene's chair and the creaking sound it made on the plain, plank floor was increasing with intensity. "His father gave him a bicycle for Christmas, last year. He liked to chase up and down the roads with the other kids his age." She picked up a ball of heavy, white string and a crochet hook from a large basket next to her chair, her shaking, brown-skinned hands causing the cord to vibrate as if it'd been strung on a harp. As she spoke in that same odd monotone, a squarish piece of white, crocheted lace began to emerge.

"As for any baby-sitters, the last I heard, Tiffany was gonna bring Billy here." She paused, thoroughly engrossed in her thoughts, her hands smoothing and stretching the doily over her knee. "Said she'd drop him off on her way to work at the casino."

This time, her pause was so long, she seemed to have forgotten that I was in the room. Finally she continued in a way that indicated that she would not be hurried and if I wanted to hear what she had to say, I would just have to wait. "Brought him everyday for about a week, then without saying anything about it, she just up and quit bringing him. Didn't even call me on the phone to say why. Just quit." Her eyes never left her work.

I wanted to comfort her. "You know, once we find him, and I really think we will, Billy's going to need you more than ever. You and his father. When this is all over, he'll need someone to take care of him and make him feel safe."

110

She looked at me then, not with a coldness but a desire to remain emotionally removed. "In our tribe, the grandmothers and grandfathers are the ones who raise the children. The elders are respected, 'cause they have a lot more experience and patience. They're not so busy trying to make a living and bringing in food and stuff to keep the home together. 'Course, the parents do their teachin's too, but not so much as the grandparents.

"Tiffany wasn't raised so much in the Indian ways. Her parents lived around the white folks too long. Working for 'em and all like that. After awhile, even a full-blood will get just like 'em. She just wouldn't believe that she couldn't do it all by herself. Was never meant to do it all by herself."

I was amazed that Darlene could say this to me, with her non-judgmental, non-condemning tone. But upon examination, her statements were neither anti-white nor mean. She simply stated the truth as she saw it, while letting me know that her views were not up for debate. And I was amazed that I did not feel put down, or insulted, or even less-than-welcome in the old woman's home.

I had asked and she had answered. Period.

The only thing that would make any of us feel better, was to catch the psychopath who had killed two people and scared a little boy so badly that he could be too terrified to come home.

Thursday. I awoke to absolute silence in the old woman's home. No alarm clocks, no TVs, no talk-show radio hosts. Not even the ringing of a phone. Listening more closely, I did discern the sound of birds singing from the hill of cedar trees out back and Blackie's restless thump as he moved under my window.

Patti and Jeff had arrived last night, and were camped out in their van which had been parked near Blackie. My briefing to her last night had been sketchy at best, as we were both exhausted. Little Sister didn't seem to be terribly surprised by her husbands' hanky-panky, so much as saddened that her own suspicions had been confirmed.

After a quick shower, I donned the clean jeans and T-shirt I'd scrounged from a tiny cubicle in the van. Hopefully, the sounds of water running in the kitchen meant that Darlene was making coffee. Outside, the van door slammed and with a sharp, warning bark Blackie scrambled to his feet, followed by a series of happy yips and much panting. Evidently, Jeffy was up and had discovered a boy's best friend.

By the time Patti appeared in the kitchen, Darlene had thick rounds of sausage sizzling on the stove and steaming mugs of coffee poured and served. She motioned that we should sit, her round face already shiny with a film of sweat from working over a wood cookstove on a morning that promised to turn into a scorcher by mid-afternoon. In a way, she reminded me of our own mother, never happier than when surrounded by her brood. A stack of pancakes, swimming with butter and syrup, had all but disappeared from the assault of Jeffy's knife and fork.

Ben also arrived, looking haggard and drawn. And smelling more than a little of horse sweat. It didn't take a brain surgeon to figure out that he'd spent the night searching far and wide for Billy.

After breakfast, while Jeff and Blackie played fetch in the yard, the four of us sat down to concoct a scheme that would hopefully produce a clue or two while foiling the plans of Junior and Dwayne. Patti worked at City Hall. She had access to innumerable public records on the countywide databases, plus valuable contacts on a first-name basis.

I had an idea. "Did you ever mention to the Mayor, or anyone for that matter, that you were my sister?"

"Uh, no. You weren't uh..."

"Uh, what? You can say it, you know. I'm not that popular around City Hall. It's no big deal. Really, it's not."

"Well, no. I've never mentioned it."

"Good," I said, rubbing my hands together. "We've got a spy. Those knuckle-heads won't know what hit them by the time we're finished."

Although Ben was supposedly on compassionate leave and couldn't use his position as Deputy Sheriff to its full extent, he had many years of law enforcement training behind him, a good working knowledge of the primary suspects and he was a highly respected member of the Bastolak Tribe. The other members and the council would not only listen to him but they would open up to him much better than they had to me. He was also one of the best trackers in the county, had worked with the Cascade Search and Rescue units many times, and knew the land.

Darlene operated our base camp. She answered the phone, kept track of the comings and goings of each of us, gave us sustenance and strength, and kept an eye peeled for Billy. She was a trusted friend to literally every member of the tribe, and could move around in full view on and off the reservation, no questions asked.

I would need to keep a low profile as far as downtown was concerned, but my handy little laptop with fax capabilities could punch some serious holes in their schemes, through my access to the media. The cellular phone from the *Gazette* had been left in the Porsche, but we still had Darlene's phone.

Okay," I said. "This is what I've got planned so far. I'm going to call Police Chief Clancey and tell him the whole story about the militia meeting and what I observed at the casino. I may be able to extract some more information, and may not.

They should have some kind of news release ready on Larson. And maybe Patti can rummage around in the courthouse in Mount Vernon during her lunch hour and find out who owns most of the property around that sewer project."

"Sounds good," Ben said, "But you'll both need to be careful."

"So what're they gonna do?" Patti asked. "Mug me just steps away from the county jail? Besides, that's the last place Dwight would come looking for me. He'd rather hang around the house, waiting for me to come home, so he can raise hell without any witnesses. Or threaten Jeffrey when I'm not around."

"Talk about raising hell, I'm about to be in deep doo-doo with Clancey for withholding evidence," I said, already dialing the police department. As quickly and as briefly as possible, I briefed our police chief on the events these last few days, including the militia meeting and Junior's gaff in the parking lot. He received the information with no comments other than gaining my permission to tape our conversation. I agreed, only on the condition that my testimony would be confidential.

"OK, I've done you some favors. Now it's my turn," I said to Clancey. "My sister, Patti Hickman, works as a clerk in the City Hall building. She is married to Dwayne Hickman. I understand that he may be a suspect for at least one homicide. Plus, he has threatened her ten-year-old son, Jeffrey. Who, if you'll remember, is close friends with the missing boy, Billy Jack.

"Now, I saw Dwayne at the militia meeting, heard him speak with my very own ears. They are threatening anarchy and treason, by the way. I'm prepared to swear to the content of that meeting. I even wrote down, at the time, a few of his more nauseating quotes. Now. Here's my question. Can you help me protect Patti and her boy? For one thing, we've got to get a protection order done *today*. Before he leaves the state. She has all the details, will be tracking down a lot of this herself. I just hoped that you'd back her up if and when she needs it. Patti tells me he's from Idaho, but their authorities may not want to release any information to her. They'll probably need your say-so."

"Let me worry about Idaho," he said. "That's my department. But a protection order in one day? No way. Not that I wouldn't want them to, but you'll never get a bunch of bureaucrats to move that fast."

"Clancey, the man my sister is married to is sick. Wacko. Stark maniacal mad. All this has put her and her son in a very dangerous position. He's already threatened to kidnap my nephew and take him over the state line. God only knows what else he may be capable of. I mean, he wants to shoot the *President!* We're talking about a real psychopath, here."

"I'll need a written statement on all this, and then I'll be notifying the Secret Service in Seattle. They'll most likely need their own statement and want an interview."

"Sure, but I can't come in there. I'll be happy to type up something and fax it to you. Do you know if Dwayne has a record in Skagit County?"

"It wouldn't look right if I released that information. Privacy act and all of that. You can try to find them in the public records yourself. How about you and your sister? I can offer you some police protection. For a period of time. We're a little understaffed, but I'll do what I can until we see if there's going to be an arrest made. Or at least until you get the order." He cleared his throat. "Miss O'Shaughnessy, I understand that this is your family and that you want to help as much as you can. But, you're getting in too deep here. This is police business and you're going to have to let us handle it."

"Naw. They may be dangerous but not stupid. Not even Junior is dumb enough to touch me within shouting distance of the major media for this state. Oh, and by the way, none of this can be shared with the Mayor, or Junior, or any of their staff. This is between you and me. Period. Okay?" In the midst of his drivel about backing off, I hung up.

Who was he kidding? I have barely begun.

"Well...," Patti said, getting up from the table and grabbing her purse. "Since I do work at City Hall and since this is a working day for all but militia members and laid-off loggers, I'll need to get going. How about I find out if they're actually going through with the late-comers agreement on that sewer project or if they've decided to keep it honest and put it out to bid. See what they've actually scheduled for the next city council meeting. I'll get every bit of information I can, then we can meet here at Darlene's tonight and go over everything. If you call me at work, and I start doing a lot of humming and hawing, it means that someone's within hearing range. No problem. Just give me a few minutes to get rid of him and call back."

Ben liked the idea. "Also, check with child protective services to see what it would take to get a warrant out on Dwayne for child abuse. And take steps to have him served with a protection order. *Immediately.* Make sure the judge understands that he is on his way out of the state, and that the FBI and the Secret Service will be wanting to question him."

I snorted. "Already tried that. Clancey said it can't be done that fast."

"Okay," Ben said, and ran a hand over his wild hair. "Let me take care of it. I know someone who works in Judge Parker's office." The four of us made a good team. The case was coming together, the loose ends being tied and trimmed, and the jackals would be punished. Even I couldn't ask for more than that.

"By the way," Ben asked. "Did I hear you say Dwayne was from Idaho? Was that his boyhood home?"

"Yes," Patti replied.

"Ah, ha. If he's wanted over there, seeing as how he *has* to cross through Idaho to get to Montana, unless he flies or goes way the hell around through Oregon and Wyoming, then this trip could be a big mistake. Let's see if he's committed to this militia group to the point that he's willing to take a chance. Call the U.S. Marshal's office in Twin Falls. See if there's any kind of fugitive warrant on him. You know, had he ever crossed state lines to keep from being arrested. Then call the state offices and see if they have anything. Warrants, arrests. Any convictions. We especially want to see if there's anything outstanding on him now."

"Clancey wanted us to leave Idaho alone. Said that was his department."

Ben thought for a minute, then said, "This request will be from the Sheriff's department. We're county. Won't hurt for there to be more than one request. Again, use Parker's office if they give you any lip. Call here at the house, once you get everything. We'll try to put together a package that we can hold him on."

There was one more villain, whom I wasn't about to let off the hook. "How about that bald dude with the red beard? Do you know his name? Anything about him? He was Junior's bodyguard that night at the casino, and again last night at the meeting. He looks like the violent sort. I know he was awfully mean to poor Blackie."

"Name's Spike Hardpenny," Patti said. "He's a logger and a subcontractor. Owns some earth-moving equipment."

"You know, Patti," Ben said. "I do want to concentrate on this Spike, a little more. Do the same on him with the Idaho authorities, although, as far as I know, he's lived in this county most of his life. Over the past couple of months, I've put together a fairly comprehensive file on him myself, but it sure won't hurt to add to it. Anything else we can find. I want to know everything I possibly can about these hoods."

Ben finished the last of his coffee, and set the cup carefully onto the saucer. He then looked at Patti, one eyebrow raised and grinning mischievously. "I've got an idea. Why don't we see if his contractor's bond is any good and if his license is still valid. Can you type up a subpoena for me?"

She nodded. "I think so."

"Good. We'll want to check the bank's records. It'd be quite interesting to see if there's any funds left in the bond account. I'll take it with me when I see Parker, tomorrow. Now, listen up, you two," he said, eyeing the both of us in turn. "Since I'm supposed to be on leave, I'd like to be the one to watch him. He lives in that apartment complex on Fir Street, and is working for a logging outfit right now. I'm telling you this so you can take pains to stay clear of him. Don't even drive down that street. Go way out of your way if you have to. The man's bad news and I'd rather you ladies didn't get mixed up with him. Just get the file on him, and bring it home with you tonight. If you get any run-around, holler for Clancey. I'll set it up so he'll know that I'm working with you, behind the scenes. Something in my bones tells me that this guy has so much hate in him, it's made him evil."

There was one item that had not yet been addressed. "Darlene," I asked. "Could we impose on you one more time

117

and leave Jeffy in your care for today?"

She looked down at her hands. "It's up to him. He can stay if he wants."

"We appreciate that, very much. He's having a ball out there with Blackie. And one other thing. The casino seems to have a fairly efficient bus service. The only bus service up here. Do they have any restrictions? Such as age or folks needing a ride besides the casino passengers?"

"They're not supposed to stop for anyone on the way into town, except to let out the passengers from the casino. But, the driver is my brother-in-law, a Swinomish half-blood from over by LaConner. If you see him coming, and start to waving real hard like it's important, he'll stop and give you a ride. I know that, cause I've seen him do it."

"Would he have stopped for Billy? I'm still wondering how in the world did he get all the way from here to the fairgrounds without being seen."

"If he really wanted a ride, he would. He knows Billy, or ought to if he don't. Lives right across the street from Tiffany's new house trailer."

The house I'd stopped in before. Dan Deepwater and his wife, Cassandra. Why didn't they tell me, then?

Probably because I didn't ask. What more did they know that they didn't tell me?

"Maybe it'd be better if you stopped in," I said, touching Ben on the arm.

He nodded, head bent, hand running through his unruly hair. "Already have. Last night." Breathing deeply, he fended off Darlene's efforts to refill his coffee cup. "It was Dan that gave Billy the ride to the fairgrounds. Took him right up to the gate. But his mother's the one who put him on the bus. Tiffany signaled for him to stop, practically ran the bus down with her car, and asked him to take Billy to the fair. Almost begged him to. Said she seemed to be pretty upset, almost cried until he agreed to do it. She must have known....," Ben cleared his throat. "...and was doing whatever she could, to save her son. As far as we can tell, Dan was the last one, except for the killer of course, to see Tiffany alive." Ben's report left us all stunned and filled the house with an uneasy silence. The spell was short-lived, broken by the shrill ringing of my cellular phone.

Gunner's sarcastic drawl could be heard, even before she handed me the receiver. "Well, well, well. The elusive reporter is alive, after all. I supply you with every communication device known to man, and still have to track you down. Do we have a story out there or are you too busy trying to be some female version of Davy Crockett?"

"Oh, we've got a story all right. But first I've got to find out how much we can print."

"Get things straight now, Kath. *You* get the story. *I* decide what to print. That's the pecking order."

I breathed deeply, *determined* that I wouldn't lose my temper. He was irritated with me, that I hadn't sent in an article for yesterday's paper or called in this morning. In an effort to lighten things up a little, I said, "Look. Things have really gotten crazy around here. I've got so much information that I'm still not sure what I can use. Give me an hour, and I'll bang out a summary of sorts and see what you think. Okay?"

"What happened to that feature you were doing on the Indians?"

"Well, actually, Gunner, I do have to check with the Tribal Council on a few points yet...."

"And what's that supposed to mean? You haven't finished *anything?* Look, Kath. Just finish the damn feature, and we'll worry about the rest of it, later. And I want it, by 1:00 o'clock. You got that?"

Now, *I* was mad. "Yes, Gunner. I've got it. And as I was trying to say, the *FBI* has insisted that I talk to them before printing *anything.* And if you think I'm going to put myself in a position to have *those* guys breathing down my neck for the sake of your precious frontpage, forget it!"

Over the phone, I heard him gasp, and pause for a minute. Apparently, *now that it was too late*, he'd finally decided to take me seriously. He breathed deeply and coughed. "All right. I was out of line, and I apologize. Okay? Now, calm down and tell me what the story is. What has happened since your last submission?"

"Don't *ever* talk to me like that again. Don't even *think* about it. And stop telling me to calm down." Taking a jagged breath, I fixed Patti with a look that warned her also to put a lid on it, and said, "So, as I was saying before being rudely interrupted and belittled, I'll be in the office sometime around noon. Given that the FBI releases me by then and that someone, such as the McDonalds down the street, doesn't offer me a better job."

 **HAPTER TWELVE**

Patti dropped me off at the Porsche, where I'd left it in Eagle Ridge. After a number of hugs and telling her to "Be careful," she went on to work and I throttled the old coupe past a few farms and dairies, and onto I-5.

The two hour drive into Seattle gave me time to think. The FBI had left word with Clancey that they preferred to interview me in their Federal Building offices, rather than at Eagle Ridge. I wasn't sure what that meant. They probably didn't see this case as having a high-enough priority. Could it be that they're pulling out of Eagle Ridge completely? That didn't seem likely. Kidnapping alone, would make it a federal case. Not to mention the fact that Indians were involved and at least part of the criminal activity had happened on the reservation, which would automatically bring in the FBI.

I walked into an office that could have passed for any other: mauve colored walls, dusty-rose carpeting, and almond-oak counter tops. The passive, run-of-the-mill atmosphere ended with the strategically placed cameras that had fixed upon my image from the first step off the elevator.

The surveillance proceeded to record my every word and gesture from then on, including the two-hour grill. Combine that with the fact that I had to pass through a metal detector similar to the type used at the airport, allow a rather macho-looking woman to search my purse and coat pockets, and fill out a questionnaire that asked for every statistic that my 30-odd years in life had produced, I would guess that they had a pretty good idea just what kind of charmer they had called in.

Their idea, not mine.

Imagine my surprise, once I had satisfied security, when an old friend sat waiting to see me. "Sims!", I cried, and would have hugged his neck except for the dour expression on the other man's face seated at the table in a conference room. *And* those ever-present camera's. "What are you doing here?"

"I work here," he said, with the same boyish charm and lopsided grin that I remembered so well. "What's your excuse?"

Sims had been the ranking FBI officer on another case several months ago, when we first met. As usual, I had blundered my way into some serious law-breaking and gotten some big-time bad guys mad at me. He was able to catch the crooks, including one of their ten most wanted. In the process, he managed to save my life and return my mother to her home and a very hungry little doggy. At the time, a rumor had been circulating that Sims would receive a promotion for his part in the caper.

After that, Sims and I had dated a few times. Even tried to form a relationship. Then he'd been called away to do a job God-knows-where, and didn't come back for months. And neither one of us was all that good at long-distance love-making. We had remained good friends.

Sims and his dour-faced pal immediately began the interrogation. An hour later, I'd run out of answers....two hours later, they stopped asking questions. I was allowed to go.

Sims followed me down the hallway. At the elevator, he punched the down button, then took me by the shoulder and said, "Look, Kathy. Things are getting hot and heavy out there in Militia-land. We've had that bunch under surveillance for some time, and from your observations, they're evidently getting closer and closer to making their move. The thing is, I'm getting pretty worried that they'll come after you next with a real vengeance."

"I can take care of myself, Sims. Been doing it for the last ten years."

"I know, I know. But we'd like to keep track of them and you, too. For your own protection. Let me tell you, I wouldn't *dream* of working out in the field without having a backup handy at all times. So, till things cool down a little, I'd appreciate it if you'd take my car for the time being." He dangled a single car key. "I'll swap with you. It's not as flashy as your Porsche, but it'll help you get around without them on your trail every minute. And the windows have a smoky tint so you can't be seen inside."

"All right. Thank you."

He punched the button for the elevator. "You'll find a cellular phone in the glove box. Keep it with you at all times. Eat, sleep, and make merry with that phone no farther than your back pocket. It's been pre-set with my number." Leaning close, his arm braced against the wall behind my head and a smile played at the corners of his mouth.

"You know," he said, nudging a curl away from my face, his light brown eyes soft and full of affection. "We had something pretty special, there for awhile. What'd you say we go out? That restaurant you like, down on the waterfront. We could grab a pizza, stare out the windows, and talk about it."

I looked down, full of conflicting emotions. "Sims, I...I'm really exhausted right now." The guilt of flirting with one man while being infatuated with another, pounded at me. I needed time to think.

It was if a curtain slammed down over Sims' face. The smile disappeared, the eyes going blank and dull. "Yea," he said. "You better go home. Get some rest." He turned away, drawing back his arm, and pretended to cough in his fist.

Knowing I'd hurt him, while hating to burn my bridges with a great guy, I touched his arm. "How about a rain check?" I also hated the hypocrisy. As soon as I said it, I knew the date would never happen, and I knew *he* knew it'd never happen. But there was no other way. It was like a pact. An unspoken agreement. Because breaking off a relationship, if that was indeed what we were doing, was just too damn painful.

"No problem," he said, jamming his hands in his pockets, easing off, backing away. "We'll see you around." The elevator door slithered open. He called from a point down the hallway. "Let me know if you have any more trouble."

I agreed, full of assurances that nothing was going to happen at home, and left. Next stop, was to run by the *Gazette* and answer most of the same damn questions posed by Gunner.

Being a journalist can make a person crazy at times, as you're constantly responding to other people's actions. Rarely does a reporter initiate a newsworthy event. And most of the news we report is the dirt. A city's tragedies laid bare, tattling on the infamous and the scandalous. Throw in a little sex now and then to keep things interesting, and we've just sensationalized another unsavory side of the human nature. Even so, I enjoyed working there... most of the time.

Gunner, the assistant managing editor, ushered me into his office. He was as tall and goofy-looking as ever, but trying to be polite. At one time, our graphics artist had circulated a picture of Ichabod Crane, a fictional character by Washington Irving's *Tale of The Headless Horseman*, sitting behind Gunner's desk. He'd placed a writing pad and pen at Ichabod's bony elbow and his size 22s boots perched next to Gunner's favorite coffee mug. Another time, during an election year, they'd drawn up some pin-on buttons, using Ichabod's face and Gunner's suit and tie, that said *I Like Ich*. He didn't appreciate it much, but we'd convinced him that it was all in good fun.

Today, I was *not* in a joking mood. Gunner got the whole story. Junior's run for mayoral office, complicated by his escapades at the casino and again in the woods during the militia meeting. He also heard all about the city council, the rich developer, and the Mayor's schemes to use a late-comers agreement, explaining that it was a document that allowed a Mayor to handpick a contractor to do a project for the city, instead of putting it out to bid. Usually, the excuse for this was that there wasn't enough time to go through the bidding procedure. The city council members would have to be convinced that this procedure was vital to the city's interests and they would have to approve it by a vote.

I summed it all up with Larson's recent demise and my concerns over Dwayne's plans to buy up a bunch of guns and form a mutinous group of anarchists to go after the President and how it was too political to be a coincidence and seemed to tie in with Junior's campaign.

Gunner had been scribbling on a yellow legal pad the whole time I was talking. He rubbed his forehead, and pinched the bridge of his nose where his heavy glasses had made dents on both sides.

"So," I said, after a few minutes of his pondering. "How much of this do I use?"

"Okay. Our last two stories were on this Tiffany Jack and the boy. Good human interest but only if we don't milk it dry. And any more on the mayor's race just means free publicity for Junior." He scratching his pointed chin thoughtfully. "Let's go with the recent death and leave the rest of it out . Do you have a report on the autopsy yet?"

"No, I don't. Clancey's office doesn't have it yet."

"Then there's no assurance that its being handled as a homicide."

"Not yet. I'm sure there will be, but as of yesterday afternoon, they hadn't heard."

"Call your Chief of Police in Eagle Ridge, what's his name?"

"Clancey."

"Find out if Clancey's got cause of death yet and if they're going to work it as a probable homicide or if they're waiting for the paperwork. Also check the next of kin, who are they and have they been notified. See if any of them would like to make a statement. Get the stats. Who is this Larson? Ever been married, any kids, what kind of work did he do. And why the hell did he ever want to be Mayor anyway? Throw in the background on Junior's campaign, but only the verifiable stuff. We don't need to be sued."

"What about this militia? Gunner, that's the real story."

"Sorry, Kath. I don't think we ought to use it. Not yet, anyway.

"Why not?"

"Can't do it, Kath. Too dangerous, legally. We could get our nuts in a real bind, over this one."

"But, Gunner. That's what papers do. They tell the people what they have a right to know. And I think, they have a right to know what these crackpots are up to."

His long, horselike face shook sadly. "That's the paper's policy, Kath. If we can't corroborate it with at least one more substantial source, and the feds aren't ready to back it up, then we sit on it till something breaks."

"Damn it, Gunner. I heard them and I saw them, myself. How much *validating* do you need? We're talking eyewitness here."

"Which is what worries me, Kath. Too dangerous right now. For you, since you are the only witness, and for us too. Keep a file going and update it periodically. Hand written notes only, don't put it on the computer where it might get into print by mistake. Let's see if they make an arrest. I want the feds to make the first move on this one."

Then, with the pink rising in his cheeks like a mercury thermometer on a hot day, he said, "You've done a fine job on this story, Kath. A damn fine job. When it's over, we're gonna talk more news stories and more money."

It took about twenty minutes to bang out a six column-inch story for tomorrow's paper. I hadn't gotten the okay to do the one I wanted, but I had gotten some long-due respect. And a possible promotion. If this militia story ever does hit the headlines, it's all mine. Including the part that Gunner was keeping to himself. I could see it in his sad eyes that he knew something about these guys that I didn't.

After making sure Gunner didn't have any questions about my story, I went home. It'd been less than a week since I'd left my humble pad. Seemed more like a month or two.

The building my apartment was in had once been a huge house on Queen Anne hill. It was built in the 1930s by a lumber baron who, at the time, had had the foresight to set up timber camps in the Cascade Mountains. So when the Department of Defense needed board feet by the billions to build ships and towers and barracks for the war effort, this very visionary businessman was ready.

Some years ago, a new buyer had divided the house into apartments. Mine was on the third and top floor. It had been a lady's parlor and bedroom and was the only one on that floor that boasted a tiny lanai.

I first thought to stop at Donna's apartment, next door down on the same side, to pick up my mail. Then quickly changed my mind. Donna was a good friend and I loved her dearly. So what if she was content to spend her days curled up on the couch, surfing through the cable channels, eating donuts and cold pizza. She was always pleasant, always returned what she borrowed and was always home.

I paused at her door, trying to ignore the yapping of that silly dog of hers that resembled an SOS pad with legs. She called the dog "Bo Jangles." I had a better name for the little rodent. He'd kept me awake more times than not, disrupted my reading and my meals. But hearing the strains of her favorite soap opera, along with being exhausted, I opted instead to go straight to my apartment, make a peanut-butter and jelly sandwich on stale toast and fall asleep in front of the TV.

I never seem to sleep when I should. My mind was racing a mile a minute, when it should have been numb from the trauma of this last week. Every creak and groan of the old house had me jerked up in bed, clutching at the sheets and holding my breath. My silk pajamas were damp from worry.

I was probably taking this case entirely too hard and needed to back off a little. Feeling guilty about leaving my sis and new-found Indian friends in the lurch. I'd definitely gotten too attached to Billy and much too emotional over the death of two strangers. *And maybe this gut-wrenching dread wasn't any kind of a premonition at all but a result of the sardines I'd eaten after the peanut-butter jar was empty.*

But something was bothering me. Something big and it wasn't going to go away.

Sims had insisted that I carry the cellular phone in my pocket no matter if I went no farther than the bathroom. I didn't argue. I got up and started prowling through the house, my link to the outside world in my pocket and carrying a hot cup of herbal tea. Easing past the drapes and the sliding glass door, I walked out on the balcony.

It was a lovely evening. Sitting in a lawn chair, feet propped up on the rail, I finally began to relax. There was little else to do out here but admire the almost-full moon and expose my neck by lifting up the length of blond hair to the cool breeze.

Suddenly, Donna's little dog ripped through her apartment in a frenzy of high pitched barking. It scared the life out of me. I jumped a good two feet high, spilled the hot tea on my lap and scalded my thigh.

I didn't scream, other than a sad whimper from the painful burn. It didn't make much difference. I could have sang an aria and hit high "C" for all the noise that mangy little rat next door was making. As I was peeling off my pajama bottoms much like one would peel a banana, I kept track of Donna's progress through her place by the heavy thudding walk vibrating the floor of my lanai.

Evidently, someone had knocked at her door. I couldn't hear much of anything but the damn dog. "Who's there?" she said, her voice quivering. "Bo Jangles, would you please be quiet a minute." It didn't help.

Donna was having a tough time, trying to get whoever he was, to declare himself. "Is there someone out there?" Amazingly, the dog's barking had become louder. He'd added some hysterical howling to the mix.

Much to my horror, a man's deep baritone answered Donna's inquiries from the hallway. "Got a message, uh, a telegram for Kathleen O'Shaw...somethin'. Shaw - nesie. Anyways, Western Union, here. It's a...really important message. Special delivery."

Western Union? I don't think so.

This was *not* how Western Union delivered their telegrams. Who in the world would be dumb enough to think this was going to work? Only someone from the sticks would....*Omigod.* He was from the sticks alright. A place called Eagle Ridge.

Meanwhile, I'd already pushed the button that would automatically dial Sim's preprogrammed number and was waiting for him to pick up.

He answered with a sleepy, "Sims, here."

It wasn't until then, I realized I'd been holding my breath. "...Uh...," was about all I could utter, feeling suddenly feint. The fear and exhaustion was taking its toll. But apparently, it was all I needed. That, and the raging rat on the other side of my kitchen wall who could be heard, not only over the phone, but halfway to Sacramento.

In my minds eye, I could see my friend instantly on his feet, awake and alert. "Kathy?"

"...Yea, ...uh....Sims?"

"Hang on. I'll be right there."

I'd been counting on Donna getting rid of our hillbilly delivery boy. But my neighbor, bless her little pea-pickin' heart, the sweet little fat girl who was always pleasant, always helpful, and *always* eager to do a good turn, would never dream of being rude. Not even to a pig who had awakened her in the middle of the night and scared us all out of our wits.

"Oh, you want Kathleen?" she said. "The name's O'Shaughnessy, by the way. With emphasis on the 'ahhh'. O'Shahhh - nessy. She doesn't live here."

Oh, no. Don't Donna, don't tell him where.... Frantically,

I began dialing her phone number.

"She lives next door. Down one, on this side."

"Hey," he exclaimed, sounding terribly put out at the inconvenience. "That ain't right. Mailbox says, it's *this* door. Number one."

"That's right. But we moved. Her and I switched apartments. Excuse me, I have to answer the phone."

I quietly closed the sliding glass doors from the outside, and backed into the far corner of the lanai. No time to worry about the circus next door. My biggest concern at this point, was to prevent an on-coming panic attack.

Deep breaths. Big deep breaths.

Head between my knees, I fought the dizziness, forcing my lungs to fill and blow out, fill and blow out.

As expected, he began to pound on my door, no longer trying to be discreet. "Telegram for Kathleen O'Shaw...whatever. Western Union."

One of the things I most enjoyed about this lanai, was the cherry tree that had been growing in the backyard for probably as long as the house had been built. Blossoms in the spring, fruit in the fall. And the fact that it had grown high enough, over the years, that I could pluck the fruit off the top branches from my little balcony.

This time, I'd be in the tree but wouldn't be picking any fruit. It was going to serve as my escape route. But wait! The branch that had offered all my goodies, was much too thin to hold my weight. Down, closer to the trunk, there was a branch three to four inches in diameter. Plenty strong enough for my measly 120 pounds.

And about five feet away. Out of reach. Unless....

The anxiety deepened, threatening to render me unconscious. *Can't worry about that right now.* I was too busy fighting to stay alive.

Next door, the circus had gone into a show-stopping act three. "Hello?" Donna chirped into the phone. "Is anybody there? Bo, would you just be quiet a minute? Hello?"

The delivery boy had given up his clever telegram ploy. He was now trying to kick my door in. Take that back, he *was* kicking my door in.

"Hello? Who is this, please?"

I climbed up on the rail, wavered....,

Breathe, lungs. Breathe, dammit.

....and literally took a flying leap into the cherry tree....my body propelled through the cool night air...., twigs scraping my sore thigh...., arms out, flailing, I grabbed the first solid thing to slap against my hands. It turned out to be a small branch, only two inches thick, dipping dangerously from my sudden weight.

It was a bad spot to be in. Swinging from a tree limb like a monkey, in my pajama tops – *with no bottoms or underwear on,* and a good two floors above the ground. I was in full view of anyone who chanced to gaze out a window.

Thank goodness, it was dark outside and I'd dropped down far enough that my trusty cherry tree branch was below the floor level of the lanai. I had another problem. I was starting to blackout from the anxiety and the sheer terror.

Look around. Be alert. Stay conscious.

He tramped through my apartment, slamming the kitchen cabinet doors and bashing through the wooden louvers in my bedroom closet. Suddenly, he stomped out onto the lanai. I could hear his heavy walk from one end to the other, his quiet curse when I was nowhere in sight.

I couldn't hold my breath much longer, and stay conscious.

I breathed softly, concentrating on being calm, on holding fast to the branch.

God help me, I don't pass out and drop to my death...and he doesn't look down.

Besides the thug who had ripped through my door and was now peering into the night only a few feet above my cold finger tips, Donna was the next best show. Evidently, she had put the phone down, nice girls would *never* hang up on a caller, and had thudded back across the room.

"Excuse me," she called, knocking firmly on her side of our adjoining wall. "That's not really necessary to, uh, do that to Kathleen's door. I don't think she's home."

Incredible. She wouldn't hang up on a phone call, so be it that they refused to identify themselves, but seemed willing to blow this guy off. Politely, of course. With all the excuse-me's and would-you-please's intact, she was actually going to tell this guy to get lost.

It only served to make him angry at *her*. He couldn't find me, after all his efforts to do so, and someone would have to pay. I could hear him curse Donna and stomp back through my apartment, kick the splinters of my door aside, and bellow at her once more in the hallway. "What the hell is going on here?"

Poor Donna was now his target. *But she had come back to the phone*!

"Hello? Is somebody there, please? I really wish you'd answer." Bo's barking was sounding more like a hoarse cough.

My body had slowed its swaying on the branch, and I'd gotten my legs wrapped around the trunk. Letting go of one precious handhold, I thumbed the cellular out of my pajama pocket and said, "Donna! It's me. Kathleen."

"Oh. Kathleen. I'm so glad you called. There's someone...,"

I could hear our friendly delivery man back at her door, banging and bellowing threats. Visions of a childhood fairy tale floated through my mind. A wolf was huffing and puffing, blowing down the house where a family of pigs lived. Their squeals for leniency sounded very much like ours.

I had to get out of this damn tree before I blacked completely out and dropped the two floors to the ground. "Yes," I whispered into the phone. "Shhh. I know all about it. Listen, Donna....,"

"But there's someone here looking for you...a man, he's right out....,"

Whispering, panting, and arguing, with the moonlight glinting off my bare buns not to mention the cold breeze, was too much to ask. "Shhh. Yes, I know. Donna, you have to be quiet."

"....and I think he's...sort of kicked at your door, uh...,"

"Donna. *Shut up and listen to me*!"

A sharp intake of breath was her only reply.

Too bad I couldn't do the same with the dog.

CHAPTER THIRTEEN

I'd gotten part-way down the tree when Sims finally showed. From my vantage point, I saw him brake in the middle of the parking lot and race to the apartment entrance.

His first act was to disarm our hillbilly friend, Donna confirmed that he was the culprit, and handcuff him to a post in the front yard. He then came around to the back and offered to fetch a fire truck with crew and ladders. I refused their assistance, loudly, adamant that I would be on the ground before they arrived. Adhered to the trunk of the tree in the juncture of a large branch and partially hidden by a spray of leaves and cherries, I implored him to evacuate all thugs, hit men and vagrants. No one had actually seen me yet, and I preferred that it stayed that way.

He agreed, although somewhat suspiciously. Hand to forehead, he stared up into the tree using his flashlight, searching for a glimpse of my form. I waved, assuring him that I was quite able to climb down on my own and would promptly do so the moment that the derelict in my apartment hall was gone. Shortly after that, the police arrived in response to Donna's call to 911. And from my lofty perch, I watched as a patrol car hauled Spike, the bald, red-bearded buck from Eagle Ridge, away to the pokey.

Thus, having finished with the preliminaries, Sims immediately tramped back around the building to the bottom of my cherry tree. He was looking for me.

It's easy to be heroic in the heat of battle. The survival instinct sets all matter of things in motion, both internally and out. Massive doses of adrenaline are released and sent valiantly gushing through the veins, converting shrinking violets into superhumans on the spot. Soldiers and warriors have experienced this phenomenon since the first cave man took up a club and bashed a lioness over the head with it.

But once the worst is over, reality sets in. For me, now that the danger was gone, I was beginning to realize just how close a call this one had been. My whole body trembled. I wanted to cry and I needed to go to the bathroom. And it wasn't over yet. Somewhere, I still had to find the strength to climb down out of this tree.

Shakily, I started down, loosing in the process, my cover of leaves. Sims was directly underneath me, head back, staring shamelessly up at my bare behind and shaking his head in wonder. "Lordy, lordy," he chuckled. "I must have done something right to deserve a view like this. Where *is* that damn camera when I need it."

I did find the strength to pluck a handful of leaves and over-ripe cherries to throw at him. "Sims, are you going to help me or not. And close your damn mouth. You're gawking and drawing flies."

When I had finally reached ground, he covered me with his long shirt and helped me up the stairs to my bedroom. And kept all of the crime scene investigators out until I was dressed. He'd taken Donna's statement while I was in the shower.

While doing my hair, Sims slow response to my call kept bothering me. It was odd and more than a little irritating, as he's usually quite dependable. There had to be something going on that he wasn't telling me about. Back in the living room, I asked him to explain. "By the way, what took you so long?

"Whad'ya mean? We're talking about driving all the way across town, you know."

I was sure of it. His expertise as an agent was being questioned, and all Sims could do was get defensive. He *was* hiding something.

"Besides," he said, drawing himself up to look righteously hurt. "I'd been sound asleep and had to get dressed."

"No, I'm not buying that. It's not like you've never done this before. You're used to middle-of-the-night calls. That's why you always lay your clothes out, the night before." The bickering had to be embarrassing Donna, but I seemed to have lost what little control I had. The trauma, the exhaustion, and the horrifying leap from my lanai had taken its toll.

"And the drive over here is a snap," I continued, coldly. "With your sirens going, and your police radio, you should have been here in under fifteen minutes. I know damn well, I was out there swinging from the trees like an orangutan a good half-an-hour. I repeat. What took you so long?"

"For one thing, your damn Porsche wouldn't start. I had to run back up to the room, and get some other keys. When I tried to call you back, the line was busy. I ended up having to take someone else's car, which meant running all the way back up to the room to get their keys."

"*The room*? What room? You live in an apartment. Wait a minute. That line I called you on was also a cellular, right? Where were you?" I pointed dramatically at a dove gray Audi sedan, crouched conspicuously amongst the gas guzzlers and rattletraps that were the norm for our parking lot. "And who's car is that?" I knew I was sounding shrill and self-serving, and would have to stop. But coming on the end of a harrowing brush with death, I couldn't bear the thought of losing him. And, frankly, the net of safety his presence cast around me.

It was a selfish thing to do and I'd feel horrible about it later on. Plus, it elicited a sheepish expression on Sims' face, making me feel even more rotten. He had the right to see anyone he pleased. Besides, hadn't I just turned down a date on the waterfront? Here, in my own familiar surroundings and in the company of friends, the fixation on Ben seemed like a old late-night movie. Poorly written and miscast.

Sims had been fiddling with his hands, when he motioned towards my neighbor. "By the way, Donna," he said. "You were great. Wasn't she great? Did you know she kept that prowler at bay the whole time? *From the other side of a door.* Can you believe it? Even had him talking in a normal tone and acting halfway reasonable by the time I got there. Saved us one hell of a chase. Guess he'd gotten comfortable and just didn't wanna leave."

"Well," she said, positively glowing from the praise. "Daddy always said that we should treat people as we wanted to be treated. That there was always some good to be found in the worst of us. You just had to look a little harder. It was one of his favorite sermons. He was a Methodist minister, you know. Preachin' the Good Word right up to the end, till the cancer took him."

Misty-eyed and pink-cheeked, she scooped the dog onto

134

her lap. "And Bo was so brave. Don't you think he was *brave*? Just like Lassy. He watches that program, all the time. Gets all excited when it's time for it to come on. How could I be any different than my little Honey Pie?" She hugged him to her ample bosom.

Time to go. I'd have to have some bit of sleep before morning and Bo had resumed his barking. I still had Sims' cellular.

Friday morning. I rolled out of bed groaning like an old woman. A pulled ligament in my shoulder was giving me fits, I'd scratched and bruised myself in a multitude of places, and the burn on my thigh needed attention. Stumbling into my kitchenette, I made coffee, fixed an ice-pack, swallowed a handful of aspirins, and located the phone under an old copy of the *Gazette*.

My next mission was to inform my fellow investigators that our friend Spike was in custody, and we could now concentrate all our efforts on finding that little boy. We finally had something to go on. By the time I'd packed a small bag with an extra pair of jeans and some T shirts, I had a call through to Patti.

"Good news," she said. "I can't really talk here, but why don't we meet for lunch?"

I agreed, and punched in the phone number of the Eagle Ridge Police Station. When Clancey wasn't there, I hopped into the Ford that Sims had loaned me and made a beeline back to Eagle Ridge.

Patti pulled into the restaurant parking lot just as I was going inside. She flopped in the opposite side of the booth and said, "How'd it go in Seattle?"

Briefing her on the questions asked me by the FBI and the meeting with Gunner, I mentioned that the red-bearded bum from Eagle Ridge must have followed me home. Her eyes widened with concern as I described the man's rampage on my apartment door. "Good God, Kathleen. You could have been killed."

"Well, I know. But I wasn't. Okay? I'm fine."

She leaned back in her seat, eyes glinting like liquid amber.

I patted her hand. "Look at it this way. The guy's been taken into custody and I've agreed to bring charges. They can ask him all the questions they need to and, with any luck, start tying him in to the Eagle Ridge murders. That means, they can use him to get to Junior. And, with any luck at all, tell us where to find Billy."

To change the subject, I waved at a passing waitress with a coffee pot. By the time the girl had finished taking our order, Patti had moved on to more juicy subjects and was prodding into my private life. "Say, weren't you dating a guy from the Seattle FBI office at one time? Did you see him there?"

"Uh, yes I did. He was the one who caught Spike."

"How's the uh, romance coming along with him? Does he know about Ben?"

"There isn't any *romance* going on with either one of them. My last date with Sims was some four months ago and Ben has a little too much on his mind right now to get involved in a relationship."

And if you think I'm going to share ALL my secrets with you, Little Sis, think again.

Cocking her head, she said, "Well, that brings up another thing. If Sims wasn't there during this guy's assault on your door, and since you only have one door, how did....?"

I just shook my head, not willing to share the highlights of my adventures in the cherry tree, and said, "Don't ask."

I knew her. The very next Christmas when we gathered at Mom's house, she'd wait until we had opened our packages and downed a gallon of brandy-laced eggnog. Then she'd just happen to "let it slip" that Kathleen had been seen swinging from the treetops in downtown Seattle, wearing nothing more than a silk pajama top and a big smile. Of course, at the first crack about my being the "butt" of my own jokes, I would be forced to choke her.

"I've got news," she said, dumping three packets of sugar and four creams into her coffee cup and stirring noisily. Iced tea with lemon was all I could handle on a hot day.

I gestured at her concoction and asked, "Are you going to drink that mess or pour it on your pancakes?"

Her lips parted to show me a teeth-clenched grimace. "Will you just listen a minute? I checked out that file on Spike. Sure enough, the dude was convicted of battery on a woman about three months ago and still is on probation. He was brought up on charges of armed robbery last year, although the charges were dropped on a technicality. There are several outstanding traffic tickets for speeding, and a warrant has been issued. Add that to the new charges in Seattle, and they should be able to hold the old boy for quite awhile." Sipping at her coffee, with half of it slopped on the table from being too full, she blinked at me bright-eyed, hardly able to contain herself.

"That's great, kid. You've done a lot of work on this since I left."

"That's nothing. Wait till you hear the rest. I went by the house last night and caught Dwayne hiding his pickup in the barn. So I called Darlene and had her give Ben the message. Of course, Ben came right over and served the big ass with a restraining order. My husband has hereby been ordered out of the house, *by the judge,* and told if he so much as comes near me or Jeff, he's going to jail. Plus, the Idaho authorities found what they called some *irregularities* that had never been resolved and are forwarding the paperwork on to Clancey."

She let me digest that for a moment, while we both ordered chef salads with vinaigrette dressing. "Which means, Clancey had to pick him up for questioning. Well, it seems that while he was denying ever having hit a woman, he was also served the papers for the dissolution of our marriage, right there in Clancey's office."

"Wow. I really am impressed."

"Plus, he admitted to Clancey that they had voted on who would be going to North Dakota. And he was one of them. Says it was just for demonstration purposes, that they had only planned a rally of some kind and never intended to endanger anybody. But I'll bet you anything that these guys can make that little nut crack."

She paused while the waitress delivered a basket of garlic toast. "Notice that what I'm telling you is all in past tense. Due to our actions, the militia's trip has been called off. Kath, you just may have saved the President's life."

"Good grief!" Head reeling and heart beating wildly, I didn't know whether to laugh, or cry, or call the White House. "Did he make that a part of his statement?"

"Sure did. Except for the last part. That was me." Downing the last of her coffee, she signaled the waitress for a refill. I ordered another iced tea. The mischief glinting from her dark brown eyes had reached momentous proportions.

"And even that's not the best part," she said. "I've submitted my paperwork to run for mayor. It seems that Junior and his pals got a little rambunctious and there was still one more day in which any Eagle Ridge resident could register. How would you like to be my campaign manager?"

We toasted her success with fresh coffee all around and a double order of fries.

Lunch over, we hugged good-bye on the sidewalk and agreed to regroup at Darlene's house around dinner time. As I prepared to crawl into the Ford, Patti turned and said, "Oh. By the way, there's some talk going around about that Indian woman's death. I'm not sure what to make of it, whether it's true or just small-town gossip."

"Well, what is it?"

"It seems that the tip of the knife that Tiffany was killed with, is missing. They're saying that it was broken off during the actual murder. And since they didn't find it in the autopsy, it has to be still laying out there in the grass where she was stabbed. And Officer Miller has claimed that they actually got some fingerprints of the murderer off the handle. If all this is true, it will be a crucial piece of evidence. But like I say, I really have my doubts."

I got into the front seat and started the engine. "See what you can find out."

"I'll try," she said, backing away. "They're keeping it pretty quiet. So far, Clancey has refused to answer any questions about it."

We waved, and I left. There was a lot of research to be done with too many unanswered questions about Junior's campaign, the militia gun-runners, and a missing boy who'd lost his mother. Somewhere, there had to be a link. And I intended to find it.

Once more, I dialed the police department. Clancey, I was told, was still at a Rotary meeting. I left the number of the cellular phone, and asked to have him call me back.

One of the stops I'd been wanting to make for some time was at the office of the town's weekly newspaper, the Eagle Ridge Report, where I hoped to speak with the editor, Andy Jones. The paper was in a dingy office in the older part of town. Andy, I'd been told, not only covered what news the little town had to offer but also sold the ads, did the graphics and layout, and took most of the pictures. His only assistants were a seventeen-year-old kid who came in and helped with the production on Tuesday nights and his father, Frank Jones.

Andy was hard at work, hunched over an old IBM word processor, eyes focused on the screen while his fingers flew over the keyboard. Knowing all too well what it was like being up against a deadline, I sat demurely on the nearest chair and waited politely for him to come up for air.

My gaze landed on a plaque hanging on the wall. It evoked my curiosity and I walked over to examine it better. It was a Pulitzer Prize, given to Frank Jones in 1968, for an article published in the *Chicago Sun* on Martin Luther King.

"Can I help you?" Andy said. He'd come up behind me so quietly that I didn't even hear the rustle of his brown corduroy slacks.

I introduced myself and told him I was in town to cover the murders. He nodded. "You and half of the country. The story has attracted a lot of interest." Up close, Andy had kind blue eyes brought out by the thick reading glasses, and thinning blond hair. "Of course, you already know that. What can we help you with?"

"I don't know. Some background, maybe? A little history of Eagle Ridge's elite?"

"That I'll leave to my dad, Frank Jones. He's out to lunch right now, but should be back soon. Now there's a piece of work for you if you're interested in the history of Eagle Ridge. Dad was born not far from here and grew up with the founding families of the town and half of the businesses, including the first bank."

"Have you always lived here, then?"

Andy had a gentleness about him that was very appealing, and he wanted to talk. I wasn't sure if it was his way of flirting with me or if he was just plain lonely. "Not really. Dad got a scholarship right out of high school, at Oregon State. From there, he went to work at various publications back East, including the *Chicago Sun* and *Life Magazine*. Dad's an old newshound whose heyday took place during the 1930s, when the law-breakers were mostly bootleggers and racketeers. He covered the rise and ultimate demise of Al Capone's war on prohibition and the authorities who enforced it. And of course, in the 60s, what with all the racial riots and the busing, he got to be quite well known."

I was impressed. Reading about the events that shaped so much of America's history, was one thing. Meeting the man who wrote them was quite another. "Yes. I saw the plaque."

"That was from a piece about the *I Have a Dream* speech by Martin Luther King and his assassination."

Assassinations. Terrorist activities. Bigotry. Not a new means of gaining power and not limited to countries outside of our own.

"Your dad sounds like quite a guy."

"He is." Andy chuckled. "Those who know him best say that he has so much newspaper ink in his veins that when he bleeds you could make a run of 30,000 copies and it'd never loose the shade of black."

Shoving his hands into his pants pockets, Andy paused and looked down. "But I'm talking too much, and not about the things you came here for."

"No, really..." I wanted to assure him that as a journalist myself I could appreciate his dad's stories. But just then an old man who had to be in his 80s, came hobbling in the door.

"Dad," Andy said. "This is Kathleen O'Shaughnessy from the *Seattle Gazette*. She's looking for some history on Mayor Winthrop and Junior. I told her that you'd be more able to give her the low-down on Eagle Ridge's elite than anyone else."

Jones was so old that time had wreaked much havoc on his body, making any movement painfully slow. Yet his lively mind still wanted to investigate, to interview and, every now and then, to write one hell of a story. He nodded to me as he came in, one quick little jerk, puffing heavily on a nasty-smelling cigar. He hobbled over to his desk with the help of a cherry-wood cane, lowered his scrawny self onto the grimy cushions of an old desk chair, and gestured that I should also sit down.

"What kind of history are you looking for?"

"Oh, just general background. What is it that makes him tick? How long has he been here? How'd he come to be elected as Mayor and keep the position for so many years? Your son tells me that his ancestors were one of the founding families not only in Eagle Ridge, but in the whole Northwest lumber community. Obviously, his name has been the major spring-board of his political success. But there's one person who hasn't been mentioned, yet. What happened to Mrs. Winthrop? Junior's mother?" I shrugged my shoulders. "I guess I'm looking for the proverbial closet skeletons. Every family has theirs and I was wondering what his were."

"Have you talked to Jebediah yet? That's Mayor Winthrop's first name, although he doesn't like to use it that much."

"I've tried, but had little success."

Frank cleared his throat, laying the soggy cigar in a filthy ashtray and settled his hunched frame into the worn cushions. "Junior came from a autocratic family that had all the luxuries that money could buy, but none of the benefits that come with life's more simple pleasures. Eating dinner together as a family, a mother to tuck him in at night, a dad to teach him right from wrong. Oh, there's no doubt that his parents loved him as their only son, but I doubt that he saw much of them. His father worked day and night at the timber camp, seldom came home unless there was a visiting dignitary to impress with a big party.

"His mother, Maggie, was a beautiful woman, grew up in a little cabin just south of here. Her daddy worked for Jebediah, till he got all busted up in a logging accident. Maggie had emotional problems and was away at different hospitals most of the time. Today, she'd be labeled a neurotic and see a shrink once a week for depression. Probably read a lot of self-help books in the winter and go to AA meetings. But back then, they didn't tolerate those relatives who couldn't conform to the niceties of society. Either hid them in the attic or sent them off to an asylum in the East.

"The first time Maggie was sent away, Junior was still in diapers. She'd get better for awhile and come home. But she'd always revert back to her old habits, drinking too much, sneaking out at night. Couple of times she was caught carousing with the men at the camp. 'Course, Jebediah wouldn't put up with it. Couldn't, I suppose, and keep his standing in the community. He sent her back East to one hospital after another. Evidently, she pulled out all the stops on that last one. Tried to burn the place down, and roughed up the head nurse on her

141

way out. Caused the hospital so much grief that *they* sent her home for a couple of weeks. She refused to go back. When her husband tried to force the issue, she ran away. Hitched a ride into town, bought a train ticket, and never looked back. If I had to guess, I'd say it was about the time Junior was entering the fifth or sixth grade. To my knowledge, no one's heard from her since."

Jones picked up the nasty cigar and sucked on it. "If I remember right, that's the same year Jebediah ran for office of Eagle Ridge's first Mayor. Just a part-time job back then; he still ran the timber company. Even started up a lumber and shake mill. Talk about power, the Cascade Timber Company offered jobs when no one else could. Fairly decent paying jobs too, considering the rest of the country was trying to survive the Great Depression. And Jebediah did all the hiring and firing. Like I was telling Andy, now that Junior's trying to fill the old man's shoes, he's probably seeing more of his daddy than he ever has. Maybe even more than he'd like."

The rest of the next couple of hours were spent perusing old newspaper copies, reading a sampling of articles that featured Mayor Winthrop. Ground-breaking for a new bank, posing with a Republican Congressman running for re-election, cutting the ribbon on the new City Hall building.

One particular piece took my eye, a story done by Andy on a City Council meeting last month. They had approved a preliminary permit for a new apartment building, to be built by Rafferty. It was on the same street as Patti's five-acre plot. At the very end of the article, it was mentioned that Gus Smith, called Smitty by his friends, was one of the sitting council members when the permit came up for a vote. Come to find out he'd owned that same property in the past, and had tried to block the vote. I showed it to Andy.

"What's the story on this?"

"That piece of land had, at one time, been part of Smitty's dairy farm. About six years ago, the city annexed it into the town, shoving the city limits out past his place. Along with a lot of heavily forested land up on Seven Cedars Hill that had been in the Winthrop family for years. Of course, for Smitty, being in town all of a sudden changed the requirements for his whole operation. He couldn't afford a complete remodeling with all new milking equipment. Barn was too old, for one thing. Taxes went through the roof. Caused him to lose a farm that had been in his family for generations.

"At the meeting, Smitty had been trying to point out that he believed, it had been planned that way from the very beginning. They wouldn't let him talk. Kept butting in, confusing him, and got him so mad that poor Smitty wasn't making any sense. To make a long story short, he was asked to step down from the vote, and to shut up or be taken in for questioning." Andy shrugged, and looked down at his hands. "I thought the guy deserved a hearing on the matter. Since he didn't get it in court, I tried to at least give him his day in the public eye."

Unknowingly, Andy had just confirmed the statement made to me by the old-timer, at that same city council meeting where I'd been standing up for Patti and Dwayne. That old man had been Smitty's friend for many years and had much of the same thing to say about that City Council meeting last month as Andy did. That made two sources by which to verify the land-grabbing techniques used by this bunch against their constituents.

When I left, Frank was in his corner, half-asleep, and Andy was on the phone, taking notes. I waved to them both on the way out. Andy gave me the high-sign.

Frank lit up another cigar.

The restaurant where the Rotary meeting was being held was just around the corner. Close enough to walk and far enough away to give me some fresh air and a chance to think. Rotary meetings, while not closed off with locks and armed guards, aren't exactly open to the public, either. They prefer to conduct their meetings with the least amount of interference as possible, and limit their guests to only those who've been invited. But no one ever said that I couldn't catch myself a cop on his way out.

As I turned off Main street onto Fir, the meeting had just ended and the members were filing out of the restaurant. Clancey had stopped to shake hands with Ethel Bowman, the owner of Skagit Fabrics and Crafts.

"I've been trying to reach you all day," I said, greeting Clancey. "How about if we touch base on a few points before you leave. You just might find them interesting."

143

"Come by my office, anytime. I should be in the rest of today."

Taking him aside and out of earshot of the others, I said, "Well, since I'm already here, and since part of what I have to say is about the Mayor and his campaigning son, who just happens to be your boss, why don't we just toodle back into the coffee shop and find us a nice, quiet corner?"

Clancey eyed me with a guarded but knowing look. He wasn't a stupid man, nor was he reckless. At that moment, I was sure that most of what I'd be telling him he'd already considered. But, as we'd already established, this was his boss and any accusations that couldn't be proved would either make or break his career in law-enforcement.

He agreed. We promptly found a booth and ordered coffee.

Point by point, I went through the same specifics of what I'd told Ben. The highlights from my FBI questioning and informing session in Seattle, and Spike's confrontation with my apartment door. The militia meeting, I covered in minute detail, including what I heard Junior say to Rafferty.

I'd already revealed that Patti Hickman was my sister and also the wife of Dwayne Hickman, one of the speakers at the meeting. And Clancey was aware of my fears for her safety. He didn't know that she had enlisted to run for Mayor. I reminded him that her little boy, Jeffy, just happened to be friends with Billy Jack, the missing Indian boy. Which meant that both boys could possibly give some valuable testimony to a prosecuting attorney, when and if this case ever goes to trial. And that Deputy Sheriff Jack and I both felt that this was the reason why they kidnapped Billy.

"I guess that what I'm asking is that you continue to keep an eye on Patti while she's at work, especially now that she's his only opponent. Even though she works in the same building as the Police Department. The people who killed Tiffany and kidnapped her son, seem to be eliminating anyone who can testify against them. Should they follow this line of attack, Patti and her little boy will be their next target."

Clancey moved uncomfortably in the booth. "Well," he said. "You certainly know how to lay it on the line. Is your sister and her boy still living in the same place? Are they still living with Mr. Hickman?"

144

"No. They're hid out, for now. On the reservation. As you already know, she's filed for divorce and has a restraining order out on him. But we can never be sure just when one of these guys is going to follow her home, after work. We try to be as careful as we can and keep an eye peeled for any tails, but it's not a situation that can go on forever."

"I'm a little limited as to how much I can do, at this stage," Clancey replied. "But, I *can* offer her an escort home if necessary. And watch for anything out of the ordinary while she's in the office. As a precaution, you might suggest that she bring a sack lunch to work, instead of going out."

"What about this Spike Hardpenny? The red-bearded dude who bashed in my apartment door? I would think you could at least take him in for questioning on Tiffany's murder. That breaking and entering charge on him in Seattle will last just long enough for us to get comfortable."

Clancey shook his head in aggravation. "I wish I could. Unfortunately, it's out of my jurisdiction. In another county, and in the hands of the FBI. They... prefer to handle that one. I will tell you that my men have been briefed on this guy. Once he's released, they've been told to report any move he makes. Evidently, Hardpenny's still locked up in the Seattle jail. We haven't seen hide nor hair of him all week."

He finished the last of his coffee and poked a sausage-sized finger in my direction. "I gotta tell ya, Kathleen, something you don't wanna hear but you're gonna hear it, anyway. This case is not your concern, other than to write your stories, *after the fact*. In my view, you've become too much of a draw for these guys. Like a lightening rod. And if you're not careful, they're gonna strike just when you least expect it. I have to repeat what I told you last time. Let the authorities handle this, before you and your family get hurt."

Clancey cleared his throat and wiped at a speck on the table with his napkin. "I've been told to give you a message. This comes straight from the Mayor's desk. My boss. We have orders to back off from Deputy Jack, don't leak any information and keep him on the list of suspects."

I was flabbergasted. "You're not serious! *Ben?* Clancey, you know darn well, that's a put-up job. And frankly, I'm getting real curious as to why in the world the Honorable Mayor

145

wants to frame a damn good Deputy. There's no evidence against Ben, and no motive. Clancey, that old fogey can't be that stupid. He's got something up his sleeve, besides Junior's political career."

The Police Chief made a wry mouth. "Like I said, that includes you. Winthrop wants you to back off from Ben, too. He's quite capable of getting a restraining order, you know."

It was almost funny. "Oh. Let me guess. He's now taken control of the free press." I snorted and pushed my coffee cup away. "No dice, Clancey. I'll fight this bastard all the way to the Supreme Court, if need be."

On that note, Clancey stood up and threw a few dollar bills on the table to pay for the coffee. As we parted, our eyes locked. And in that moment, I knew what he most wanted to say but in his situation didn't feel it was prudent to do so. Yet. It was the same thing that I'd been thinking all along.

Junior's already made some big mistakes. Eventually, he'll do something that we can use against him in court.

The next thing was to get my hands on the details of Larson's autopsy. It probably wouldn't be finished for a couple of days, unless someone managed to light a fire under the coroner's behind. I intended to call him this afternoon.

It was only after Clancey was out of sight, that I remembered one other little piece of information that he might want to take into consideration. I'd forgotten to warn him about the upcoming City Council meeting. The special one, at which the proposal for Rafferty's late-comers agreement would be voted on. And one which, we intended to show up for in force.

On the way to Darlene's house, I stopped and picked up a cartfull of groceries. The makings for a spagetti supper including hamburger, sauce, rolls and a large salad. It was enough that Darlene had opened her home to this horde, but she didn't need to feed us all, too. When I walked into the house, Patti had already peeled a five-pound sack of potatoes, Darlene had prepared a large salmon for the oven, and Jeffy had flopped on the couch, watching TV. Ben hadn't arrived yet. No problem. I placed the groceries in a corner of the kitchen and offered to help. Darlene could always use them tomorrow or the next day.

As he had before, Ben came in just as dinner was going on the table.

It was a delicious family-type meal, as if we'd been doing this forever, and was incredibly comfortable. After dinner, the dirty dishes were quickly swept away with each of us washing and drying and we sat back down for more brain-storming.

Since Patti appeared to be bursting at the seams to tell her all of what she'd learned at the city hall today, Ben asked her to start the discussions. She passed out photocopies of a land deed and several other documents, stamped by the courthouse.

"I found out that the property up the street from our place had indeed been owned by Junior. Oh, he did a pretty good job of using a non-registered company name and an address of his attorney's, but the paperwork shows that the Cascade Timber Company paid cash for it at a Sheriff's auction. For an amount which barely covered the back taxes. Later on, it was quick-deeded to Junior's company for the price of one dollar. Junior sold it, through this fictitious company, to Rafferty, just months before he filed to run for Mayor. Now, it seems that this same developer not only got his permit to go forward with a big apartment complex on that land, but is also on the agenda this next Monday night to be the contractor who'll put in the sewer on a late-comers agreement. Which means, the sewer project won't even go out for a bid. It's being handed to him on a silver platter. It's not even a regular meeting night and I doubt that the public will receive much prior notice."

"I cannot believe the gall of these people," I said. "What do they think this town is? Their own private kingdom? You know, that's exactly what I overheard Junior offering Rafferty, if he forked over the money to pay Junior's gambling debts. He promised him the project for a ten-thousand dollar kick-back." Looking around the table, I offered a solution. "What do you say, we all show up at that meeting. As a property owner on that street, Patti has a right to insist on being heard."

Andy, from the town paper, would most likely be there, covering the meeting for next week's front page headlines. Unless he hadn't heard about it, either. I made a mental note to inform him of the meeting and what I'd heard at the militia meeting.

"And, while we're on the subject, this is a copy of an article done by the Eagle Ridge Report. It details the comments by one of the City Council members, Smitty, who had owned this same property for many years. The land that was in that Sheriff's auction had been his dairy farm. We're talking about your property, Patti, and your house and barn. And where the new apartment complex will be going in, not to mention the new sewer line. As soon as I have time, I'll try to pay a call on Smitty."

I also briefed Ben on the events in Seattle, including the gist of what the FBI had wanted to know and the destruction of my apartment door by one red-bearded logger. I left out the part about my pajama bottoms and former flirtation with Sims. While I was wondering whether or not to mention my conversation with Clancey, Ben interrupted my thoughts with news about his search for Billy.

"By way of the process of elimination," he said. "It doesn't appear that any of the militia members have Billy. I've checked out every one them. Studied their habits, searched every possible place they could have used to hide him. They're hiding a lot of stuff, but not Billy. I have to wonder if they're not running scared because they *don't* have him, and that's the reason for such ill-advised behavior. Could be that Billy has slipped away from them all.

"On the other hand, I've tracked him to the point that he's either on this reservation, hiding out somewhere, or is long gone, many miles away from here. But, knowing Billy, I can't really believe he'd do that, either. If he had a choice. Which is why he bummed a ride with you back to town. He doesn't really want to go too far away. He's just running scared right now."

Ben sighed, rubbed a spot on his forehead, and looked at each one of us in turn. "Let's just hope that we find him before they do something really drastic."

"Do you think he actually saw his mother, Tiffany...," I asked.

"I think it would take something that traumatic to make him stay away from his own family. His grandmother, his father, everyone he knows and trusts....,"

Ben shook his head, the muscles in his jaw beginning to bulge. "They've done something to scare him. Badly. Who knows what Billy has seen or what he knows."

Jeffy was pulling at his mother's shirt-sleeve, bored with

the talk of grown-ups and begging, in a quiet but insistent whisper, to be allowed to go outside for a romp with Blackie in the back yard. Patti, not wanting to be distracted from the conversation, simply nodded and sent him on his way. As the kitchen door slammed behind him, Darlene moved to the window where she could watch them play.

With the kitchen quiet once again, Ben continued his theories on Billy's disappearance. "I believe his mother was scared for him, telling him to run like that. Maybe she saved his life and maybe she didn't . Maybe she didn't have time to do anything more. But she must have done whatever she felt she had to, in order to keep him safe.

"Which only reinforces my belief that she knew her killer and knew that they were coming after her. It's a shame that she couldn't trust anyone. Not even me." Ben stared sadly down at his hands, lost in remorse. I gently touched his arm.

He never did look up.

CHAPTER FOURTEEN

Darlene was still at the window and was the first one to spot Jeffy, running and yelling for all he was worth, with Blackie in hot pursuit. She darted to the door and yanked it open, as an excited Jeffy came sliding in. In his hand was a baseball cap. A cap that I had seen only once before but for which I had filled out innumerable forms in describing a little boy's appearance. No doubt about it. It was Billy's baseball cap. The same one that he was wearing the day I gave him a lift home from the festival.

"I found it in the back," Jeffy said. "Or, I should say, me and Blackie found it. It was hanging on a low branch, under one of those big cedar trees."

Ben had hunched down, in order to be on an even level with the boy. Jeffy handed him the cap, his young face beaming with pride. "You've done well, Jeff," Ben said. "You have good reason to be proud."

Jeffy blushed, looking from Ben to his mother to Darlene. "It was Blackie that took off running," he said, almost apologetically. "I went after him right away, so's he wouldn't get lost in the woods, it being almost dark and everything."

"It's good that you've found this," Darlene said, with a soft smile. "A sign that Billy will soon be home."

On his feet now, staring into the woods as if to implore the spirits of the cedars to reveal their secrets, Ben laid his hand on Jeffy's shoulder. "Can you show us where you found the cap?"

"Sure."

Blackie's leash was brought out, and within minutes, we were off, racing past the barn and corral, across the pasture and into the forest.

This was a tribe that held the cedars in high regard, as they did all living things, but the cedar tree seemed to be special. Enchanted. Almost mystical. As we entered the woods, there did seem to be a larger-than-life presence in the hushed whisper of the cedar needles as a slight breeze swept their graceful boughs.

Patti and I were out of breath and lagging behind, by the time we heard Jeffy exclaim, "It was here, we found it. Blackie was kind of snorting around, sniffing at everything. Like he's doing now." The dog's nose was to the ground, and he'd begun to whine.

"That dog smells something. Or someone," Ben said. "Let go of his leash, and stand back . Let him find their trail."

Nose to the damp earth, dog began to paw at the ground, frantically sniffing as he recognized a scent. Suddenly, he stopped in his tracks, the ruff on his back standing straight up, and growled softly. Panting, he then came up to each one of us, shoving a wet nose into our hands, then returned to the same spot, digging for all he was worth. Now and then, he would stop, sniffing at the air around him and the leaves within reach, and howl.

"You know," I said. "That poor thing is trying desperately to communicate with us. If he could just speak English."

Ben caught Blackie by the collar and peered deeply into the dog's eyes. "Don't need to speak English," he said.

Patting Blackie's massive head, Ben promptly let him go. "Blackie has found the scent of his owner. Or at least, the man who raised him. And, he thinks he's also found an enemy. If not an enemy to us, at least an enemy to him."

Ben caught a cedar branch in his hand and stroked it as he stared at his mother. An unspoken understanding seemed to pass between them. He then dropped the handful of earth he'd been crumbling, and said, "I believe the man is dead and this is the spot where he was killed. And the dog just may have been an eye witness to the murder."

He looked at me, and I instantly knew what he was thinking: *Billy!*

Growing more and more agitated, Blackie darted around the spot where Billy's hat had been found, growling softly to himself. His search widened into ever-larger circles. Suddenly, he raised his muzzle to the skies, let out a loud yip and several long, sad howls. It was a cry of mourning and had to be the most heart-rending sound I'd ever heard. He then took off deeper into the forest. We followed as best we could, Ben leading the way with a flashlight.

Sharp rhododendron leaves scraped our arms and cedar branches whipped our faces, as we plunged headlong through the forest. Racing against time, trying to keep the dog in view, scrambling to keep up. Some twenty minutes later, I was stumbling. My side ached, and my lungs were heaving for air. But we had come out on the other side of the cedars....and in the back yard of a trailer park.

The park where Tiffany and Billy had once lived.

Nose to the ground, Blackie seemed to have momentarily lost the trail of his prey. More people meant more footprints and more scents to sort through. He yelped and trotted into the street. Sniffing eagerly, he ran to each parked car. When the scent wasn't there, he moved on the next. Into every yard and up every walkway.

A slight breeze had picked up, blowing briskly now. Blackie turned his nose to the wind, snuffled a time or two, and yipped happily. He'd caught a scent. He dashed over to Tiffany's trailer, under the yellow crime scene tape, and pawed at her front door.

I clutched Patti's arm, whispering that it was Billy's old house.

Ben, reluctant to break the yellow tape and spoil any evidence, stood outside the tape, watching Blackie closely. Evidently, as the tape was still up, the police had not yet finished their search and may possibly come back. With Winthrop on his heels, adding Ben's fingerprints and hair follicles to the mix now, would not be beneficial to him or to the investigation.

"Billy," he called. "Are you in there, son? Billy?"

We waited, holding our breath. Praying. Darlene had moved over next to Ben, standing expectantly. Many of the neighbors were watching, creeping onto their front porch steps in order to see better.

"Billy. Is that you in there? Whoever's in that trailer, I'm asking them now, to please come out.

Darlene took up the call. "Billy? Come on out. Your father's here. We've all been hunting for you for days. Please.

This is your grandmother, asking you to come out. It's alright. You're not in trouble and nobody's going to hurt you. Or me either, or your dad. Just come out. We need you out here."

Again, we waited. Was Billy really in there? Was anyone really in there? Or were we all standing around like fools, shouting at an empty trailer.

Blackie had no such doubts and he had no qualms about yellow tape or crime scene disturbances. He clawed the front door, leaving great gouges in the thin aluminum. His barking turned into a worrisome howl, hyphenated now and then with happy little yips and powerful lunges.

We held our breath. Darlene stepped closer to the tape. Any minute now, she'd be going in after that boy, everything else be danged. Slowly, it began to dawn on me that although Blackie was making one hell of a racket, he was not making all of the barking noises.

There was another dog inside, answering his barks with sharp little yaps.

I looked at Ben. With finger to lips he gestured that we'd best not speak. The handle turned, the door cracked open, and a little black-headed, black-eyed boy peered around the door-jamb.

Darlene was the first one to his side. She ran to the child, trampling the tape, and scooped him up in her waiting arms. Ben was right behind her and the three of them hugged and sobbed, assuring one another that all would be okay. And since Patti and I needed hugging too, we clasped Jeffy and each other and cried.

As Billy emerged from the trailer, the reason for Blackie's odd behavior came to light. The dog paid little attention to the boy. A Husky with one blue eye and one brown had followed Billy out of the trailer, creating chaos with Blackie.

He literally went nuts.

Within minutes, the two dogs were showing a total disregard for any human contact. The Husky was a female. She was in heat, and Blackie was in love.

Amid the tears of reunion and the antics of the dogs, we all trekked back to Darlene's house. First Billy would eat and be fussed over by his grandmother and dad. The questions would have to wait.

An hour later, the boy had finally finished his meal and was rested. Ben took him onto his lap. "Son," he said. "I know that whatever made you run away is very painful and hard to talk about. But we're going to have to. I will need to know who you're so frightened of and why."

The fear in Billy's face was a painful thing to see. "Mama told me to run, and not to come back. She made me promise, over and over, that I would. To run as far as I could and not let them see me. She said that those guys were coming after her and that I had to run away or they'd get me too. But it was too scary and I ran out of the money she gave me, and there wasn't any place to sleep. And then, when I saw on TV that they really did...., you know, what Mom said they would, I ... didn't know what to do." He was trembling. "I was gonna stay away but I wanted my Nintendo set. It was boring there in the stockroom."

"I know this is hard, son. But you must tell me who the men are. And where you've seen them before."

"That dumb guy, you know, the one who likes to pretend he's got no hair? Only he's got this big beard? Right. He's the one Mom was fighting with. She hollered at me to get in the car, and was driving really fast, man. I mean, *really fast.* And this dude was behind us, acting like he didn't know how to drive at all. I mean, this dude was all *over* the road. Practically pushed our car off into the ditch, a couple of times. Musta been drunk or somethin'."

"Where did your Mom take you in the car?"

"Well, we were going down the road. I mean, like *fast*, man. Really *fast*. Then she sees the bus, you know, the one from the casino and did this really cool wheelie, right there in the street. Then she gets out and makes the bus stop. And tells me I have to get on. She was talking to Dan. You know, the neighbor guy? And said I had to go to the festival at the fairgrounds. And that's when she said that they were after her and that I had to run as far and fast as I could."

He sniffled, shaking as he remembered.

Did he realize that that was the last time he'd ever see her? A little boy, caught up in the corrupted elements of an adult world, trying to understand an inconceivable act.

In a little-boy voice that was trying hard to sound grown

154

up, he said, "Brian told me that the reason Mama died was because she wouldn't listen to anyone and do what she was told. He said I had to hide in the stockroom, you know, the one at the casino, or the same thing was gonna happen to me."

Brian? The cook from the casino kitchen? Of course. The day I interviewed him, he'd acted awfully funny. It was Billy all along, making those scraping sounds in the stockroom, right off of the kitchen. With Brian lying to whoever was on the phone, that he was there alone.

"Is that where you've been all this time?"

"Yea. I had to stay in the stockroom during the day. Either that, or up in the hotel room. Sometimes, I got to run around at night in the woods with Sheba."

Without asking, I decided that "Sheba" was probably the Husky.

"It got really boring in there. And I wanted to get my Nintendo."

"Well," Patti said. "I'm so glad that everything turned out. We were really worried about you. But Jeffy and I better get going. I still have to work tomorrow."

Ben stood up. "Where are you going?"

"Home. It's okay. Dwayne's been served his restraining order, which means that he can't come anywhere near me. And Spike's in jail down in Seattle. We'll be fine."

Shaking his head, Ben spoke quietly but with great intensity. "I wish you wouldn't. We just got one boy home. I'd hate for them to kidnap Jeffrey as another hostage."

"But, how can I possibly..."

"That restraining order simply tells him not to go home or around you at work. The penalty for breaking that means he'd do a little time in the county jail, probably no more than a week or two, with the rest of it relegated to community service. And be fined. That is, if we catch him at it. It doesn't guarantee that Dwayne won't go after the boys, if he decides that he's in even more danger by what they know. Up against murder one, it's a small price to pay.

"And there's something else. Just this afternoon, I got word that Spike has posted bail. Actually it was his employer, Cascade Lumber Company, that put up the money. He's out. Roaming the streets."

Chills ran through my spine. Spike out on bail? "But I thought....,"

"Oh, he'll have to appear before a grand jury. And there'll probably be a trial. But until he is tried and convicted, they can't keep him."

Ben flipped his long hair out of his eyes and cleared his throat. "What we've got to do, here and now, is to decide how we are going to protect these children. Of course, we all want them home with us, safe and well looked after. But, I wouldn't put it past Spike and probably Dwayne, to do everything they can to eliminate these eyewitnesses. They've probably already learned that Billy is gone, and will come here looking for him. Oh, not while we're all around. They'll wait until we've all gone to work and Mom is here alone with them.

"We can't take any chances with these boys. I say, we take them completely out of the county, and keep them in a safe place until this all blows over. Frankly, they're not safe in this house any longer. It won't take long before these guys add two and two together and follow somebody here."

Once again, a look passed between Ben and Darlene, a voiceless communication. She had been standing at the window, looking out. She turned, and directed her verdict to Ben. "Take them to the peak," she said. "There, the *t'ku`ba* will help us protect the boys. And the white men will never be able to find it. If they try, they will only get lost, chasing their tails around in circles."

My curiosity peeked. "What is that?"

"The *t'kulba*? It's a spirit that legends say, lives on the highest peak of Mount Baker. It's a place where our people used to go for spirit quests."

Ben then directed his comments to Patti. "I don't want to frighten you any further. But I do believe Billy is still in great danger and they'll probably go after Jeffrey too. This is a hard decision for you to make. But I ask that you make it, soon. We'll be leaving here with Billy within the hour and Jeffrey is welcome to come."

She looked at me, and all I could do was try to show support and comfort. As hard as it was for me to not interfere, I had to keep quiet. As Ben said, this was a hard decision to make and she was the only one who could do it.

Looking at her son, Patti huddled in her chair, and said, "I don't think I could go through what you have with Billy. Especially now, since the stakes are even higher than before." She shrugged her shoulders, and wrapped Jeffy in a bear hug.

"There's nothing to decide. If that's what it will take to keep my baby safe, then that's what we will do. In fact, why don't you take my van? It'll sleep all three of them, and there's a tiny stove and sink that pulls out. They can at least get inside in case it rains."

"Okay," Ben said. "Here's what I think we should do. Mom will drive your van up to the scenic drive, on Mount Baker, and park the van. From there, the lake is a two-hour hike. I'll stay with them tonight and help them pack into the lake in the morning. I'll be pulling the horse trailer. The horse will be corralled about ten miles from camp. I'll be back, sometime tomorrow night and from then on, I'll go up every other night. Check on them, make sure they have plenty of groceries. Drive my car to the farm where the horse will be kept, and ride over this rocky trail the rest of the way. That way, they're sure not going to follow me. I'll hear them. For the kids, it'll be like summer camp."

"What kind of a place is this?"

"They'll be camped alongside a small, little-known lake, up on Mount Baker. To get to it from the lodge where most people go, you have to pass through this real different kind of place. Scientific explanations have shown that it's an electro-magnetic field that's been turned on its kilter. Certain mineral content in the rock reacting to the natural minerals in our bodies, alters our sense of direction. Combined with the high altitude and decreased oxygen levels, it causes this horizontal surface to feel kinda like its perpendicular. Makes you dizzy if you're not used to it. And like Mom says, the white men will end up chasing their own tails around in circles."

Ben ruffled Billy's hair and moved his arm so that his son could sit next to him on the couch. "You know, when I was a kid and had a problem that was too big for me to handle by myself, my grandma used to tell me a story. It's an old legend that's been told in our tribe for centuries, about how the Creator made the world.

"You see, long, long ago, our people knew that they lived

157

in a beautiful place, with just the right amount of trees and rivers and salmon to eat, but they weren't happy with where the Creator placed the sky. It was too low and the tall people kept bumping their heads against it. And some of the people could actually jump into the Sky World and get lost. It was the Changer's job to make the land more livable for them. After all, he was the one who turned some of the animals into People. But when the Changer came out from the East he saw our beautiful valley and wanted to go no further. There was no better place to live, than right here. But he still had all these languages to pass out. Well, he ended up giving every group of people he met a different one.

"So, some of the elders got together and talked about what they should do about the sky. They would have to push it up above their heads. But none of these groups were large enough to push up the sky alone. So, these same elders decided that if all of the tribes tried to communicate and they all worked together, they could push with long poles and move the sky up above the tree tops. There was one word in all the languages that was the same. *Ya hoh.* It meant to go forward. To do it. It was decided that that would be the signal in all the land to push. They would all shout at the same time, *Ya hoh!* "

Ben looked at each one of us in turn. "Let's see if we can do it. On the count of three, let's all say, *Ya hoh.* One, two, three....,"

The boys were tickled. "Ya hoh," they said, grinning sheepishly.

"Oh," Ben said, nose wrinkling. "That was an awfully puny one. Come on, put some feeling behind it. You too, Kathy and Patti. Again...,"

"Ya hoh!"

"That's better. But I still think we can improve on it. Everybody, come on now...,"

"Ya hoh!!!"

"Much better," he said. "But this time, I want you to feel like you're really pushing up the sky. One more time..., PUSH!"

"YA HOH!!!!!!"

"Excellent. Well, the different tribes worked and worked and worked, and they all pushed on their long poles at the same time and they all shouted *Ya hoh* really loud, and they did it. The sky was pushed up above the treetops. 'Course, there's always somebody who doesn't pay attention, right? There were a few hunters who hadn't heard about the sky pushing, and happened to chase four elks into the Sky World. Also, some fishermen in a canoe floated up there. The Changer turned them all into stars."

"This particular place where we'll be going, is so far up the mountain that a loose translation from the Lushootseed language would call it, 'The Place Where The Earth Meets The Sky.' And if you believe the stuff of legends, and you were to get lost up there and wander into the Sky World, the Changer would turn you into a star."

He grinned and said, "Ya hoh. Let's all work together and there won't be a thing to worry about."

I was struck by the innocence of this tribe. Even their legends were of a non-violent nature. And I was impressed by this wonderful thing that Ben did. The whole atmosphere had gone from a fear-charged horror to one of anticipation. They were going fishing on a real "Indian camp-out."

While Ben was talking, Darlene had been packing the food from the kitchen to take with her. An hour later, they were ready to go.

To Ben, I said, "There's one more question I'd like to ask Billy, if I could."

He nodded, and said, "You'll have to ask Billy if he wants to answer any more questions. It's up to him."

My chair was directly across the room from him. I bent over slightly, and smiled. "Billy, you remember me, right?"

"Sure. Jeff's Auntie."

"Would you mind telling me how your baseball cap was found in the cedars out back?"

"It was Zeke that took me there. Really late, one night. We snuck out when Brian and Junior weren't watching, and got all the way to the cedars before they caught us."

"Zeke? You mean, Zeke Larson? The guy who was running for Mayor against Junior?"

Junior's only opponent, at the time, and the only thing keeping him from running unopposed. The same one who suffered a fatal accident himself, just three days ago. Ohmigod! I had to wonder if he had yet realized, with Patti in the race,

159

he'd still not be running unopposed.

"Yea. Well, I don't know anything about elections and stuff. Junior used to talk about it all the time to Brian like it was a really big deal. But I think they're all pretty stupid. One time, there was this big party or something in there. Brian said for me to help, but I had to stay quiet. Making some of those little sandwiches and loading the dishwasher and stuff. It was okay. A lot of work but at least I wasn't so bored. Then after everybody left, I had to back to the stockroom.

"Then Zeke comes back there and says how would I like to go to my grandma's house? I said, *cool*! Then I told him what Junior and them said about how I had to hide or the guys that got my Mom would come after me. But Zeke said that I'd be even safer at home, since my dad was the Deputy Sheriff. And I went, *duh,* that's the same thing I was trying to tell them but nobody would listen. So, we got as far as the cedar trees out back before Spike and Junior comes after us. That's where I first saw Blackie."

"Blackie? How did Blackie get involved with Zeke?"

"Didn't you know? Blackie's Zeke's dog. Belongs to him. Do you think we oughta call Zeke and let him know that Blackie's okay? He really likes his dogs."

Ben swallowed, his arm moving instinctively to protect his boy from the malignancy of a man gone mad. "Son, this is important, so I want you to be very careful in your answer. "Who was it that took you back to the casino? Did all three of the men go back with you, including Zeke? And what did you see and hear, there in the woods?"

"That's easy. Junior made me go back, by himself. Spike stayed with Zeke. They were arguing when we left. He didn't like it that Zeke had been taking me home."

Patti was visibly shaken. "And Jeffrey? He hasn't wanted to talk about anything you might have told him, because he was your friend and didn't want to be a snitch. But did you ever say anything to Jeffrey about Junior? Or any of the other men?"

A look passed between the boys. Every inch of Jeffy's body language pleaded with his friend. *I stuck up for you, now it's your turn.*

"Uh, yea. I guess so. Just...talking and stuff." Billy's reply to his friend, was a wide-eyed shrug. *What'm I supposed to say?*

My sister cast me a look of pure horror. Taking pity on her, I took one of Billy's small hands and said in as calm a voice as I could muster. "Billy, what did you tell Jeffy, at the time?"

"Uhm, I guess I told Jeff about Junior coming over all the time." Once again, he looked to his pal, to see if this testimony was what had been expected of him. It was met with Jeff's tiny nods, encouraging him to go even further.

"Junior used to come to our house and argue with my Mom. Making her cry. I didn't like that, at all. And before, he used to come over and they'd talk *business*. I always had to go outside or to my room when that happened. But Mom said it was worth it, because he fixed it so we could get a new mobile home. She paid for it, though. She made sure that everybody knew about that. Junior just did some...kind of business with these other guys and helped Mom talk them into it. The guys that she bought it from."

From the looks of Ben and Darlene, they knew what this meant. *No doubt about it. Billy was the next best thing to an eyewitness and Jeffrey could collaborate his testimony. Because of their young age, it probably wouldn't be a pivotal part of the case, but it could inflict some heavy damage if packaged with other, more concrete evidence. Not to mention the fingerprints on Zeke's car, and my observations from the militia meeting and at my apartment. Put all of that together with any evidence the FBI has gathered, including whatever Sims was able to pry out of Spike while he had him in custody, and the case could very well be ready for trial. Therefore, Spike and Junior have very little to lose. They'll be doing all they can to eliminate these kids now that Billy will be available to testify.*

They were ready to go. Darlene was making a last-minute check. Each of them would need a jacket and the dogs would need extra dog food. Patti was stuffing the last of the dry milk, the peanut butter and a loaf of bread in a bag.

It was obvious that Ben didn't like leaving Patti and I alone, either. With worry lines etching permanent grooves between his brows, he took us both aside. "Stay inside and keep the doors locked. If you hear anything, your best bet is to pretend that there's nobody home. I don't have an extra gun to leave with you, but I do still have the cellular phone. Call me on that if you have to. And the Tribal Police will respond to a call to 911. Otherwise, I'll be back tomorrow." He hugged me good-bye. I had to fight the instinct to hang on and beg him not to go.

"Since there really isn't room for two dogs and the boys in the van," he said. "I'm going to leave Blackie here with you. Keep him with you, everywhere you go. Even in the car. He's a good friend to have. "

The van was packed, and idling in the driveway. Billy was the only one who hadn't boarded for their trip up to the mountains. After a panicky moment of searching, he was found in a corner of Ben's old bedroom. He was crying. "I guess I'd forgotten about....I was looking for Mom. But... it's true, isn't it? I mean, about my Mom getting killed and everything. I really do miss her."

**HAPTER FIFTEEN**

After they left, the house was eerily quiet. Patti and I tried talking a bit; she'd become teary-eyed over Jeffy having to leave. Then there was her breakup with Dwight to worry about. It was a heart-breaking time, discovering that she'd been married to a lunatic, and promised to turn into a bitter court battle. We were both too edgy to sit around an empty house that just hours ago had bulged with the energy and the sounds of two young boys, not to mention Ben and his mother.

In addition to the loneliness, it infuriated me that a murderer, with each passing day, was running around free. And Brian needed to pay *dearly* for his part in kidnapping Billy. He had to know by now that Billy had been found and had implicated him. Though Ben had made some calls before he left that I took for granted were to Clancey and the Sheriff, I was extremely curious to know just how Brian had decided to handle it.

"Hey, Kiddo," I said, nudging Patti with my elbow. "How about if we go to the casino?"

"The *casino?* I don't have any money. And I'm hardly dressed....,"

"Not to gamble, silly. There's a guy there I'd like to talk to. And I'd like to see how Brian's taking Billy's absence. The little creep. He lied to me."

"Do you really think we should? I mean, Ben said we should hole up here and pretend that nobody's home. What if Junior and Spike show up? For crying out loud, what if *Dwayne's* there?"

"So what, if he's there. So what if *any* of them show up? We'll be a lot safer with all those people around us, than here alone."

She sighed. "I don't know, Kate. Having Jeffrey go off in the middle of the night has just about done me in."

I took her by the shoulders and forced her to look at me. "Jeffy is fine, and you know it. He's much safer up there in the boonies with Darlene than here in town. He hasn't been safe, you know, for quite awhile. And Billy's back. What more do you want? Those boys are having the time of their lives. Now, come on. Where's that mischievous spirit of yours? You used to *love* this kind of sport. We'll wrap some scarves around our heads and take off all the make-up. No one will ever recognize us, with no mascara and no kinky hair blowing all over the place. Let's face it. When was the last time *anyone* saw either one of us without make-up? We could even wear some of Darlene's old dresses and pretend we're from the janitorial service."

At last, Patti began to respond. "We'll have to take your car."

"All the better. They won't have a clue if we go in a car they've never seen before."

It took longer to don our cleaning lady disguises than it did to drive to the casino. Once there, I drove directly to the rear of the building, acting as if we'd been doing this for some time, and backed up to the rear door marked *employees only*. When one of the security guards answered our knock, I said, "We're the first shift from the janitorial service, Clean Livin'." I edged around him into the hallway.

"This early? You ain't supposed to start till after we close. About 3 o'clock."

"There's extra work tonight. Hafta inventory the kitchen panty and scrub everything down special. Has to be sanitized. Health Department is comin' tomorrow. Boss said for us to start early."

He shrugged, "As long as you don't get in the way of paying customers, I guess it's alright."

"Don't forget to unlock the storage room for us." Armed with squirt bottles filled with foul-smelling cleaning supplies, I had filled them half and half with ammonia and a strong pine-scented antibacterial, I hefted a bucket with a wet mop, added an over-sized sponge, and led the way to the kitchen. About midway down the hallway, we hurriedly whispered our plan of attack.

"You go in first, make sure Brian is gone," I said. "He won't recognize you. If he's there, give him the story about

164

tomorrow's surprise visit from the Health Department."

"No problem. I'll ask him to stick around and help us clean. That request has sent more than one male scurrying for cover." Patti snapped her fingers. "He'll be gone so fast, to quote young Billy, *he be smokin'*."

The kitchen was closed, the dining room doors locked and Brian was nowhere to be found. We begged the use of a key from the same security man who'd let us in, then proceeded to secure the swinging kitchen door that led to the dining room by stacking large cans of tomato sauce and 20 pound bags of pinto beans against it on the inside. A small aluminum ladder was balanced over the top in a way that would send it clattering to the floor should anyone barge in through the dining room, using their own key, and force the kitchen door open from the other side. As good an alarm system as any. That left only one way in or out: by the rear kitchen door that opened into the same hallway.

The security guards looked askance at us, muttering and complaining a few times. But whenever one of them looked as if he might object enough to get in the way, we pleaded with him to help us. "Could you do us a favor? We can't reach the top shelf very well. Maybe you could scrub it down for us?"

Finally, when they had all decided it'd be best to ignore us, I ventured forth to find an old friend. Peering around the corner at a spot where I could see most of the casino floor, I spied Montana at the bar. While I was wondering how in the world I could discretely get his attention, he got up and headed for the men's restroom. I darted after him. By the time I reached that part of the hallway, he'd already gone inside.

My cleaning lady equipment in evidence in case I was spotted, I edged along, listening with every inch of my being for the sounds of another man's voice.

Lord, please let him be in there alone. Hearing nothing, I rounded the corner and darted into the latrine.

Drats. Montana was not in a stall, but standing in front of a urinal, doing, I supposed, what all men do in that position.

"Pssst," I whispered, and thumped my trusty mop against the aluminum pail. "Montana."

He jumped, fumbling at his trousers, face turning a beet red. "Hell, hold on, lady. I'll be through here in a minute."

The disguise as a cleaning lady must have worked. He'd only seen me once before, all decked out in a black party dress. He didn't recognize me. Come to think of it, *I* didn't recognize me, with my head wrapped in a silk scarf and wearing a shapeless rag complete with tattered slip and baggy support hose.

"No. Montana. It's me! Kathleen, the journalist. Remember?"

His back to me, he did a funny little squat then whirled around and fixed me with a frosty glare. "What? *Kathy?* Jesus, girl. Get out of here. This is the men's *john.*"

"Dammit, Montana. I have to talk to you." I shivered. Those piercing, green eyes of his had chilled me to the bone.

"Not in here, you ain't. What if somebody comes....?" He made a self-affirming motion, checking that all was tucked in, zipped up, and dry. It was probably not often that somebody unnerved Montana to this extent. He'd lost his cool and was getting hostile.

"Never mind," I said, backing into the hallway. "I'll meet you in the kitchen pantry. Okay? This is important. I wouldn't be doing this otherwise."

When he finally entered the kitchen, my friend had recovered most of his cool but still a little agitated. It had to have been his curiosity that brought him.

"So," he said, straightening his tie. "Are you gonna tell me what the hell is going on?"

Quickly, I introduced him to Patti and offered a cup of coffee. "Here's the deal. It seems that they've been keeping Billy right here in the casino. Mostly in the pantry and stock-room. Evidently, they had the kid scared to death and convinced that they were protecting him. Told him that even his Dad had gone into hiding, disappeared into the mountains, and nobody had heard from him for weeks. Billy knew that his mother had been killed, and he was terrified. They even let him call the Sheriff's department and the dispatcher confirmed that Ben was on compassionate leave."

"Ah, the lying bastards," Montana said, running a jewel-bedecked hand over his smooth blond head. "You know, I saw a kid once, playing around the trees out back. Chasing this big dog. So it was Billy, after all. I asked Brian about it, but he swore to the heavens that it was some kid who belonged to one of the top floor maids. Said she didn't have a babysitter so Brian was watching the kid for her. Made him a hamburger and some fries." Montana's pale features seemed frozen in place, consumed with a cold fury. "I damned near called you then, but Brian insisted that it would just cause problems for the kid's mother. Said she needed the job and showing up with a kid in tow could get her fired."

I nodded. "I believe you. Okay. Next question. You said when last I was here that Junior's lover worked in the kitchen and that he had to hide that fact from his dad, Mayor Winthrop. Did you mean Tiffany? And why in the world did he have to hide the fact that he was dating a beautiful Indian woman? Are the Winthrops really that bigoted? Or just plain snobs?"

"No. Tiffany didn't work in the kitchen. She was a dealer. Everybody knew she was his cover-up. Tiffany was just *pretending* to be Junior's date and getting paid quite well for it, I might add. Until she paid with her life. And yes, he *did* have to go to some pretty extreme lengths in order to keep his Daddy happy." He looked down at his hands, cleaning a perfectly manicured fingernail. "As for his being a snob, I wouldn't get my feelings hurt over him, if I were you. He's not a snob, he just ain't interested."

"Heh. Don't do me any favors. My feelings aren't hurt, just awfully curious." Taking a deep breath, I tried to put voice to my confusion.

"Then he was actually *dating* someone else. Do you know who? She must be married. One of the waitresses, maybe? That's an awfully elaborate scheme just to keep his Daddy from finding out about his extra-marital affairs. But, there again, this guy *is* in the middle of a campaign, isn't he? And he continues to carry on like this? Talk about compulsive behavior. Lord knows, he's in a lot of trouble with gambling debts in this casino, yet he keeps coming back. I don't know, Montana. There's just something....strange about this whole setup. I can't seem to get a handle on this guy."

Montana shook his head. "Tell you what. You want to know Junior's little secret? Come with me, both of you. " He plucked a large, serrated knife from the wooden block that held an assortment of cutlery and handed Patti a long meat fork. "Bring

167

those mops and squirt bottles with you. Good disguise, you damn sure fooled me," he said with a grimace, and pushed the muzzle of my squirt bottle so that it was facing away from him. "And they look like they could inflict some serious bodily harm."

We strode to the elevator in the hotel lobby. We landed on the third floor and in the wing that held the hotel rooms. At the near end of the hall and around the corner, he gave Patti and me a wink and opened the maid's closet with a tiny file on his fingernail nippers. Peering inside, he snatched a key ring from a peg and continued down the hall.

Patti and I hurried after him, the carpeting covering the sounds of our footsteps. There were some twenty rooms. Ten on each side. Huddling in front of the last door on the left, weapons at the ready, Montana inserted the key into the lock.

"When I jerk this door open," he whispered. "Stand ready to beat them back with your mop handles if necessary. I'd like for them to stay here for awhile. Let *them* find out what it's like to be taken hostage."

He opened the door quietly, although he really needn't have bothered. The two lovers on the bed were conscious of little else but themselves and their culminating passions. In the dim light of the hotel room, their bodies heaved in a frenzy of carnal desire.

Was I really that naive? I turned my face away, ashamed of myself for watching, as they deliriously murmured their love for each other.

A quick flick of the switch, and the lights revealed Junior's most vulnerable frailties. A weakness so risky to his election that a beautiful woman had died over his fear of being exposed and a little boy had been kidnapped and frightened half to death.

The lovers were Junior and Brian.

Montana had gone into a crouch much like a large cat. "Sit tight, fellas," he said, brandishing the knife from the kitchen.

Junior jumped up from the bed and retreated to a corner. "What are you doing here? Get out! Before I have you thrown out!" He'd managed to grab his trousers and held them in front like a bashful schoolgirl.

"Don't try to run," Montana snarled. "... you little son-of-a-bitch. "Don't even move or I'll slit your boyfriend's innards like a pig at pork-curing time." He jerked off his own tie and forced Brian to the floor with a head lock and the kitchen knife. Brian whimpered, but sat perfectly still as the edge of the knife was lodged against his throat.

"I don't like assholes that kill innocent women," Montana said, allowing the tip to lightly prick a piece of skin. A tiny drop of blood rolled down his neck. "...and I particularly don't like the ones who'll kill the mothers and then go after their kids."

Brian immediately swore he wasn't a murderer.

Montana wasn't listening. He proceeded to bind Brian's hands and feet with his tie and belt, and pointed to the phone with his jaw.

"Kate? Get the downstairs pit boss, on the phone. I saw Mayor Winthrop come in, just about 20 minutes ago. Tell him that the Mayor needs to come up here. Right away. Give him the room number. Have him say that Junior's upstairs, waiting to come out of his closet. He wants to confess his dirty little secrets to his Daddy."

I punched out the lobby number, my heart beating like a pair of tom-toms. Patti alone, was standing guard at the door. Wielding the meat fork much like a small spear, she jabbed it in Junior's direction just to let him know she meant business. She'd skewer the first man who tried to pass her.

But Junior was after all, a Winthrop. And as such, obviously felt he had faced much tougher adversaries in his day than a carving knife and an oversized meat fork. Brian was struggling, as it became apparent that Montana's tie and belt weren't going to restrain him for long. With me on the phone, and Montana trying to subdue Brian, it fell to Patti to fend off Junior's attempts to escape.

Undoubtedly, Junior preferred a confrontation with just about anything, including Montana's blade and Patti's spear, than to face his father, fresh from the throes of a homosexual tryst. He bolted for the door. Dropping the phone, I dove onto the end of the bed and thrust my mop handle between his legs. He went down, rolling over on the thick carpet. I pounced on his back, trying not to think about the fact that he was naked.

We grappled, mostly a lot of pushing and shoving and cursing. At one point, he called me a nasty name. Scrambling on all fours to the corner where my squirt bottle had been dropped, I grabbed it, rolled over, and leveled a shot of cleaning liquid at him as he was getting up. Front and center. A direct hit to the nasal cavities.

Gagging and spitting, he kicked me in the teeth. A desperate, dangerous man, he'd grown rabid with his need to escape. Holding fast to his bare foot, I caused him to stumble but he continued to kick and claw his way to the hall.

I couldn't hang on.

Back on his feet, he lashed out at Patti, bouncing her head off the doorjamb. Recovering quickly, she lunged at his midriff with the fork. Fearless in his hysterics, he swept past her too, the fork barely grazing his side. From there, he quickly dashed headlong down the hallway. I ran after him, grabbed a handful of bare, sweaty skin. He easily broke my hold with a crude, karate chop to my wrists.

Finally, Montana secured Brian's knots and sprang to our assistance. But he was too late. By now, Junior was halfway down the hall, fleeing for the elevator which had just arrived.

As the elevator dinged, the doors separated, revealing a contingent of senior citizens. As they spilled out into the hall, their chattering and laughing was soon replaced with frightened gasps. They retreated back into a corner of the elevator much like domestic sheep being herded by a well-trained dog. One of the men hurriedly thumbed the close button from the inside.

As the four of them waited for the doors to close, they were left with little to do but stare, dumbstruck. I could imagine how it must have looked. A naked Junior, chased by two screaming, cleaning ladies, all of whom were bounding at breakneck speed directly at them. The man with the thumb on the close button began tapping furiously.

With only mini-seconds left and an inch or two of open space, Junior threw himself the last ten or so feet and thrust a hand between the doors....dislodging the sensitive rubber edges and causing them to reopen. Panting victoriously, he easily elbowed the guests out of the elevator and pushed one of the women, a short, plump one who had been screaming incessantly from the start, hard enough to sprawl across me. By the time I had untangled myself from her clutches and incrimina-tions, the doors were closed and the elevator had begun it's descent.

The last thing I saw, hoping I'd never be forced to gaze upon it again, was Junior's bare behind.

Montana didn't even slow down. "Stairway's over here. Hurry."

Tossing squirt bottles and mops, I followed him. From there, it was a race down three flights; our feet and lungs against modern technology.

We were in luck. Junior had managed to beat us to the lobby, but a force even mightier than my trusty ammonia mix stopped him dead in his tracks. Mayor Winthrop had received a message of sorts from the casino floor manager and was on his way up. Mayor and son had met, or rather collided, at the elevator as Junior was getting off. By the time Montana and I burst upon the scene, Daddy Winthrop had already briefly in-terrogated him, had a long rain coat delivered to cover his son, and had Junior in a state of stutter.

The red-neck voters in this district would never under-stand Junior's choice of a life-style. If news of his homosexu-ality ever leaked out, heads would roll. Daddy Winthrop would have to keep it quiet and I couldn't help but wonder how he'd manage it. Probably, most all of it would be denied before the night was over, covered up by morning, and lied about for the next decade. That done, I also had to wonder what Winthrop would have to say to his only son, in the privacy of their home, tomorrow? Or the next day? And how much farther would he go to keep it covered up?

And what in the world was Tiffany doing, hanging out with him?

The danger, as I saw it, was that Junior would be pun-ished for his sexual preferences, which in this country remained a person's right, instead of his real crime. Involvement in the death of two people and the kidnapping of a little boy. But Daddy Mayor had spent a lifetime dodging, sidetracking and skirting issues. He had already come to his son's defense and spied a handy place to lay the blame.

Speaking to the small crowd of onlookers, he puffed up his chest and bellowed. "Hell, you can't blame a young man for sowing a few wild oats from time to time. Not a criminal offense, last time I checked. Don't know many men who haven't flirted a little in their day. Best they get it over with and out of their system before they settle down, I always say. And if this young lady is," he cleared his throat and eyed my sack dress. "...a little on the wild side, at least she's willing enough and doesn't need much convincing."

At this point, he pulled himself up with all of his mayoral stature, the result of which left him sneering at my cleaning lady rags. "Momentary object of his affections, I presume. Strictly momentary. Although, next time, son, I might suggest you select one more fitting to your station. Nevertheless, I suggest we leave this young woman to her own devices and call it a night." At that point, he began propelling his son through the lobby and towards home.

I'd been trying to keep up with Winthrop's line of reasoning, when I suddenly realized he was talking about me. I was offended....Patti would be furious. But, this time I'd have to bite my lip, declining the instinct to defend myself lest I blow the cleaning-lady cover. After all, Patti did work for City Hall and could possibly lose her job over this.

Plus, Little Sister had yet to come down. When I had followed Montana down the stairs, I'd taken it for granted that Patti would also be following on *my* heels. I was wrong. And beginning to worry about her.

But Montana wasn't just mad. He was getting even. "Are you kidding? What's it take to make you realize, man? Your son's gay! *He's a homosexual.*"

"That's not true," Junior whined, clutching the raincoat about himself as if afraid that someone might want to extract something from under it as evidence.

His father was immediately incensed. "Just a minute, young man. That is a bald-faced lie and I insist that you apologize to me and my son. Or see yourself in court in a big slander suit. And don't think I won't do it, and win it to boot. Take your pick."

Winthrop and Montana were arguing *loudly* when to my surprise, Ben entered the hallway and walked toward us. I was never so glad to see anyone in my life. And even though I didn't dare draw attention to myself by running to him, I mo-

172

tioned by way of a set of grimaces that trouble was a-brewing. He didn't seem shocked, as much as tickled with my costume when he realized what I was wearing.

Mayor Winthrop saw him and gestured wildly. "Deputy Jack. I demand that you witness the sick accusations of this man. They are vicious lies. Why he would slander my son with such a thing, I can't imagine other than for one reason and one reason only. It is clearly a disgraceful attempt to tear down his campaign for the mayoral office."

Once again, the elevator chimed. And as we had come to expect the unexpected, all eyes turned it that direction. I breathed a sigh of relief. It was Patti and she had Brian in tow. Trussed up like a pig with Montana's tie and belt, she was leading him by way of her cloth belt around his neck.

Hunched over his leg, which was connected to his neck by way of Montana's tie, Brian hobbled along behind her using tiny, mincing steps. Each time he'd pull back, wailing and making excuses, she'd prick him with the meat fork. He also was partly naked, but she had thrown a bedspread over his shoulders.

She shoved Brian against Junior, who reacted by catching him. She then sneered and said, "Your lover was getting lonely for you, Junior."

Meanwhile, we had gathered quite a crowd. To keep the eavesdropping to a minimum, Ben ushered us all into the museum for the Coast Salish Tribes, and made gestures that we should keep our voices down. Once he'd closed the door behind us, he moved over to stand next to the glass case that held the Bastolak tribe's *s.gwedilic* board. The carved cedar board I'd seen when I first interviewed the assistant personnel manager. It was the same one that claimed to be imbued with spiritual powers, and had been used for settling disputes. The sign next to it still proclaimed that the tribal members had believed, at one time, that anyone who held it was bound to tell the truth.

Mayor Winthrop promptly launched into a tirade that found fault with most every one there, including Junior. While he harangued and ranted, I motioned to Patti to watch Ben. He took the carved cedar out of the case, holding it by the handles, and blew the dust from its smooth wood. His finger ran affec-

173

tionately over the grooves that had been carved so many centuries ago, with symbols that looked half-man and half salmon.

The Mayor didn't miss a beat. Having reduced his son to a sobbing mass, he moved on to Brian, blaming him for Junior's present fall from grace. He was berated, and vocally sliced and quartered for attempting to lead his son into a (quote), "life of sinful atrocities against the Lord." He then demanded that Junior denounce this man's flirtations and reclaim his manhood.

"This blasphemy must stop. Tell them, son. You are *not* one of those," here, he stuttered and stammered. "You're as much a man as anyone else. Easily swayed at times, I'll admit. But you've never sunk to the level of depravity as this one."

Brian shrank even lower to the floor as the mayor leveled a bony finger. "It's gold-diggers like you that make a tough job even harder. Trying to tempt a young, impressionable boy like that? You should be ashamed of yourself." And though it was a charge so ridiculous it didn't deserve an answer, no one seemed willing to stop arguing and simply go home.

At that point, Ben did something totally amazing. He handed the *s.gwedilic* board to Junior, and said, "Here. Hold this."

Suddenly, all hell broke lose. Junior began to cry. Not on his dad's shoulder but on Brian's. And he shouted back at his father, "Why can't you accept me like I am? I'm still your son. All I ever wanted was for you to just accept me. But no! You had to make me '*normal.*' You could never just let me be who I am, but I had to get '*healed.*' Just like you did with Mama. You drove her out of the house because she couldn't measure up, either. Well, I'm tired of it. Do you hear me? *I'm tired of it.* Do whatever you have to, but I'm not going to deny who I am any longer. You want to disinherit me? Go ahead. But Brian and I love each other and we're going to stay together, no matter what!" He kneeled to the floor where he could reach Brian better. They then hugged, and stared defiantly at the Mayor.

Of course, this set off a battery of accusations and finger-pointing. Ben helped the process along, by asking a well-placed question now and then, receiving a torrent of screaming confessions and justifications in return. But through it all, the real story began to emerge.

Mayor Winthrop was from a fundamentalist background and simply could not bear that his son was gay. It was not the first time that a parent had seen the homosexual tendencies of a son or daughter as "sick." A condition which, by its description, suggests that the offspring needs to be "cured." To get "purged" of their abnormalities and be made well. Unfortunately, such attitudes are fairly common.

On the other hand, poor Junior tried to obey his father. Needed his approval, and desperately wanted his dad to be proud of him. Therefore, Junior felt his only recourse was to hide his true self.

Soon after his affair with Brian began, Junior started dating Tiffany as a cover-up. She knew what he was doing and agreed to go along with the charade only after Junior began bestowing presents upon her. Tiffany was a single parent who wanted the very best for her son. When her salary and questionable credit rating, combined with Ben's child-support, still couldn't qualify for a loan on a new mobile home, she was forced to ask Junior for help.

But it didn't stop there, and she found herself embroiled deeper and deeper into Junior's ambiguous lies. Eventually, she couldn't take it anymore and begged Junior to tell his father the truth. And that was when Junior panicked, and swore her to secrecy with threats that she'd not only lose her job, but also her home and car. Even hinted that he would hurt the boy. When even that wasn't enough to keep her quiet he felt that he had to take more drastic action.

"Sure, after Tiffany was killed, we hid Billy out," Junior said, after he had quieted down. "It wasn't hard, you know. He came right up to the kitchen's back door about noon the next day and asked Brian to make him some french fries. Brian had done that many times before and they were friends. We did it to keep him away from whoever had killed his mother, mostly. And yes, to keep him quiet about his mother's and my business dealings. But I didn't kill Tiffany, or anyone else. I swear to God I didn't."

Mayor Winthrop wasn't finished. But he had stopped shouting. "My son may be easily swayed at times, and he might even have gone along with that boy being hidden in the casino pantry. But that doesn't mean he is a killer. Someone else killed that woman and Larson, too. Probably ambushed her on the way home from work one night. Raped her and left her for dead. You might want to finish this investigation before you do something you might regret....and while you're about it, try checking out some of your own people. Let us not forget that these Indians are only one generation removed from wild savages."

That was the last straw for Benjamin. He'd taken an immeasurable amount of grief from these bigots and, by the look on his face, he wasn't taking any more. He pinned Winthrop with a look of subdued fury and said, "No Indian I know would commit a crime like this. Tiffany had no enemies here on the reservation, not even with the casino customers." Ben paused, looking away from Winthrop to address everyone in the room. "First, we need to look at what kind of crime this was. And we can do that best by showing what kind of crime it was not.

"This was not a crime of passion. There was no semen found in the autopsy, *at all*. And this was not due to the use of a prophylactic by the rapist. She simply was not raped. Nor was she was on any type of birth control pills, and didn't appear to have been sexually active for some time. She had a young boy at home. Evidently, Tiffany felt that she needed to raise him without having any boyfriends hanging around.

"No, this was a white man's crime. A crime of greed. And it has to have been done by someone with the gall to think that they are above the law. Untouchable. A *gambler.* The Coast Salish tribes do not believe in greed. They are the potlatch Indians. We have special ceremonies where we give away most of our possessions, simply to remind ourselves not to become too attached to them. To divest ourselves of material matters.

"Kill the mother of a small child? Never. Only an evil person would harm a child or kill a woman. Someone capable of evil for the sake of evil. There's no one in our tribe who matches that description. If there had of been, we'd have barred him from the reservation and sent him away a long time ago. Kidnap the young son of a Deputy Sheriff who just happens to be a member of your own tribe? That's stupid. Besides, we've already established the fact that Brian and Junior had been holding Billy prisoner in the pantry. No, these homicides were committed by a white man. Done as a matter of improving the odds against failure. A matter of winning an election."

Junior looked as if he was ready to run. "I'm telling you that I didn't kill anyone. Why won't anyone believe me?"

"We'll see how all that pans out. If nothing else, you are responsible for setting up the atmosphere that got her killed. Could even have promised or at least insinuated that the killer would receive a bonus or a payoff of some kind if she was out of the way. And, you covered up the identity of the true killer to keep yourself from being incriminated. You're the true gambler here, and you've taken the biggest gamble of them all. That your soul and those of the men who associate with you will survive the evil you have wrought in your quest for greed and power."

At that point, Brian was read his Miranda rights and taken into custody for false imprisonment of a minor child and a list of other charges that went along with that. Everything except murder. Junior, after much bellowing by his father, was left to his own recognizance but warned not to leave town as he'd be answering to a Grand Jury within a few weeks.

As they left, Montana leaned against the wall for support. Although Ben had replaced the *s.qwedilic* board long before he left with Brian, Montana seemed as if he too were suffering from the confessionary mood of the moment.

I placed a hand on Montana's shoulder and said, "You were in love with Tiffany, weren't you? And you were the one who saw Tiffany climb into Junior's Honda."

He nodded, caught a tear as it formed in the corner of one eye. He'd been in love with her, all along. Probably still was. Before she'd started dating a worm called Junior, before she'd given up on the love of her life and settled for easy money, and before she'd gotten herself killed.

"Months before any of this happened," Montana swept his hand to the area where Junior had been standing. "Ben would come after Billy for the weekend, and Tiffany and I would take a run up to Victoria for a few days. Stay in a nice room, relax, and get to know each other." He sniffled, and wiped at his eyes. "She was so...beautiful. It was one of the best times, I've ever had."

Patti and I exchanged looks. Enough truth-telling for one night.

"Come on, you too," Patti said, "How about a drink? Loser buys the first round."

With our long faded dresses rustling just above the support hose, the klunky leather shoes making a "ker-flopping" sound with each step, my sister and I whipped off our head scarves, took the arm of our very suave and polished escort and marched onto the casino floor.

The craps table was first in line.

CHAPTER SIXTEEN

Saturday. The next morning, I was up early, had my daily story written for the *Gazette,* and engaged Gunner in a verbal conflict by 8:00. The story centered on the discovery that Billy had been held hostage in the casino's pantry. But Gunner cut out any reference to Junior, pleading the case that he'd not yet been charged with anything. He also wouldn't allow any reference to Junior and Brian's sordid affair, saying it was an invasion of their privacy...even though they'd kept a young boy hostage, against his will, in a disturbingly close and questionable manner.

"Plus," Gunner had added smugly. "We're a family newspaper and I don't see any way to both delicately report what you saw, and evade a lawsuit."

Which was all fine and dandy. But it rankled me, to no end, that once again, Junior's money, when heaped upon the best attorney in the county, had given him an out. And the ability to forge ahead with his campaign, in his slash-and-burn style, with little or no consequences for his deeds.

It continued to worry me that Patti was his last remaining obstacle.

Even so, we at least, seemed to be headed in the right direction. Brian had been arrested for kidnapping and Junior had admitted in a statement, *some* knowledge of the boy's abduction. They would both appear in front of the Grand Jury, as soon as it was scheduled.

Later that morning, I paid Clancey a visit. When I walked into his office, he was rubbing his right temple with a hairy fist, the other curled tightly around the phone receiver as if to choke out some desperately-needed information. He grunted a sharp retort into the receiver and gestured to a high-backed wooden chair.

I would have my interview, but only if I was willing to

wait. I cleared it of an official-looking manual, sat down, crossed my legs, and folded my hands demurely.

This was going to be interesting.

The Police Chief was bleary-eyed and in a foul mood. His desk was cluttered with stacks of letters, faxes and messages taken by his receptionist. An open bottle of aspirin reposed on the highest peak.

Suddenly, there was a flurry of activity in the hall. Doors opened and were slammed shut. A uniformed officer with heavy shoes thudded by, a shout sounded, and a woman in the front wailed and cursed. It wasn't clear if her venom was directed at them, life in general, or the world at large. Within minutes, Officer Miller poked his head in the room, causing Clancey to look up expectantly.

"Just a drunk," he said. "We got it under control." The Chief made another motion, as if to say 'carry on', and grunted again into the phone receiver.

We had a lot to catch up on, Clancey and me.

When finally Clancey slammed the phone down with a flourish, we were both close to exhaustion. But even though the lights on the phone continued to blink, signaling even more calls with an alarming persistence, the receptionist was told to hold them for the time being. I whipped out my notebook, preparing to divulge some notes taken days ago and possibly jot a few more.

He already knew about my visit to the FBI. And Spike's temper tantrum at my apartment in the middle of the night. He wanted my version of them and everything else I'd been up to. Painstakingly, we went over every detail of the past week, including the scene in the casino/hotel lobby. Ben's report, from when he'd arrested Brian and put Junior on hold for assisting the alleged kidnapping, would have contained the charges and the facts as we knew them to this point.

I told Clancey everything I could, other than the part about Junior's choice of a sexual experience. He'd have to dig that out of somebody else.

Clancey knew I was holding out. Faced with his anger, I made a real effort to explain my position. "Clancey," I said. "I am a newspaper reporter. And as such, there are certain ethics to which I must abide. Not to mention my own conscience.

180

And revealing the details of another person's sex life goes beyond the pale of disclosure, even to you."

He moved uncomfortably under the table, mumbling something about paperwork: his superiors were leaving no rock unturned, no matter how revolting the life forms under it might be. We quickly went on to other subjects. Such as the whereabouts of one Spike Hardpenny.

"Do you think he's gone, never to return? Is he speeding through Montana, or Wyoming, or New Mexico as we speak?" I asked.

"Hard to tell. Spike has dropped out of sight. Hasn't been seen since the FBI let him go. If you want to know what I think," Clancey again rubbed his forehead. "It looks to me like his options aren't pretty. His best bet would be to eliminate as many witnesses as he can, destroy as much evidence as possible and *then* take flight across the state lines. And who is his biggest threat?"

"Billy."

"Yes, Billy's one of them. And so is Deputy Jack. But, you....Kathleen, are probably his biggest threat. Your testimony would be very damaging, to say the least, but consider this: you have an unlimited access to the local media. And your newspaper could hype this story to the point that the national media might take an interest. Especially as the militia-movement is concerned. It would create a media-orgy - we've seen it happen before - which would plaster his face across every newspaper and TV broadcast in the country. Thereby, hounding the FBI into taking steps that they would otherwise not have the recourses to handle. You could create an atmosphere in this whole country that would leave him absolutely no place to hide. And don't think that he's not aware of that." Clancey paused, scratching the stubble on his chin. "I'm tempted to put you into protective custody, now. Give us time to find him without having to worry about him finding you and your sister, first."

"Clancey, that's not fair and you know it. My sister and I have contributed significantly to this investigation. Just because we're not handicapped by a City Hall that's working against itself and don't have to worry about displeasing the damn mayor if we get too successful too fast, there's no reason for banning us from this project. Our goals are different and we have a much lighter, less threatening approach. Besides, you don't have the manpower to follow us around."

He thought about that a moment, knowing what I said was true. He could neither deny it nor could he stop me. By now, both burly fists were digging at his eyes and massaging his forehead.

I felt sorry for him. "Why not let me help you?"

"And just how, pray tell, will you do that," he snarled, and swallowed a handful of aspirins that was washed down with coffee from a chipped cup with the insignia, *Defenders To The End,* emblazoned on its front in fading red and blue letters. He grimaced and almost spit the brew back out. It was obviously cold and probably tasting like it had been boiled with battery acid.

"Look. I'll keep in constant contact with you with periodic updates and messages. I keep my cellular with me at all times and you can call me day or night. Patti and I seldom go anywhere alone, especially after dark and half of the time either Ben or Sims is with us."

I paused, letting it sink in that both Ben and FBI agent Sims were communicating with me on friendly, in fact, sometimes *very* friendly terms, in total defiance of Mayor Winthrop's demands.

"What can go wrong?" I added, as a shiver ran through me, a haunting reminder that there were indeed a number of things that could go wrong: trying to outguess the fanatical actions of a superpatriot bigot and a murderer to mention a few. Clancey didn't look convinced, but he did seem willing to re-think his position.

"Well, at least Ben has been cleared," I said, and sighed audibly. "He'll still have his good name and his job when this is all over."

Clancey harumphed and stared at the swill in his coffee cup. "We're holding all our options open at this time."

I wanted to kick him. "What," I screamed. "Billy's home, in case you've forgotten." .

"That's true. But Tiffany's murderer is still running lose." He frowned, and moved uncomfortably. "We'd have brought Ben in for questioning by now, but he's too damn hard to find."

Simmering, I forced myself to keep quiet on the matter. If Ben was being framed, my protestations would only anger Clancey and make things worse all the way around. The best thing to do at this point, was to change the subject. "How about Dwayne? Has anyone seen him lately?"

"From what we've heard, he seems to be moving out of county, probably up into northern Idaho or Montana with the militia movement. The FBI is tracking him, just in case he goes forward on this assassination plot or finds any other mischief to get into." He moved his huge feet around under his desk, kicking the side of his desk in the process and knocking over a stack of print-outs. A handful of coffee-stained papers floated to the floor. "By the way, what I'm telling you at this point is off the record. I'm mentioning it to you only because you've already become painfully aware of their operations and you need to be warned of the consequences. But right now, I'll have to ask that you not mention any of this in your paper."

"Oh. Thanks a lot. I get to know about it but I can't write about it. Talk about a coverup." I immediately regretted my flippant remark, but by then, it was too late.

"Young lady," the Chief said, banging his coffee cup on the table, and causing the rest of the papers to slide fluttering to his feet. "You can call this a coverup if you want. But if you're going to play with the big boys you better damn well learn the rules. This is a case of national security and there are some pretty important lives here on the line." Clancey was heating up, his blond head looking like an oversized thermometer on a hot day.

"I'm sorry. I didn't mean that." Now we were both upset. Taking a deep breath, I tried to get back on friendlier terms. "Are they going to arrest any of the militia group?"

"Can't talk about it right now. You'd better go. If I get anything else in that you'll need to know about, I'll give you a call." The expression, *That'll teach you to get smart with* me, *Big Mouth,* was delivered with great, although unspoken, dispatch.

It was just as well. Tonight was the emergency City Council meeting, when Junior would spring his proposal for Rafferty's late-comers agreement. Notices of the meeting had been hand-delivered only to the homes directly affected. And even though Ben had asked us to stay out of trouble, hinting broadly that we shouldn't show our faces around there *at all,* I couldn't see Patti having to lose everything she owned to satisfy the monetary appetites of the city's governing officials.

Evidently, she felt the same way. "So," Patti said. "Are we ready to go to the meeting? I'll be damned if I let them get away with this without a fight." Within minutes, we were in the car and on our way.

Driving through the familiar streets, Patti surprised me with a question of concern. "That Deputy has really gotten under your skin, hasn't he?"

"Am I that obvious? You know, I've done everything in the book to get the man's attention." I sighed. "But he just isn't interested. Looks like I went knocking on the wrong door, this time."

"Give him a chance, Kath. He needs to settle things with his family and grieve for the woman who gave him a son. Remember, he's from a different culture than yours. One that just might still believe that it's a man's perogative to chase the woman. Back off. If he's ever going to come to you, it'll have to be his decision."

I nodded, wishing that the knot in my chest would stop hurting. "Maybe you're right."

"I know I'm right," she said. "Give him time."

Once inside, we took seats on the second row. The council members were lined up as before, some of whom looked at Patti and me as if seeing a pair of witches intent on casting spells over the lot of them. Others were taking our presence as a matter of course. Smitty, the old farmer who'd lost his dairy farm to the city's greed, was in his seat. The look on his face could have sliced raw liver.

The mayor and his son were off to one side, in deep discussion. Junior glanced around, his gaze lighting on me with a look of sheer horror. I had an idea that the casino was after him *big time*, if he was willing to go through with his charade, after all that had happened. Junior still seemed to feel that he was above the law, not to mention the free press.

I'd called Andy from the house, shortly before we left. As I'd guessed, he hadn't been notified of the meeting. The fact that he was editor of the town's paper made him the least likely participant in any kind of a bureaucratic cover-up. He walked in with his usual long-gaited shuffle, smiling and nodding at those with the courage to look him in the eye. This time his dad, Frank, was with him. Frank could still smell a hot lead a mile away, and recognizing this as a milestone for the city, wasn't about to let this one go by without a front-page story.

Tonight's attendance was poor, to say the least. Meetings on Saturday nights were almost nonexistent; evidently, the Winthrops wanted this vote out of the way before news of Junior's tete-a-tete in the casino got out. And they wanted work to start on the project immediately.

As for property owners directly affected, only Myrtle Pearson and her kids were there. At the last meeting, she'd testified that her toilet was flushing into their front yard and needed this sewer to prevent their home from being condemned. And, of course, Rafferty was there, grasping his leather briefcase with both hands, his shoulders eternally hunched.

The meeting was called to order. As the only item on the agenda, they went right to it. Junior was the first one to speak. "Mayor, Council members, I'd like to thank everyone for coming on such short notice. I hope it's not been inconvenient. The reason we've called this meeting is because a matter has come to my attention that the sewer situation on Pine Street has become a health risk. There are families living there, and, to be frank, the city is in grave danger of being sued.

"Also, this is September already and, though we are still enjoying summer weather, I've checked with the weather bureau and rain is on its way. Those of you who've lived here for some time will agree with me that once this weather breaks, we are in for it. The project will have to be put off until next spring at the earliest, and this family," he indicated the Pearsons four children. ".... will have their home condemned and they'll lose everything they own. Winter is coming, and a storm is the way. We have no choice but to make our move now. Tonight. While there is still time."

He turned to Rafferty, as if introducing a knight in shining armor who would save their fair city from financial ruin. The developer then stepped up beside Junior, put some papers on the podium and straightened his tie. No one could have guessed that, only days before they'd been at each others' throats over the money needed to pay Junior's gambling debts. Evidently, robbing the city's coffers still seemed to be their best bet.

Rafferty cleared his throat. "When I spoke to you last week," he said. "I mentioned the growth opportunities available for Eagle Ridge. Growth that can still occur with good planning and foresight. And I want to reinforce that statement, and assure you good folks that those opportunities still exist, today. The businesses I mentioned, when last I checked, are still interested in relocating here. Provided there is adequate housing.

"And yes, these businesses and additional development will create more jobs at higher pay. A priority which has long been a Winthrop benchmark." This was said to the mayor, for which he preened like a bantam rooster.

"But tonight, I bring another, more urgent matter. As my friend, Junior Winthrop has just explained, winter is approaching with distressing certainty. If this project is to be completed, it needs to go forward. Now. The weather service assures me that this sunshine we've been enjoying, won't last much longer. Enjoy it while you may, as fall is on its way. Which means, as you all well know, that the rain is right behind it.

"Now, what does all this rain mean to us? Normally, we accept the seasons as they come and go. All part of God's great plan. Turning the leaves from green to gold and back to green again. But this time, we don't have that luxury. Our fair city is under the gun, folks. The County Health Department has already made samples of the soil in this area and along the ditch that carries the run-off water. One family suffers most from this calamity."

He paused, his eyes going to each council member, his long arm indicating the same woman and kids. "Let me digress a moment and introduce the Pearson family. Would you stand up, please?"

The mother had each one of her children stand, with the youngest on her arm. In an obviously staged performance, she called out each of their names.

Content that he'd milked *that* family of all possible drama, Rafferty continued. "As you all can see, there are four father-less children here, including three grade-school kids and a toddler. All of whom will soon be on the street if we don't move soon. In the winter and in the rain. And who will be to blame for this? Some attorneys will place the blame at Eagle Ridge's door, folks. And I have no doubts they will try to prove their case in the courts. Not only driving up the costs of this project, but taking up valuable time and resources."

Rafferty unrolled a large paper, of the type that engineers and drafters use to display drawings and details of future projects. "I have here a set of plans already drawn up and approved by the city engineer. Ready to go. We could start working tomorrow morning. The only thing lacking at this point is your okay. I understand that Junior here is prepared to introduce a measure so this problem can be resolved tonight. Please, give it your full appreciation. Otherwise, as much as I'd hate to leave Eagle Ridge, my plans, my equipment, and frankly, my line of credit, will have to go on to other projects in other places. So. Without further delay, I'll hand you back into Junior Winthrop's capable hands."

Junior adjusted the mike, a pitched whine interrupting his efforts. "On the table in front of you you'll find a late-comers agreement. It's the same one that was delivered to your homes this last week for your review. I apologize for springing this on you so suddenly, but all of the discussions in the past have not rectified the situation, only made it worse. And we have very little time left before it will be too late.

"There is a grant attached to this proposal for matching federal funds that our able engineer has obtained. A grant that will soon run out if it is not used, expeditiously. Let me repeat that. This grant will help *tremendously* to pay for the project, but it won't be available forever. Another reason, my friends, to go forward on this, immediately. Mr. Rafferty and I stand ready to answer your questions and then I will be asking that you vote for this measure, tonight."

I stood up and waited to be recognized. After a moment, when it became obvious that they didn't want to acknowledge me, I spoke up. "Mr. Mayor. I'd like to approach the mike, but the area around it is a little crowded right now. Could I respectfully ask for a few minutes to speak?"

Junior immediately turned to the front and, forgetting that he was at the microphone, began to whine. "Dad....,"

Mayor Winthrop banged his gavel. "Miss O'Shaughnessy, this meeting is closed except for those Eagle Ridge residents whose homes are directly affected by this proposal. The reason Mr. Rafferty and Junior are at the mike is because Rafferty is a property owner on Pine Road and my son is running for Mayor. And, since he is running unopposed, it's quite obvious that he'll be the one to officiate over this particular project. Now, if you will please sit down and allow us to finish our business, we might get out of here before midnight."

At that moment, Patti moved up beside me. "Mayor Winthrop, if what you say is true, then surely, I should be given a chance to speak."

"Patti," he snarled. "I'll say the same thing to you. Property owners only, on Pine Road."

Her face blanched, but she held her ground. "Which I why I'm standing, Mayor. I have property on Pine Road, at 1412 Pine Road, sir...., that will be directly effected by the vote tonight. And your notion that Junior is running unopposed is a little premature. As I am also running for mayor, I seem to be your son's last remaining opponent. Therefore, since I qualify to speak at this meeting at least as much as your son and Mr. Rafferty, I have a statement to make as to this sewer project. And, I would like for it to be a part of the record."

The mayor quickly covered the mike with his hand and consulted with the city clerk, the city attorney and everyone else in whispering range. By their expressions, they'd all been too busy working - trying to prepare this project for the vote. There hadn't been time to keep up with the errant son's election concerns. Winthrop gestured at a few of the council members. None of them seemed to have any answers either.

The Mayor addressed Patti, again. "Let me get this straight. You're saying that you live at 1412 Pine Road? That deed is filed under the name of Dwayne Hickman, a single man."

She nodded. "My husband. We were married only days after the escrow was closed. If you want to be technical, my salary was in consideration when he qualified for that loan."

"And this other thing. Young lady, in order to run for mayor, you have to file with the State Auditor's Office before a certain date. And that date is long past."

"I'm aware of that. And I *did* file, your honor. On the very last day. The day *after* Mr. Larson was killed. Which was," she looked at her watch. "....last Tuesday. Three days ago."

Again, the mayor consulted with the city attorney who simply shrugged his shoulders, indicating, without saying it out-loud, that it was not his job to run Junior's campaign. The Mayor was confused and close to hysterics. I also noted that, he didn't deny the charge that Larson had been *killed*. Had Winthrop been on the ball, he should have corrected her and stated that Larson had simply *died*. And the investigation had not yet revealed just exactly how this sad event had occurred.

"Mr. Mayor," I said. "All Patti wants to do, at this point, is to speak. She just wants to *speak*. Politics not withstanding, she is a land-owner on Pine Road, and I believe she has proved herself worthy to do that. And since you're concerned about it being late, could we please proceed?"

With pursed lips and a tiny, mocking bow, the Mayor motioned to the microphone. I raised one brow and winked at Patti as she straightened her shoulders and stepped up to the mike. "Thank you, Mr. Mayor," she said. "I'll try to be brief. City Council staff and members. Some of you will recognize me from my job at City Hall. A job that gives me many opportunities to grow and to gain in experience."

Holding in a chuckle at her subtle sarcasm, I cast a sidelong glance in her direction.

"In reference to this sewer project," she said. "I'd like to go on record as saying that I am not against having this sewer put in. Let me repeat that. *I am not against this sewer project.*" She banged on the podium with one knuckle for emphasis. "I *am* against losing my home and that of my family members. By the way, I wasn't aware that the plight of homeless children would be on the agenda tonight, but I also have a ten-year old son. A *fatherless* son whose name is Jeffrey. And according to the game plan already laid out by Mr. Rafferty, this is of primary importance."

"To begin, I'd like to refer to the letter from the building department, stating that this sewer will stretch across the front of my property and that the city will be asking for some $30,000 in assessments. It also states that they'll give me only 90 days to hook up to it and that the hookup is mandatory. Mr. Mayor, as our house is some 500 feet removed from the area where the sewer will be, I respectively submit that we be allowed to waive that requirement. We are too far away from the sewer, and our septic system is in fine repair and quite capable of handling its task. I believe our house should be left out of the equation."

"Young lady, as of today, this city has no ordinance stating that a home owner can refuse hookup, simply from where it is situated on the lot. Be it 100 feet, 200 feet or 500 feet away from the sewer line," Winthrop replied. "It's unfortunate, but that is the law. You therefore, will be expected to comply the same as everyone else."

"I beg to differ with you on that too, Mayor. As I said earlier, my job gives me many opportunities. One of them is the ability to research the Eagle Ridge records for any old ordinances." She whipped a paper out of her folder. "Here is a copy of an old ordinance that became law in Eagle Ridge some forty years ago. It obviously hasn't been used in some time. Never-the-less, unless it's been overridden by another ordinance, this is how the law stands."

"Let me see that," the Mayor demanded.

"I have a set of copies packaged up for everyone, to pass out. If I may?" She immediately moved to the council members' table. "Oh, and by the way, in your package, you'll find copies of the Sheriff's sale when Smitty over here lost his farm for the price of a few years' worth of taxes to a company that bought it and the next week transferred it into Junior's name for the price of one dollar. And, of course, the deed showing where only a week after that he sold it to Mr. Rafferty for $247,000." She paused, then looked directly at Smitty. "My husband and I are buying the house, the barn, and five acres of that farm."

Rafferty glared at Junior. It appeared that Junior had not been totally forthcoming in their business dealings.

Patti was not finished. "Another copy is the application for a permit, made out and signed by Mr. Rafferty, to build a multi-family apartment building down the road from us, contingent of course, that a sewer be installed before any construction takes place. The construction company listed here, to build that particular apartment complex, is *also* owned by the brothers Rafferty. One of whom sits tonight as a voting council member. And, this same construction company, once again owned by the Rafferty family is the same one to which we're talking about handing over a million-dollar project *to-night* on a late-comers agreement, without it even going out to bid."

Patti paused, relishing the growing look of panic across the room. "If this is not a conflict of interest, I'd be hard pressed to find one." She was in her glory and it was high time something went her way.

By way of an additional jab, I thought it time to remind the council members that the Eagle Ridge Report was present and taking notes. I leaned into the mike and said, "Andy, did you get your copies of this?" Andy and Frank both grinned as I walked over to them and hand delivered their copies. They knew exactly what I was up to.

"Oh. By the way....," Patti said, as if the little pixy had just remembered her last and most devastating line.

The Mayor couldn't stand it. "Young lady," he said. "I think you've already said quite enough."

"I'm almost finished, Mayor. This afternoon, I noticed that the sub-contractor for the earth-moving equipment is none other than our infamous Ralph Hardpenny, known as Spike to his friends, and who is in partnership with our same Mr. Rafferty. And yes, the brother to Councilman Rafferty. And, before I forget, I'd like to remind everyone that Spike won't be around for awhile to drive the bulldozer. It seems he has skipped out on a warrant for assault and battery, among other charges. He is also wanted for questioning on another case and *that* warrant has been issued...." She paused dramatically. "For homicide in the death of one Tiffany Redbear Jack."

After a moment in which whispers erupted, chairs scraped the floor, and the council members stared and shuffled their copies, Patti gathered up the last of her paperwork. "I guess that's all I have to say. Uh, Mr. Mayor, Smitty looks like he's gonna choke if he doesn't get to say something. Maybe he ought to speak next."

It took the Mayor awhile to get it together. This meeting was *not* going the way he'd planned. He'd lost control of the entire proceedings. And once started, certain protocols of running a City Council meeting were expected even though it was working against his own son. He had to go through with it and finish as if none of it had anything to do with him. Oblivious to it all. I had an idea that if he was forced to choose between going to the mat in support of Junior's shenanigans, or retiring from office with his own reputation intact, the favorite fledgling of Eagle Ridge was about to be edged out of the nest and left to fly on his own.

The Mayor banged with his gavel and said, as pleasantly as you please, "If that's all of the speakers for tonight, I'll hand it over to the council for questions."

The order of questioning started with the man in the first seat. Brother Rafferty. "Your name is....Patricia Hickman, is that correct?"

"Yes."

"Mrs. Hickman, you have made some pretty serious accusations against me, my brother, and my associates. I hope you're ready to back up every damn one of them."

"I am. If you'll refer to the packet, each point I made is backed up by a document." Alert, almost as if she were standing at attention, Patti awaited other questions.

The other council-members were already submerged in their packets, looking over each of the documents. They took their time, reading most of them carefully.

Councilman Rafferty glanced casually at his, his mouth pulled down disdainfully.

"This is all very interesting," he said. "But I have to say that there's nothing illegal about buying land at a sheriff's auction and turning around and selling it. This was all done, not by the Mayor, but by Junior Winthrop. A businessman. And whether Spike is going to jail or not, has nothing to do with this meeting. This is a small community, isolated from the rest of the state by geography. Most all of the businesses around here have dealings with each other of one sort or another all the time. Including me. If being a successful businessman in this town is suspect to a criminal act, then I guess I'll have to plead guilty.

"The thing is, *if* Spike is actually in trouble with the law, this here just says that Clancey wants to talk to him, he's not been arrested or even charged with any wrongdoing. Nevertheless, *if* Spike can't fulfill his contract for whatever reason, we'll simply hire someone else." He cleared his throat, eyeing everyone there except his brother. "And, as Patti Hickman has just admitted, she is also running for Mayor and I have to wonder if this whole shebang here tonight ain't getting just a little too damn political." He thumbed through the copies as if they meant next to nothing, then tossed them aside. "The facts remain the same. A sewer is badly needed on Pine Road, even Mrs. Hickman would like to see one on her property: think of the development possibilities for *her* as Mayor Elect. She just doesn't want to have to pay for it."

Finally, Smitty spoke up. "This business about Junior buying up the land and selling it to Rafferty is quite interesting. I congratulate this young lady for her diligence and hard work. And I agree that when some land comes up for sale a man has a perfect right to step forward and buy it. Where I tend to get my hackles up is when they also want to give him the late-comers agreement on a silver platter. Without giving anyone else a chance to bid on it. *Now* we're talking taxpayers' money. This is not business as usual. And another thing that's giving me some trouble is the price on this bid. I can't see what the money is being used for. Not broken down enough. Why are we paying so much? Normal installation for a sewer line runs about $200 a foot. This bid, is three times that much. Something is wrong. If we're going to put in a sewer on that property, I say we should put it out to bid."

Rafferty, the developer, jumped up and pointed dramatically. "What about this family?"

"What about any of the families in this town?" Smitty asked. "Why are we singling out just one of them? I can point out a number of people who are going to be hurt by just about all of the decisions this council makes, without a backward look. Sewers are damned expensive. For the town, and for the folks that got to pay for them. Like those other families who already said that they can't afford the assessment. Let alone the hookup fee. That reminds me." He faced the family in question, and directed a question to the woman. "Mrs. Pearson, is it?"

She got up, looking nervously to Rafferty. "That's me."

"You're the one who Rafferty's been referring to. Ain't that right?"

"I reckon."

"Tell me, on this plat map that Mrs. Hickman has so kindly made available for us tonight, why is your name not on that particular property? Do you own this house yourself?"

"Uh, no. I don't own it. If it were mine and I had the kind of money they was charging me for it, things wouldn't be in nearly as bad a shape as they are. Plumbing going bad, roof leaks and the septic ain't been pumped since they first dug it, far as I know." A hush fell over the room.

"I see. So, you're *not* the owner," Smitty said. "To whom do you pay your rent?"

"Eagle Ridge Realty is the one collects the money and takes down any requests for repairs. I'll be glad to see the sewer in, myself. One less headache, that's for sure. I just hope they don't plan on raising the damn rent on it once things are all settled."

"How long have you lived there? With how many children?"

"Seven years and four kids. Course, Mary Elizabeth come along just this last year. And little Joe, he's just three and a half. But the other two, they been in that house most as long as I have."

"You mean to tell me that the septic tank hasn't been pumped in all that time?"

"Hell, it ain't my place to have the thing pumped. Or to replace the damn roof when it leaks or to shore up the rotten floorboards in the bathroom. Long's I pay my rent, seems to me that the owners ought to be takin' care of things around there instead of galivantin' around in the Caribbean. Or where ever it is that they've run off to this time."

She thought about it for a minute, jaws working, then continued. "Welfare check, it don't cover no extras you know. Some months, I don't know whether to pay the light bill so's we don't hafta sit in the cold and the dark, or put food on the table so's the older two don't hafta wait till lunchtime at school in order to eat. But let me be three days late on the rent and I'm lookin' at an eviction notice by nightfall."

Smitty slapped his hands on the table and stared directly at the Mayor. "Jebediah, I thought you were a better man than this. You ought to be ashamed of yourself. Dragging that poor woman in here, subjecting us all to this kind of malarkey. All

194

in an effort to set us up for a money-gouging, late-comers agreement with your cronies. One that you know damn well is three times too high. That house and its septic tank is your responsibility, Winthrop. And don't think I don't remember when you and Maggie had that place built. Right after you was first married. Called it his little love nest. Sure, its been quick-deeded over to some business that nobody's gonna lay claim to 'cause you never registered the name."

Thrusting his craggy chin forward, the old-timer stared menacingly at the Mayor. "Caribbean, my foot. I say you own that company and you still own that little house. And I challenge you here and now to prove me wrong."

The place went wild. The Mayor banged the table with his gavel, and roared, "Quiet! Give me some order in here." When his demands simply increased the uproar, he banged again shouting, "This meeting is closed."

They didn't even bother to vote.

CHAPTER SEVENTEEN

Andy was the first one to reach me, after the pandemonium had died down. "Kathleen, you were just great!" He said, shaking my hand, grinning like a kid in a candy shop. And why not? He'd just been handed a front page scoop that would keep his readers talking and buying more papers, for the next year.

"This is your sister?" I introduced them, hurriedly, while trying to keep an eye on the movement in and out the building. If we were going to walk through the parking lot within the safety of a group, we had to go right away.

But as I turned to Patti, hoping to hurry her along, she was being interviewed for the paper. Clasping his set of copies under his left arm, Andy snapped her picture while asking some pointed questions. I moved aside, trying not to reveal a feeling of urgency about getting out of there. She was, after all, in the midst of a campaign.

Once when Andy referred to her marital status, Patti corrected him, making it clear that Dwayne was her soon-to-be *ex*-husband. She and Andy were becoming fast friends and I couldn't be happier. I just wished they could do their bonding in a safer place and at a better time. Although grateful for the new friends we'd made, we had also acquired some nasty enemies.

The biggest surprise, and what proved to be the biggest delay in leaving the meeting hall, were the well-wishers and other council members who wanted to meet her. Mostly, they wanted to ask her position on certain up-coming issues in town and to make their case for a few favorite projects.

Smitty had stopped by to clap his old friend Frank on the back, causing the ancient journalist's cigar to be spit out in a fit of coughing. The stub popped out through the door and rolled into the flower beds outside, thereby endangering the life of countless petunia's but, mercifully, sparing our own.

The reason for Smitty's hearty greeting, was that he'd seen the feature in last week's paper highlighting the chain of events that had resulted in the loss of his dairy. He wanted to thank Frank and Andy for writing it. Already hyped from the emotion of the meeting, he immediately launched into a detailed explanation of the troubles he'd had with a family-owned farm in the technological age of the 90s.

While Smitty prattled on, Frank immediately produced a new cigar and offered one to his friend. The new ones, having been sufficiently slobbered and sucked on, were then lit. And in less time than it took to stagger outside into the clear night air, two evil-smelling curls of cigar smoke spewed forth, seeping into our hair, our clothing, and most everything in the Community Hall including the woodwork.

"You know," Frank said to Patti, between lung-wrenching wheezes and gasps. "It's been a long time since this paper backed a mayoral candidate. Maybe it's about time we did that."

There was hardly anyone left by the time we were ready to leave. As we said our good-byes, Patti suddenly stopped at the hall entrance. Her normally pale skin went chalk white.

"Don't anyone go out there," she whispered and grabbed my arm, pushing me back inside.

"What do you mean? We can hardly spend the night in here."

She was adamant, though trying hard not to alarm everyone. She shook her head, a tiny, intense shake, and said, quietly, so that only I could hear. "Don't go out there. Listen to Blackie. He's barking from inside the car. Something's wrong."

I looked at her more closely. *She meant it.* "What do you suggest?"

For a moment, she listened intently, staring out into the night. Then turned to the friendly farmer-turned-council member. "Smitty. Would you mind doing us a little favor?"

"Don't mind a bit. You little gals in trouble of some kind?"

By then, we were all peering through the open door, leery of going out. A lump had emerged in my throat and seemed to be growing.

"It's probably nothing," she said. "But we don't want to walk into that dark parking lot alone and find out the hard way. Would you take the car keys? It's that cream-colored Ford, over on the far side of the parking lot. Just open up the door and let the dog out. Keep him on the leash, but let him out and bring him to us. If there's somebody lurking about out there, he'll let us know long before they get close enough to hurt anyone. We'll wait here for you. Mind you, he's excited about something and may be a bit of a handful."

As we waited for Smitty to come back with Blackie, Andy mentioned an upcoming Chamber of Commerce luncheon to Patti. Evidently, Andy was going to cover it for the paper and thought she should also be there. And though she pretended to be interested, I had an idea that she was more concerned with the situation outside.

Smitty was having trouble with Blackie. The dog had no interest in the hall where we stood waiting, but wanted to pursue something in the shadows, back of the hall. A small grove of birch trees and rhododendron bushes made up most of the landscaping back there and offered a dusky playground for any number of raccoons, squirrels and pussycats. All of which would have excited him beyond belief.

But I was getting to know Blackie's barks, and he wasn't just excited about a raccoon. He was mad. Enraged. He lunged against the leash, snapping and howling at the darkness as Smitty tried to lead him.

I stuck my head out and whistled to the dog, then called his name. "Blackie. Come here, boy. Come on." He turned his head, barking directly at me as if to communicate his concerns, then lunged again at the shadows. When that didn't work, I ran out into the parking lot and tried to help Smitty hold the dog. But it was too late. Blackie snarled and lunged in a fit of rage, ripping the leash out of Smitty's hands. The last we saw of him was a black streak, charging into the night.

Less than a minute later, we heard the creak and slam of what sounded like an old pickup and a roaring take-off. As it sped away, we could still hear Blackie barking. He was chasing the truck!

Patti and I dashed for the car. As we piled in, Patti said, "It sounded like they headed that way." She pointed east. The hair on the back of my neck was at full mast as I started the engine and threw it into reverse.

Suddenly, a man's head leaned over the back of my car seat. I first felt his hot breath, then heard his voice in my ear. "Hello, sweetheart. I see you're up to your old tricks again." Patti squealed and jumped a foot high. I grabbed her arm to keep her from flying out of the car.

"Sims," I said. "Man, am I glad to see you." I quickly introduced them, explaining to my sister that the FBI agent was an old friend.

"For crissakes," she scolded. "You could have warned me. I almost wet my pants."

Sims apologized to Patti, adding that he was in the midst of a covert operation and had to stay out of sight. While they talked, I threw the clutch into first gear. Wheeling out of the parking lot, gravel skittering, I would have given anything to be driving my Porsche. This clunker Ford would have a tough time keeping up with anything larger than a lawnmower, and our prowler already had one hell of a head start.

I took a second to grab Sim's hand. "I'm not even going to ask you how you found us." After all, it *was* his car that I was using. "I'm just glad you did."

"Me too," he said, and winked. At the stop sign on Highway 20, Sims made an odd request. "I'd rather you wait here for a minute before we take off."

Frustrated beyond belief, I slammed on the brake and glanced in the rear-view mirror, eyeing Sims as he fiddled with the contents of a large briefcase on his lap. "You don't seem to understand what's happened here," I said. "The driver of that truck has to be Spike. Blackie recognized him. In fact, we think the dog was there when someone killed Larson. That's the guy who raised him." This garnered no reply from Sims. He was too engrossed with the briefcase.

Again, I tried to make him understand why we needed to hurry. "The dog's done that before. You see, we think that the reason the dog hates Spike so much is because he saw Spike kill Larson."

Sims nodded, calmly. "Don't worry. We're going after him, I just don't want him to know it. Just hold it, another couple of minutes." It was already too late. Spike had to be miles down the road by now. I set the emergency brake and leaned over the back seat to take a better look at his gadgets. Inside the briefcase on his lap was a black box, with knobs and little colored lights around a small screen in the middle. He was watching a little red dot move across the screen, beeping as it passed through the cross hairs.

Sims looked up and grinned boyishly. "This is called a 'bird-dog.' I put a tracking device on his pickup, while he was lurking around the community hall. A transmitter that sends a signal to this box. With each movement of this little blip across the screen, I can track a vehicle's course within a radius of five to ten miles. He's not going to get too far." He paused. After a few minutes, he pointed east, and said, "Okay, let's go. This way." From then on, Sims watched his box, giving directions of when to turn and in which way.

"How well have you been keeping up with this case?" I asked, as we sped down Highway 20.

"Well enough. I know just about everything you do, plus a bit more."

I thought about that for a moment, and the fact that either he or Ben always seemed to show up at the most appropriate times. "Do you, perchance, have a device on this car? Is that why I've been driving it all this time instead of my own car?"

"Yep. That's one of the reasons. It does have a tracking device. Too damn hard to keep up with you, without it. Plus, in case you've never noticed, it has bullet-proof windows and the gas tank is lined with lead to help prevent explosions. You won't stay out of trouble....the idea of minding your own business is just not in your vocabulary. We're just trying to keep you alive, Kath. What else could we do?"

I could see now why this car drove like a tank. It *was* a tank.

What other gadgets does it have? Could there be microphones in here with someone be listening to our every word? Good grief, I'd just revealed my most personal feelings about Ben in here. *One of these days, I was going to learn to keep my big trap shut.*

About two miles out of town, we turned onto a dirt road. Sim's device showed the pickup to be dead ahead. Minutes later, we drove past it, pretending to be headed to a destination somewhere down the road. It was the same red truck I'd ridden in the back of, to a militia meeting. It was parked on the side of the road with no driveways, houses, or even people in sight. Sims ducked down below the window while Patti casually glanced at it on our way by.

"There's nobody there," she reported. "Spike's gone."

Sims cursed under his breath. "Are you sure about that?"

"Yep. I'm sure."

We parked the Ford some 500 feet ahead and around a bend in the road. Sims wouldn't let us out of the car right away. He wouldn't even let me pull off the road, but kept the car tires on the well-worn grooves in the road. "Stay here for a minute. I can't be letting you two go charging off, when they're supposed to be paying me to do all that."

He began fiddling with the same box. "By the way, I can give you an exclusive, if you want it. We'll be putting out a news release, probably in the morning, but you will have it first."

"What do you mean, *if I want it.* You're damn right I want it. What's it all about?"

To Patti he said, "I take it, you are Mrs. Hickman?" She nodded. "Your husband's name is Dwayne Hickman?"

"Ex-husband...almost. But yes, that's his name."

"Well, your husband's been busy these last few months, gathering stuff to build bombs and storing it. We've discovered some of the bomb-making equipment in your garage and in a storage unit rented in his name, with his fingerprints all over it. Some chemical compounds and wiring, typically used in the making of explosives."

She looked horrified. "Oh, God. What if he comes after me? Or Jeffy? Like they did with Billy, for a hostage?"

"Don't worry. We'll get him. We would have brought charges against him earlier, but there wasn't quite enough to make it hold. Now it looks like we can."

"Where's he at?"

"Headed for Montana, near as we can tell. "But that could be a maneuver to throw us off his track. There's evidence that he was supplying some of those nuts in the Freemen holdout up there, with weapons: assault rifles and handguns, with the ID numbers filed down. And we think he's learned how to make a type of remote-control bomb. There was some literature in the storage unit, directions on how to build one. Looked like it was copied right out of an Army explosives manual.

"You see, when one of these fruitcakes makes a mass-killing device, they're so damn proud of themselves that they all have to have a symbol on it, somewhere. Some kind of mark, like a signature. Or a logo. Something that makes it personal. Like it's not enough for them to commit the crime, they just can't resist that one last chance to rub our noses in it. Believe it or not, they do it time and time again. And that's when we get 'em. There's proof that this last bombing, the one in Oregon, was at least partially made from his stock. We'll get him. I just hope he doesn't kill anybody in the meantime."

I felt Patti's hand on my arm. This was not good news.

"So, anyway, you can call Gunner tonight," he said. "But only after we make our arrest. We plan to pull him over at the state line. Then I've got to take you two ladies to a safe place until we pick up Spike Hardpenny and a few of his buddies."

"You mean I have to wait until he's actually behind bars? Why can't I fax in the details now, so the public will at least be notified that there is yet another lunatic out there. We can even run a picture of him and an 800 number for people to call."

"Can't do that, Kath. You know the rules. We can't release any information about a pending investigation, before the actual arrest takes place. That's what happened at Waco, and four ATF agents got killed."

Frustrated, I scribbled an outline for the article on a pad....should we ever get a chance to run it.

Patti had been so quiet, I'd almost forgotten she was there. It startled me when she turned to Sims and said, "Can I ask a question?"

"Sure."

"We seem to be talking about two different things. On one hand, there's the militia guys and their stupid antics. And on the other hand, there's the two homicides. Are you saying that the militia members didn't have anything to do with Tiffany's murder or Billy's kidnapping? Was that strictly Junior and Brian's handiwork? Aren't they part of the militia?"

"Not really, from what we could tell. They all knew each other of course, but that's not exactly a crime. And they'd all gone to a meeting now and then, trumping for votes more than anything else. But I don't think Junior had anything to do with the bomb-making. Or Brian, or even Rafferty. None of them fit the profile at all. No, these kooks are the kind that like to stockpile weapons. Your husband, Dwayne, is a good example. They know every crook and pin of any gun made. Get their rocks off by shooting them. The disenchanted Viet-Nam vets are another type, especially those who received training in explosives when they were young men and extremely impressionable."

"Dwight was never in the military."

"No, but he tried to enlist. Rated a 4-B. Which is pretty demoralizing to an ego that's already fragile. That's another fairly typical case. Kind of a war-veteran wannabe." Sims fiddled some more on his little black box, then switched it off. "Right now, I've got to get you two to a safe place. Any preferences? You know this area a lot better than I do."

"We can go on back to the reservation," I said. "To Ben's mother's house. His car is parked outside and although he kind of comes and goes, nobody will be able to know if he's there or not. We can always call 911 if we hear anything."

"I don't think so. Just cause you haven't seen anyone around there yet, doesn't mean that you won't. I'll contact the agency and get you into a safe house by tomorrow. Plan on staying there for awhile. I can probably get Ben to bring you your son, but you won't be leaving to go *anywhere*. You're too vulnerable out there driving around and getting yourselves in the kind of trouble you two seem capable of. Just wait until you hear from me."

Patti balked. "You mean, hide until you find Spike and Dwayne, *both*?"

"Until Spike's in custody, at least. And we're sure Dwayne is out of the state."

"What if it takes you days to get him? Weeks? I can't lay low that long. Besides holding down my job and trying to raise my son, I've got a big speech coming up tomorrow night. Don't forget, I'm running for Mayor."

"If you get beat up or killed, the election won't make much difference, will it?"

She frowned at him, obviously mulling over the pros and cons. "Let's see how it goes. I can take a couple of sick days without getting into too much trouble, which brings us right into the weekend. Kathleen and I could go up to Mt. Baker and sleep in the van for a little while. Spend some time with Darlene and the boys tomorrow and come back on Sunday night. Then, if things are still pretty scary, I'll see about taking a leave. But I'm not sure they'll give it to me. You have to remember one thing, the Mayor is my boss. And simply put, I've already gotten the old boy mad at me. I don't think he'll give me very many chances to screw up before I get canned."

It was a tough call to make, for all of us.

I turned the car around, then drove slowly back the way we came, stopping to observe the pickup from about 30 feet away. By that time, Blackie was getting hard to hold. We'd stopped on the way here, and picked him up on the road. I let him go, hoping he'd scout out Spike's trail, watching him circle the pickup, sniffing, barking and peeing on the tires.

"I have an idea," I said. "About halfway between here and the murder site, there's a little fort. Built by Jeff and Billy, last summer. Let's take Blackie on in there, just to see if there's been anyone around since we last looked."

Sims was adamant about us getting out of the way. "I'll do it," he said. "You two start packing. Leave the dog with me and I'll check it out. Be sure to keep the cellular phone with you at all times."

"Do you know how to find it? It's not like there's a street address with a mailbox in the driveway, you know. The trail is hard to find, even in the daylight. Impossible in the dark, and there's no way I can explain how to get there. I'll have to show you."

"Look, Kathy. I've worked with dogs before. And if Spike's been anywhere around there the last few days, I can tell by the dog's reactions."

"Yes, that's true. But Blackie's not a trained police dog. He won't understand any of your regular commands and even if he did, he won't mind you because he doesn't know you. This is no ordinary dog, you know. He's half-wolf and very sort of ...let's call it independent. If he smells Spike, he'll go off after him all right. Leaving you in the dust. And no amount of calling will make one bit of difference. I know you hate having to admit it, but you need me, Sims. Not only to help you with the dog but to show you how to find that fort."

"All right, all right. Gawd. I think I'd rather face the whole frigging bunch of them bare-handed than argue with you any longer." He fiddled with the box another minute, then motioned that he needed a private moment to make a call on the portable phone. Patti and I got out of the car and fussed over Blackie while we waited. Minutes later, he joined us and said, "Let's go."

Holding Blackie's leash and hoping he wouldn't bolt, we set out. Armed with little more than a few flashlights and Sims pistol, we approached the fort from the upriver bend. Each time before, we'd come up from the downriver direction. Which meant that it'd be even harder to spot the tiny trail leading to the fort. Heading in a somewhat southerly direction, we picked our way over the narrow beach. The River's Edge Park would be on the far side of that bend in the river, down about a mile and a half from where we were.

Sims had brought along the portable phone. Disconnected from the black box, it looked like a cross between a walky-talky and a cellular. Every ten minutes or so, he mumbled into it. A couple of times, I heard it beep and saw a tiny light flash on. He obviously didn't want to answer any questions about his conversations and, for once, I didn't ask any. But it did leave me to wondering who was on the line and exactly what they were planning.

CHAPTER EIGHTEEN

It wasn't long before Blackie darted into the brush, sniffing at a slow trot, the ruff on the back of his neck raised, like a sign. Something was amiss. At one spot, he growled low under his breath. He was getting harder and harder to hold, darting into the brush with no warning, yanking me along. Sims noticed his agitation and motioned for us to be as quiet as possible. He took Blackie's leash, but even he had trouble holding him with the dog straining against the thin leather. Spike had definitely been here. Although it was hard to tell how long ago or if he'd had anyone with him.

At the opening to the trail of Jeffy's fort, Blackie lunged up the bank. Evidently, the scent was much stronger here. Climbing furiously, we raced to keep up.

We reached the fort out of breath, the dog fully alert, snuffling at the scent, prepared to attack. But Spike was no longer there. Blackie scoured the immediate area, growling, digging at times in the soft earth. At times, Sims pointed out certain spots to him. Finally, Sims tied Blackie's leash to a tree. "Everyone stay back," he said. "We'll need to keep this area as uncontaminated as possible until the lab guys can make a thorough search."

Now came the fun part. We needed to go back to the river and continue tracking Spike. But how in the world would we ever explain this to the dog?

"Blackie," I said, petting the scruff on the dog's neck, wishing Ben was here to better communicate with the animal. Kneeling, I took the dog's head in my hands the same way I'd seen Ben do it before and looked him straight in the eye. "Go get him, Blackie," I said, pointing back out toward the river. "He's this way, boy. Go get Spike, this way." He whined, pulling away from me and barked softly, trying to escape my hold and dig around the area of the fort.

"No, Blackie. This way," I said, running a short ways down the trail. "Come on, Blackie. Go get him. *He's out there, Blackie. He killed Zeke, and he's this way.*" I wasn't sure if the dog understood what I said, or if he simply didn't want to be left behind. But once I started down the path, Blackie took off after me. And though Sim's shoulder had to be hurting by now from the constant pull and strain of the leash, we were headed in the right direction.

At the river's edge, we turned again to go south, away from where we'd parked, but toward the River's Edge Park about a mile downriver. The same park where Tiffany's body had been found. We sneaked through the darkness without seeing anyone. Once started, Blackie seemed happy enough with the direction we'd taken, picking up fresh scent as he trotted beside the bank.

As we walked, the river sloshed and gurgled like a living thing, a snake-like monster slithering through the valley that drenched our shoes each time we wandered too close, and crashed against large boulders and fallen logs to shower us with icy spray. As the light from a full moon lit up the water, it shimmered invitingly as if beckoning us into its frigid depths.

As we approached the path leading up to the park, Blackie suddenly became very excited and lunged up the bank. Sims tried to pull back on Blackie's leash to give us time. But Blackie wouldn't stop or even slow down. Ears up and fangs bared, he wasn't waiting around for anyone. Sims couldn't hold him. The only thing left to do was to follow the dog, trying with little success to run with him.

At the edge of the park, Sims got a headlock around Blackie's neck and motioned for us to duck down below the bank. Patti and I crawled up close enough to hear his whispers. "You two stay here. No arguments, this is as far as you go. And don't let them see you. I can't be worrying about keeping you out of the line of fire. *Stay here, or I'll be forced to handcuff you. Okay?*"

"Sure," Patti said. "Do your thing. I'm not prepared to tackle those guys."

I agreed, as Sims scrambled up the bank.

Out of the corner of my eye, I thought I saw a shadow moving parallel to Sims. It came from a grove of trees off to my right, fleeing toward the building where the restrooms were housed. To one side of the building, the roof had been extended about 12 feet, supported by posts on each end, creating an open-air shelter with picnic tables and a barbecue pit. The lights in the shelter were on and portable floodlights were pointed strategically, lighting up the crime scene area.

Blackie had pulled out of Sims' hold. He burst upon the scene, racing across the grass, his leash flapping uselessly behind him. He didn't bark, just a deep-throated growl. Sims scrambled after the dog, while Patti and I peered over the bank. It wouldn't have helped to call to him, but would have alerted the men sooner than necessary.

It was an odd sight. Spike lowered to his knees, in line with two or maybe three other men. Crouched on all fours, faces to the ground, they were performing a methodical search of the grounds around the crime scene with a fierce intensity.

They were looking for the knife tip.

In one leap, the dog had his man by the neck and they were wrestling on the ground. The other men hollered, jumped up and ran. Sims had drawn his gun, and shouted, "Freeze!"

I held my breath, scared that he'd hit Blackie.

He ran after them for ten or twelve yards, but it was too dark. They were gone, quickly disappearing into the shadows around the corner of the building. Finally, Sims walked back to Spike, grabbed Blackie's leash and pulled him off in time to keep him from ripping through the man's throat. He then tied the leash to a tree.

Spike was momentarily grateful to have been rescued. But his relief was short lived. Too late, he realized why the law had so conveniently turned up in time to save him. From our hiding place, Patti and I watched as Spike curled up into a fetal position, seeming to shrink before our very eyes. He'd been caught, and he knew it.

Sims handcuffed Spike to a park bench. Spike coughed, called Blackie a mad dog, insisting he was rabid, and demanded that he be protected from the beast.

Sims ignored him, did a fast turn-about and dashed for the building that housed the restrooms. He bashed through the door in the men's room and, a few minutes later, came out with Rafferty in tow. The others had gotten away.

I felt bad about their escape. Knowing I'd be asked to name them later on, I was worried about making any identifications. Even with the lights in the shelter on and floodlights concentrated on certain spots in the grass, most of the area was too dark to see very well and I'd only glimpsed the back of their heads. I couldn't be sure who the other ones were.

But I had a damn good idea.

Sims was searching Rafferty for weapons and handcuffing him to a picnic table when two more men strode through the tree grove and walked over to the shelter. My heart lurched and I almost cried out.

I thought so. It was Ben. And he was pushing Junior in front of him. Evidently, Ben had been communicating with Sims on the portable unit. And Ben had to be the one who'd been running parallel to us, through the trees. He'd known that we were coming and had positioned himself to catch Junior as he fled. I began to relax. Patti and I moved closer to the shelter. Just having that big, brown-skinned Deputy close made me feel safer. Feeling better about our relationship, what little there was of it, would have to wait.

Once all three of prisoners had been searched, handcuffed, and read their rights, they were told they were under arrest for conspiracy in the murder of Tiffany Redbear Jack and Zeke Larson.

Up close, it was amazing to see what these jackals had been up to when we stormed upon the scene. Lines of string had been laid out, crisscrossed about every 6 inches in a kind of grid, across the length of the crime scene. As each quartered-off square was minutely searched, the closest string was picked up and placed yet another 6 inches ahead of them. Spike, Junior, and Rafferty had been on their knees, thumbing through the grass, searching every square for that knife tip. Inch by inch and square by square. If DNA tests on the knife tip linked Tiffany's blood to the fingerprints on the knife handle, it would be hard evidence to overcome in court.

Waiting for Clancey to arrive with a vehicle in which they would be carted away and we would be returned to our car, Sims felt that this case had proved some theories he'd studied in a class on criminology. "Couldn't help but come back, could you," he said, terribly pleased with himself. "Besides having to find the knife tip, you also had to see your handiwork, didn't you? Check the area out? Gloat a little, that you'd gotten away with it?"

Rafferty was hunched over, shriveled up like an old man. Little good his money would do him now. By the time the lawyers and courts were paid, there wouldn't be much of it left.

Patti had not only survived the onslaught but was snuggled up against Blackie, under the tree, and actually had him calmed down and quiet. I patted the dog's head and told him he was a good boy. Sims was back on his walky-talky, and as we were still waiting for Clancey to arrive, I took the extra time to visit the ladies restroom. The entrance was on the other side of the building with a dirt path leading around the shelter.

Evidently, the park's budget didn't include a lightbulb on that side of the building and I'd lost my flashlight somewhere along the way. A little spooked, I strode quickly up the darkened path. To one side, I briefly noticed a small building tucked beneath the fronds of a Chinese maple. Probably a storage shed, no more than ten feet by twelve, it was also without lights. The shed's door had been left ajar, and I made a mental note to report it to the park supervisor.

About ten minutes later, on the way back to the others, the shed door creaked...swinging on rusty hinges. *Someone was opening it from inside.* I shivered, goosebumps erupting on my arms. My fast walk broke out in a run....but it was too late.

Suddenly, all hell broke loose. At a point on the path nearest the shed, a man's arm circled my throat, a knife poised to slash my windpipe.

Terrified, I would have screamed, but my supply of air was already shut off.

Mayor Winthrop.

I knew it! There had been a fourth man. Wily as he was, when Rafferty took off to the men's john, Winthrop had hidden in the storage shed. He walked me around the corner and under the lights of the shelter.

"Everybody on the ground," Winthrop bellowed. "Now! Or I'll kill her, and let you watch her die."

Sims had been facing toward the road. He now whirled, gasped, and stared at the Mayor. "You'll never get away with it, Winthrop. It won't work."

"Drop the gun, and get down the ground," Winthrop replied. "Or I swear to God, I'll kill her."

With all eyes on Sims and his slow withdrawal of his pistol, Ben slipped behind a rhododendrum bush. But Winthrop seldom let anything slide. "Deputy Jack! You too, ya damned Indian. Gawd, I hate you sneaky bastards. Get out here or watch your little girlfriend die."

Ben stepped out. Black eyes glittering, he lowered to the ground, watching Winthrop intently.

Either by accident or design, Winthrop's knife nicked the skin on my neck. I winced and tugged on his arm. The cut stung, and blood dripped onto my shirt.

The Mayor's other hand had pulled my body in close to his. As it roamed freely across my breasts, his breath caught and his chin nudged the edge of my ear. "Mmm," he mumbled. "Very enticing. Too bad I got to tend to business first."

At this, Junior sneared, and looked away.

A few feet away, his old pal Rafferty didn't miss a lick. His eyes constantly on the move, he monitored every flinch and grimace in the group with hooded little darts.

I felt sick, my skin popping with sweat. To speak or even to move, meant certain death.

"Toss those guns over here at my feet. Gently! No funny business, or your girlfriend dies." To me Winthrop said, "Don't kid yourself, Honey. One sudden move, and I swear to Gawd, you're history." He reached for one of the guns, forcing me to bend with him. His hand was no longer clamped on my breast, but I now had a .357 Magnum aimed directly at my temple. The knife was in his pocket.

He glared at Sims and Ben. "Which one of you has the keys to the handcuffs?" Neither one of them moved. "Who's got them? Tell me or I'll kill her here and now." He jerked me up, feet dangling, tightening the grip on my throat.

It was getting harder and harder to breathe.

"Over here," Sims said, and stood up, dangling them on one finger.

"Good. Now unlock my son. Careful. You better know that I'd just as soon kill this nosy bitch as not." Sims did as he was told, watching Winthrop from the corner of his eye.

"Junior? Pick up one of those handguns and make him put the handcuffs on himself. Hurry up! Same thing with our Indian Sheriff. Unlock Rafferty and have him handcuff Ben."

The sudden appearance of the Mayor had excited Blackie. He was growling, feet set and ready to lunge. Only the thin, leather leash and Patti's soothing hand held him at bay.

Winthrop swung the gun at my sister. "Patti? So much for giving you a job. Traitor! After all I did for you, this is the thanks I get. You get over here, too. And don't try letting that damn dog loose if you want your sister to keep breathing." She got up, nervously.

Blackie went nuts, snapping the leash and lunging straight for the Mayor's throat. Winthrop leveled the gun, and fired twice. At least one of the bullets found their mark. The dog stumbled and slid nose-first into the picnic table.

I screamed. "Blackie." Sprawled across the cement floor, he twitched a few times, trembled and moaned.

He didn't move again.

Using every bit of strength I had left, I kicked at Winthrop's ankles and screamed again. "You bastard. You killed Blackie."

My kick glanced off the side of his shin as the Mayor pulled me off balance, squeezing my throat, hard, effectively cutting off any speech and most of my air.

"Damned right I did," he said. "And you're next if you don't shut up. Okay, fellas. Now that I've got your attention, I want to make you a deal. Rafferty, bring the van around where we can load up. Junior, go get the kid."

Omigod. He's got Billy.

Minutes later, Junior brought him out. The boy was white as a sheet but walking on his own. It didn't appear that they had harmed him too much, physically.

Who knows what they've done to his mind.

Billy stared at his father. On his feet, swaying like a large bear ready to charge, Ben nodded to his son and winked. Jaws clenched, he janked on the handcuffs, scooting the picnic table a few feet across the cement floor.

Winthrop chuckled, his bulging belly jiggling against my back.

"Ben," the Mayor said. "I've got a deal for you. A tradeoff. Thanks to you and your friends, my son has damned near no

212

future left here in Eagle Ridge. But your son has his whole life ahead of him. So, I'll trade you. Since you think you're honor is so damned important, give me your word that you'll let my son go. You won't go after Junior or testify against him. Or me for that matter. And you'll do everything I tell you to see that he gets off on this rap. Plus, you'll find that knife tip and deliver it straight to me. Like I say, it's a tradeoff, you see. My son's life for yours. What'd you say to that?"

The upheaval of emotions were causing havoc on Ben's stolid features. An honorable man in league with the Devil in order to save his son's life. He gritted his teeth and narrowed his eyes. "All right," he said quietly. "You've got a deal. I'll do anything you say."

"I thought you'd see it that way. Don't disappoint me, boy. The county'd hate to hear that a father and his boy had a terrible accident. Not to mention, these two little ladies." He adjusted his arm on my neck, and for the first time, I realized that his arm was getting tired.

"You," the Mayor said, indicating Sims. "I guess you think you're pretty smart. Well, Smartass, I've got a job for you, too. You're going to take us for a ride. No problem, everybody'll have a seat. If you'll notice our new vehicle, we got lots of room."

About then, Rafferty drove up with Patti's van! The last time we'd seen it, Darlene was driving, taking Billy and Jeff to hide in the mountains.

Patti was shaking. "Where's my son, you pervert. And Darlene. What'd you do with them? Where's Jeffrey?"

"Watch the name-calling. They'll be fine, as long as you behave yourself. As I was saying, you're going on a little trip. The agent here is going to drive. Spike, you sit up front and keep an eye on him. The rest of you, including this nosy bitch," he squeezed my neck for emphasis, "...and her traitorous sister, will ride in the back. Long's you don't give Spike any reason to kill you, you'll eventually by given a chance to make restitution. We'll let you go at that time.

"Deputy Jack, you'll be turned loose as soon as the hostages have been dealt with. Remember, total cooperation and no testifying. Plus, I want that knife tip by next week. Remember, there's two women in this van, plus the kid. And don't forget your sweet Mamma. I'll be staying here to see that things go as planned."

Moments later, Sims was at the steering wheel, staring straight ahead. Spike was in the passenger seat and had trained a gun on him. Junior, using yet another gun, began to round us up like cattle. He waved the pistol at Billy, ordering him to get in the van and pretending indifference to Ben's steely glare.

The Mayor walked me up to the van's door. As I was getting in, Patti directly behind me, I glanced one last time at Ben. He was still shackled to the picnic table, eyes intensely black and shiny, trying to comfort Billy. The boy's face was buried in his father's shirt, sobbing quietly.

"Go ahead," Ben said, and bobbed his head feebly. "You'll be okay."

I shook my head, indicating that I didn't share his optimism as Winthrop shoved me inside. Billy was dragged to the door and shoved in behind me, and then Patti.

The van had small windows in the back, similar to portholes in a boat. Placing Billy in the farthest corner, I sat next to him with my sister on the other side. This arrangement put Patti next to one of the windows.

She looked out, then nudged me with a sharp elbow. Her eyes widened, and she pointed her chin to the porthole. Knowing something was up, I nonchalantly glanced out as if waving good-bye, and barely suppressed a gasp.

Clancey was here! The van door slid shut, and he came up behind Winthrop, his huge frame surprisingly agile, and clapped the Mayor's head between his two huge paws. It knocked him out. Winthrop crumbled, going down with almost no sound.

From the other window, I spied Ben going to work on the picnic table. He didn't even wait for Clancey to unbind him from the manacles. With one huge roar and a twist, he raised the table in mid-air and smashed it against the shelter's post. The roof trembled, as table and posts splintered like kindling. Taking up one of the table legs for a club, he advanced to the van.

The thugs inside hadn't noticed. Spike had turned on the radio to a nasty acid-rock station, loud enough to do permanent ear-drum damage. He was leering at Sims while waving the gun like a baton, in keeping with the beat of the music. The man was in hog heaven. He had a heart full of hate, a handgun with a full clip, and an FBI agent at his bid and call.

Junior was also incensed. He'd been given the Magnum and told it was okay to threaten women with it. The fact that we peeked out the window a few times didn't seem to bother him, as long as we sat where we were told and didn't openly rebel.

An odd sinking feeling in the back of the van gave me a clue as to what Ben was doing. He'd punctured the van's tires and let out the air. The van wouldn't be able to pick up much speed without going off the road.

With Spike's pistol being tapped rhythmically against his temple, Sims was ordered to start the van and head toward Highway 20. Somehow, I would have to warn Sims that Clancey was in operational mode and Winthrop was out of the picture.

The only thing left on my person was a piece of paper in my jacket pocket and a short pencil. "Spike," I said, getting up to walk to the front. "You'll probably want this," and thrust the folded paper in his direction. Junior immediately threw a temper tantrum, thrusting the gun in my direction and ordering me to stay where I was.

"Well, for crissakes, I was only trying to help. If you don't want it, fine with me." I shoved the paper back into the pocket.

It had gotten Spike's attention. "What is it?"

I threw my hands up and cocked my head. "Never mind. It's not worth getting shot over."

I paused, waiting while their thoughts moved like sludge through their thick heads. "It fell out of the Mayor's pocket." More pause. "I just thought you'd want to know what they've been saying about you. Figured that you and I could, you know, talk. Maybe work something out." At this, I moved my shoulders suggestively.

"Lemme see that."

"No way. Not until you tell Junior to stop jabbing me with his stupid gun."

"Junior. Put the damn gun down. And get me that paper."

I didn't give Junior time to demand it from me, but jumped up and bounded to the front. As I moved, I dropped the pencil in Patti's lap. She would know what it was for. I flopped into

215

the space between the front bucket seats, as if it was terribly necessary that Spike look directly at me while I handed him the folded sheet. Doing so, my body became a shield, cutting off Spike's view of Sims.

It was all Sims needed. The agent kicked out at Spike, grazing my head and knocking the gun toward the van's ceiling. It went off, blowing a hole through the roof. At the same time, Clancey yanked at the van's passenger door on Spike's side. It was locked. Ben also tried both the drivers' and the side door. They were all locked.

In the front seats, Sims and Spike were engaged in warfare. Spike smashed Sims in the jaw, gaining the upper hand. As Sims fell back, Spike pounced, effectively wedging them both between the steering wheel and the seat. With Sims on the bottom, Spike used his weight to jam an elbow into his throat. The gun had fallen to the floor.

As expected, Patti made short work of Junior. She jabbed the pointed end of the pencil into his thigh. "Pervert," she cried. "How dare you prey on little boys."

While he screamed, clutching the wound, she slid the door open behind him. With one well-placed shove, Junior tumbled backwards to the ground. He went willingly, expecting to be met by his father. *Too bad.* Clancey was officiating in this reception.

With her free hand, Patti gingerly picked up Junior's gun and placed it carefully against Spike's temple. "Your turn, you sonofabitch."

Spike froze. Sims slid out from under Spike's weight, staring up at Patti with a new appreciation. I reached over and pulled the door handle. Both men spilled out onto the ground. Moving quickly, Clancey shoved a number 12 boot into Spike's windpipe. I thought it to be an appropriate move.

With the no-longer threatening threesome off to jail, we headed toward home. Sims was beginning to settle down, but still needing to vent.

"You know," he said. "Normal people may feel a morbid kind of curiosity at an accident scene, but unless the victim is a relative or a loved one, no one wants to hang out for very long in a place where somebody died. Not so with a criminal mind. Killers will usually want to congratulate themselves, to show off. If at all possible, they'll go back at least once and lots of times they'll take someone with them. To brag about how clever they are and how they managed to outsmart the authorities."

Sims snorted and breathed heavily. "They think they're so damned smart. But they're not. Animals are smarter than they are. They'll return to their kill only when they're hungry." He shook his head, disgustedly. "The only hunger here was greed and Blackie's thirst for revenge."

CHAPTER NINETEEN

Sunday. The next day, Patti and I were too bummed out to do much but drink coffee and sprawl across the couch. It felt like we'd been out on a four-day toot, and suffering from a serious hang-over. We both needed to go back to work, but neither of us could be sure if we still had jobs waiting for us.

Having to bury Blackie didn't help. We'd laid him to rest under a large cedar, where the breeze whispered and the tree boughs sighed. I would have played taps if I'd known how. He'd been incredibly brave and deserved a hero's sendoff.

Ben had gone after Darlene and Jeffy. He'd said that finding the van must have been fairly easy as it had been parked in the hunting lodge's parking lot. With the Mayor's connections, a conscientious night watchman at the Mount Baker Lodge had discovered it in the parking lot.

Finding Darlene and the boys in those mountains, hadn't been easy. It took the whole Skagit Search and Rescue team working with half the Whatcom County Sheriff's Department. She'd run them ragged, but there was just too many experienced woodsmen among them. Evidently, Winthrop's men had asked that they be released to his custody, then hidden her and Jeffy somewhere else.

Poor Patti. She was distraught, red-eyed from crying and worried sick about Jeffrey. "I should have gone with Ben. This sitting around, waiting, is getting on my nerves."

I hugged her, my forehead brushing her dark curls. "Don't be silly. Ben will be on horseback half the time and we'd just be slowing him down. And Clancey said that if he could get anything out of either Winthrop or Spike, he'd call us. The waiting is hard, but it's the only thing we can do right now."

I'd finally gotten ahold of Gunner and dictated the events of last night. He was delighted.

I was scanning yesterday's story in the *Gazette*, about the militia. That finished, I automatically began reading the local paper, the Eagle Ridge Report. Frank had done a nice feature on Patti's campaign, mentioning her experience with civic matters, by working at the City Hall. He even reminded the readers that they could meet her at the Baptist Church Open House, on Sunday night.

That was tonight. If Jeffrey wasn't back by then, she'd be hard pressed to go on. Even so, today was Sunday, the bells were chiming in the church steeples, and the citizens of Eagle Ridge would be all decked out in their finest.

As if she'd been reading my mind, Patti was the first to mention our concerns out loud. "You know," she said. "Tonight's my talk at the Baptist Church. How am I ever going to get ready for it?"

"Oh, you'll do fine."

"What if ....?"

"You mean, what should we do about Jeff and Darlene?" I rubbed my temple, and shuddered. A total recall of Winthrops gun pressing against that same spot, flashed through my mind. "The only thing I know to do, is to take it one minute at a time. One hour at a time. And trust Ben's abilities to track them down."

We were interrupted by Sims arrival. He pulled up in the driveway, driving one of Clancey's patrol cars. We had a lot of questions and he had a lot of answering to do. He was served coffee and a bite to eat.

"So," I said. "What is the connection between you and Ben? There's some sort of communication going on, and I doubt that you're that psychic."

"As you've probably guessed, Ben has been our contact with the militia members for the last couple of years. We've been gathering information on them for some time. So, when his ex-wife was killed, we asked Ben to go along with them on the compassionate leave thing. Since it was the FBI's case all along, Winthrop's insistence about his staying on the suspect list didn't really make much difference, other than keeping the old boy quiet. It would give Ben the time he needed to find his kid and feed us what information he discovered on the way. That way, he could help us monitor Spike, the Winthrops and Dwayne, and they'd never be the wiser. It was Ben who found the bomb-making equipment.

"Remember all those nights that Ben was out on the horse? He grew up in this area and knows it like the back of his hand. It was a perfect setup. The militia members relied on the roads much too heavily. With his knowledge of the terrain, Ben could move literally undetected around their perimeter, riding horseback. It was great."

"I was there one night," I said, ignoring my sister's questioning stare. I hadn't told her about my adventures with the militia at the mountain cabin yet.

"Yea, I know. I almost shit when you turned up under that window. I was also there in disguise. Wearing a body wire. Ben was on the other end, handling the receiver. After he set the dog loose and you took off, I did what I could to put them on the wrong trail and give you some space to run in. At least, temporarily."

I closed my eyes and rubbed a finger over the lids. *All that effort and risk-taking, for nothing.* "Great. Now I feel like a total fool."

"Now, don't talk like that. You helped us a lot. That dog of yours was a real jewel. We're trying to get to the point where we can intercept any really aggressive behavior on the part of these militia groups, before they hurt someone."

"Why don't you just haul them all in and throw the whole bunch in jail?"

"Can't do that. There's what we call *civil rights*. Even for the crooks. We can't take them in until we're sure we've got a solid case."

We were interrupted by Billy, who'd wandered into kitchen. Patti had saved him a double serving of breakfast and delighted in serving it to him. By unspoken consent, all discussion of the case stopped until he was fed and told where his dad went and how soon he'd be home. An hour later, the boy had finally had enough to eat, and was rested.

"Billy," I said. "I know that what you've been through was very painful. We just want you to know that the bad guys who did this to your family are in jail, and can't hurt you anymore. You're safe." I indicated Sims. "This man is from the FBI. He and your dad are the ones most responsible for catching them."

Sims offered the boy his hand, and shook it. "You know, Billy. You're one brave dude. What you told your dad earlier is important, and it'll help us when we put these guys on trial. Before I leave, I'm going to ask you to tell it again on a tape recorder. And you'll probably be asked to tell it again several more times before it's all over. Can you handle that?" The boy nodded, stating that he understood.

"That's great, kid. Meanwhile, your dad and grandma oughtta be showing up any minute. And they've got Jeffy, too. Why don't you go out front and watch for them?"

We watched him run out the front door. "He is quite a kid, isn't he?" I said, fondly.

"Tough as nails," Sims replied. "By the time he gets his full height, Spike's going to be glad he's in prison. Keep that young man from coming after his sorry ass."

I was still trying to get the people and events unscrambled. "So, wasn't it Ben that you were talking to the other night by the river? On that fancy phone of yours?"

Sims nodded. "Ben and Clancey, both. We also had a few undercover agents running around out there, who didn't want their identities revealed. Once they've lost their cover, it's pretty tough trying to work in the field anymore. You see, this was what you might call a sting operation. We had microphones set up in the shelter, picking up every word they said, both before we got there and afterward. Plus, it looks like we interrupted the payoff, or what should have been the payoff. From what we can tell from the recordings, Spike still hasn't been paid for killing Tiffany and Larson, and he is pissed about it. And, the casino ran out of patience with Junior long ago. They want their money, too. Nobody's been paid. Which was why they'd been arguing, when we arrived on the scene."

He paused and refilled his coffee cup. "The Winthrops screwed the deal when they failed to get tonight's late-comers agreement passed. That's where the money was supposed to come from, for the payoff. The taxpayers owe the both of you gals a big debt of gratitude for that. Saved them a ton of money. I'll see to it personally that a press release goes out about the part you two played in that."

There was one other player who I wanted to be totally

clear on. "So, what you're saying is that Clancey knew all along what they were up to."

"Sure he did," Sims replied. "But his hands were tied until we had the goods on them. In fact, the knife-tip sting was mostly his idea."

Patti was visibly trying to be more optimistic about her son's return. She'd set out two extra place-settings; determined that they would arrive in time for breakfast. "You know," she said, puttering around the kitchen. "I never have understood the panic over that stupid knife tip. From what I saw when they first drug it out of the river, there wasn't any tip missing. It didn't even have fingerprints. There was a lot of rust, which meant it had probably been there for some time."

Grinning sheepishly, Sims stared at her profile. "And you were right. It was probably dropped by a fisherman, years ago. But they didn't know that. Ergo, the sting operation. We planted that story about the knife tip, to draw them into the shelter. It's been wired for sound since the investigation began. Get them all together, fighting among themselves. Arguing. You'd be amazed what people'll say out loud."

She smiled sadly. "So what happens to them now?" That china-doll complexion of hers, framed by the soft auburn waves, was already weaving its magic on our illustrious agent. He was spellbound. And in my heart of hearts, I couldn't really blame him. Even after the horror of this last week, she was still *gorgeous*.

Sims cleared his throat. "The case against Spike, Rafferty, and the Winthrops is going to trial."

"And the militia members?"

"That one's not ready yet. It'll be going to federal court. You see, this whole militia movement is a tricky situation. Ever since the Randy Weaver case, and the Waco disaster, they've been feeling their way around these self-proclaimed patriots with velvet gloves."

With that, Patti pulled a baking sheet of hot biscuits out of the oven and served them with a bowl of sausage gravy. We were just digging in when Jeffrey burst into the living room. He was followed by a tired-looking Darlene and a triumphant Ben. And before we knew it, the make-shift, oddly-matched family had chattered, hugged and laughed away the rest of the morning and most of the afternoon.

Darlene had seen the men looking for her and hid herself and the boys in the woods. And as she'd prophesized, they'd ran circles around her like a dog chasing its tail. Blackie would have been delighted. But there were just too many of them. One of the Search and Rescue people, also an Indian and a member of the Lummi tribe, had spotted them under a cliff in an overhang of grass and weeds.

"He was just doing his job," Darlene said softly.

It was time to get ready for Patti's stump speech at the Baptist Church. The boys would stay here with Ben and Darlene, and get to bed early. Sims had to get back to Seattle, which meant that I was the only one going with her.

It had been awhile since I'd been to church services and it was surprisingly comforting. The sermon centered around love and healing. We'd been so wrapped up in the case that none of us had realized just how much the recent deaths and destruction of lives, had unnerved the citizens who lived here.

When the regular Sunday night services were over, the Pastor Hill called for a twenty-minute break. Patti was to begin her speech, immediately afterward. Her hands shook only slightly, as she climbed the podium. Frank, from the town paper, showed up as the Pastor began her introduction. His arrival reminded me that I'd forgotten my camera in the car.

This night would mark a life-changing event for her. It could not go by without a picture. I held up one finger to indicate that I'd be back in a moment, slipped out the side door and dashed to the car.

As I wrestled to get the glove-box open, I happened to glance in the rear view mirror. The street was mostly empty, except for an old Toyota pickup. Parked about a block away, the driver was leaning against the steering wheel, staring at the church building. There was something familiar about the sour set of his jaw. As I pulled the camera out, checked it for film, a working light meter and batteries, a nagging anxiety squeezed the pit of my stomach.

Another feeling of deja vu swept over me. I'd never been here at the church before. So why did that pickup and driver bother me?

Suddenly, it hit me. *That driver was Dwayne.* And I'd seen

him drive that truck a dozen times. The most recent one, was backing out of his driveway last week when he almost plowed into my Porsche.

So. Either the little creep had followed us here, or he'd seen the notice in the paper. Hopefully, he had no plans to spoil Patti's speech by making a big scene. I doubted that he had the nerve to do anything outright in public. The squeamish little runt preferred sneaking around at night, then running away before the fireworks started.

Wait a minute! I'd seen that pickup since then. He had pulled into this church parking lot, the same day that Larson was killed. And put something in the storage shed, in the rear of the church building. I had taken it for granted that they were having choir practice. But according to the Eagle Ridge Report, in the same issue that publicized Patti's speech, their choir practice was on *Tuesday* night.

Omigod. Sims' warnings about Dwayne's abilities to build bombs echoed through my mind. He knew Patti and me would be here tonight. And his hate was so sinister, so viscious, that he could very well blow the church and all its members sky high.

I froze. Behind me, Dwayne had started the pickup, and was backing it down the street. Putting more space between him and the church building.

Patti. And the church members. I had to get them out of there.

I started the Ford, giving thanks for Sims' foresight in giving me a tank to drive in place of my thin-skinned Porsche. There wasn't time to explain and have everyone evacuated. Petal to the metal, the Ford had barely reached 30 miles an hour as it rumbled up the church steps. It smashed through the front double doors at about 25 mph.

Doors can be replaced. People can't. And I only had one sister.

Amid their screams and crying babies, the frightened audience scattered. Pastor Hill immediately took the microphone, directing them to the exits.

The tank bumped to a stop, fender grinding against the podium. Without a word, a white-faced Patti ran down the stairs and jumped into the passenger seat. Folded her arms and stared straight ahead.

I slammed the gear shift into reverse and we hurled back out through the hole I'd just made in the entrance and jostled down the same steps into the street. Speeding backwards away from the building, I was happy to see the congregation fleeing to their cars and racing down the sidewalk to their homes. Surely, they were convinced that Satan himself had entered their midst and Armageddon was nigh. I didn't really care what they thought, as long as they were safe.

Dwayne had planned it well. The building blew about the time Patti would have entered into the part about her plans to stamp out crime and violence in Eagle Ridge.

Monday morning, I was back at the *Gazette*, pounding out the story of this last week on my computer keyboard. These lunatics needed to be exposed, along with the militia movement they had created. Hopefully, I wouldn't get any flack about getting it into print.

Finally, Gunner called me into his office. "Sorry, Kath," he said. "I can't run this particular story at this time. It'll hurt the FBI's case, as they'll be using some of this information for all kinds of different warrants."

"But, Gunner....,"

He held up one hand to ward off my arguments before they even started. "I've already pitched your side of it. And you're right. The readers have a right to know. But the Feds have asked me not to run certain details, most of what you uncovered. A potential juror could read it, giving the defense good cause to petition that a well-deserved guilty verdict be thrown out the window. And the policy of this newspaper is to cooperate with the state and federal authorities whenever asked."

He looked at me, long and hard. "We will be doing a more general kind of expose on the militia members in the Pacific Northwest. What their main beliefs are and their beef against the government. How many there are and run a few pictures of their weapons inventory. I'd like you to be in charge of that."

I slumped in my chair, defeated and too tired to be angry.

"Look at it this way. You'll be a part of something larger than yourself. Do you realize that you could very well have saved the President's life, by informing them of certain details? Early enough to give them time to adjust their plans? How many people can actually say that?"

That night in my apartment, Donna brought over a pasta salad to share while I told her of Spike's fate and his reason for having been here. We ate out on the lanai, plucking the last few cherries on the reachable branches.

After she left and as I prepared to go to bed, Ben called me. Midst much stammering and clearing of throat, he asked me if I'd be willing to go on a picnic next weekend. It was good idea. Spending a day together without a crisis of some kind driving our every move, we might be able to talk a few things out. I was no longer sure how I felt about a number of people, including him.

That next Saturday, we met at the lake. The same place where we'd walked before. And as before, he was having a tough time finding the words to express himself. I looped my arm through his, in no particular hurry as we strolled. Who said that all communication had to be done with the spoken word? He patted my hand as we walked along the shore, listening to nothing but the birds, the lap of the water, and the beating of our hearts.

He cocked his head as if to speak, and for once I gave him the time and the space to say what he needed, in the way he needed to say it. He paused a long moment, then said, "You know, growing up, it was always hard for me to talk to girls." He pulled on his ear, sheepishly, and kicked a small rock into the water. "Still not very good at it. Probably the biggest cause of my breakup with Tiffany."

I leaned against him, and chuckled. "Looks like we're even. I'm the one who never knows when to shut up." I could tell he felt comfortable, and for once, I felt at ease in a man's presence. Nothing to prove, nothing to gain. Just a good friend who'd been there for me and my family, when it counted.

He pointed out a nest of bald eagles across the lake. As we watched, the female soared in and landed. "Before I forget," he said. "I wanted to invite you to a potlatch, in November. My potlatch, and we'll have a winter dance ceremony."

He grinned, "My mother's finally consented to the idea that I've become a man. I'll receive a name in the Lushootseed language. The name of one of my ancestors. Perhaps even my grandfather." He cleared his throat. "A potlatch, among other important functions, used to serve as a distribution of wealth. In the old days, it was a way to circulate blankets and coiled baskets to those who didn't have the resources to hunt or make their own. It also reminds us that we shouldn't get too attached to material objects because we might be asked to give them away at any time. "

His goodness was a godsend. It was also an incredible turn-on. I tipped my head and he bent to kiss me. I wanted to have the touch of him...the forestry smell of him on my lips and to blend a bit of my passion with his. He moved to hold me, his arms incredibly strong, protective and engulfing. We kissed again, only this time, it was deep. And passionate. And Ben didn't break away, but wanted more of me as I had been wanting him. And when our clothes were in the way, they were removed. And when our bodies could get no closer, he went inside me.

Later, as the birds sang overhead and the sun warmed our bare bodies, Ben turned to me, his face full of love and concern. "By the way," he said. "I thought you'd like to know that Blackie left his calling card in the world before he left it."

I went up on one elbow. "Calling card?"

"Yea. Sheba. You know, the blue-eyed, brown-eyed husky? She'll be having puppies. Blackie's puppies. We thought you might like to take first pick of the litter."